D0882450

MEAT THY MAKER

MEAT THY MAKER

Tamar Myers

SEVERN
HOUSE

First world edition published in Great Britain and the USA in 2023
by Severn House, an imprint of Canongate Books Ltd,
14 High Street, Edinburgh EH1 1TE.

Trade paperback edition first published in Great Britain and the USA in 2023
by Severn House, an imprint of Canongate Books Ltd.

severnhouse.com

British Library Cataloguing-in-Publication Data
A CIP catalogue record for this title is available from the British Library.

ISBN-13: 978-1-4483-0866-8 (cased)
ISBN-13: 978-1-4483-1008-1 (trade paper)
ISBN-13: 978-1-4483-1009-8 (e-book)

All Severn House titles are printed on acid-free paper.

Typeset by Palimpsest Book Production Ltd.,
Falkirk, Stirlingshire, Scotland.
Printed and bound in Great Britain by
TJ Books, Padstow, Cornwall.

This book is dedicated to my best friend and husband of almost half a century, Jeffrey Charles Myers. I met him when I was fifteen, and for me it was love at first sight. It was my first day attending an American high school, and I was in eleventh grade. He is the kindest man I have ever known.

ACKNOWLEDGEMENTS

I would like to thank my publisher, Kate Lyall Grant, at Severn House for the opportunity to write this book. I would also like to thank my editor Sara Porter for her wisdom and skillful guidance. I also wish to acknowledge my copyeditor Anna Harrisson for a bang-up job, and of course, the art department for a scrummy cover.

In addition, I am very grateful to my literary agent of twenty-nine years, Nancy Yost, of Nancy Yost Literary Agency. I want to give a shout-out to the entire team there, most especially Sarah, Natanya, Cheryl, and Christina.

Last, and certainly least, I would like to acknowledge Alexander Byrd Myers. He is the worst secretary this side of the Atlantic. He simply cannot focus on his duties. Besides that, he is a frightful speller, and utterly incapable of typing a single word, no matter how vigorously he pecks at the keyboard. Then again, it's perhaps understandable, given that he is a three-ounce parakeet (budgie). However, he does cheer me on all day by saying 'I love you, sweetheart' and 'I'm a happy bird, because I'm your little baby'.

ONE

The truth is that not all men are created equal. To my initial surprise the Schmucker men and their monstrous sausages were a huge hit with the ladies of Hernia. 'Bigger is better,' is what I heard over and over again from my friends. Personally, I preferred to place bite-size bangers on my breakfast plate alongside my scrambled eggs.

But like I said, Jacob, Solomon and Peter Schmucker (three very handsome brothers), had somehow stumbled on a winning product. Schmucker Brothers Sausages went from an obscure brand to one that had customers begging their favourite stores to keep it in stock. This all happened in just a few months.

Sceptic that I am, and one who loathes following trends, I finally capitulated and bought a package of the much-coveted breakfast meat. I am ashamed to admit that I had to snatch it out from beneath the reach of a slower-moving woman with shorter arms. In my defence, that woman was talking on her phone at an ear-splitting decibel level about arranging a 'Bazillion wax' that day. She was so upset that I got the last package of sausages, she dropped her phone in the meat case. For all I know, she may not have been able to get her floor shined that afternoon.

My beloved husband scoffed when he saw me unpack the prized sausages.

'Following the crowd now, are you, Mags?'

'Absolutely not!' I said. 'I simply want to see just how wrong everyone is.'

Gabe laughed and kissed my cheek. 'You're still the same, humble woman whom I married twenty-five years ago.'

'Not quite,' I said, as I continued to unpack groceries. 'I finally have a streak of grey running through the mousey brown hair.'

'What's a mouse without a grey streak?' my husband said, and gave me another kiss.

'*And* I've put on a little weight.'

'Well, you always complained about being thin as a beanpole, and what did I tell you?' Gabe said.

'That you liked women with rail-thin figures,' I said, as I put away the frozen goods.

'Yes. But I also said that you were in danger of blowing over in a stiff wind, because your head made you top-heavy, despite your enormous feet. However, since the weight you gained is all in your ankles, you now have a good shot at remaining upright in even the most inclement weather.'

'Thanks, dear, you say the sweetest things.' I tossed him the package of sausages, which were now lying on the counter. 'Here, since you're just standing around dishing out compliments and kisses, fry these up for supper.'

Gabe gasped. 'Breakfast for supper? The label says that they are "breakfast sausages".'

'Let's break some rules. After all, I'm seventy-four – you're seventy-five. How many more good years can we expect? Ten? Twelve? The children are grown and on their own, or away at university. Eat breakfast sausages for supper, I say. Eat ice cream for breakfast.'

'Who stole my wife,' Gabe demanded, as he stepped away in mock fright, 'and replaced her with this wanton woman?'

'Now, now, dear,' I said, wagging a long, knobby finger at him. 'Let's not get carried away. The rules that we break will only be societal conventions; they certainly won't be anything that leads us into sin. Or anyone else into sin,' I hastened to add.

Gabe grinned. 'Does this mean that you're going to shed your dowdy conservative Mennonite garb, and start dressing in something more – uhm – alluring?'

'Absolutely, dear,' I said. 'Tomorrow I'm going to run out and buy a low-cut dress with a mini-skirt. Given my beanpole figure, it will slip down to my chunky ankles and puddle there, just inches off the ground. Then you can spray me with blue paint and enter me in a snobby art show someplace like New York, or Philadelphia.'

'Sounds like a plan,' Gabe said, as he reached for a skillet.

I grabbed another skillet for the eggs, and a pot for the tin of baked beans that invariably accompanied this meal for us. Some toast with butter and thick-cut marmalade, along with some milky tea – now *that* was supper.

Gabe got halfway done cutting the package open with the kitchen scissors when he let out a howl of derision.

'What now?' I said.

'Mags, did you read what's written on here before you bought this stuff?'

'You mean the list of ingredients?' I said sweetly, for I knew exactly to what he was referring.

'No, those seem to be on the up and up. It's this stupid claim under the logo that these are hand-crafted sausages for the sophisticated consumer. I mean, are they implying that they fill each sausage casing by hand and personally tie off the ends? And if so, how does that make them any better than if a machine did the work? I think not! I know that I sure don't want some stranger's hands messing with my sausage.'

'It gets cooked,' I said. 'Read there at the bottom – in big red letters. Unlike other sausages, these sausages must be cooked until a dark golden brown.'

'Dark golden brown?' Gabe echoed. 'Is there such a colour?'

'Just start cooking, hon, because the eggs will take only a few minutes, and I don't want them to get cold. How many slices of toast do you want?'

Thank heavens my Sweetie Pot Pie, whom I often refer to as the Babester, shut up and began frying, and I was able to coordinate all the dishes to be ready when needed. The sausages contained sage, ginger, cloves, red pepper, black pepper and brown sugar, and although they were a tad spicy, they were a perfect complement for the otherwise bland eggs. However, I think that young children, and some of our elderly citizens, would be put off by the two kinds of pepper – at least in the amounts that these bangers contained.

The Schmucker Brothers Sausages by the way, came in two varieties: 'Breakfast' and 'Dinner'. They didn't sell a 'Lunch' variety, probably because no one in their right mind would eat sausages for lunch. At lunch a thinking person should eat either a peanut butter and jelly sandwich, or a tomato and cheese sandwich. No salads, ever! Salads are just an excuse to pile on all sorts of toppings and caloric dressing to make the rabbit food palatable. In the end the salad ends up having twice as many calories as a sensible, and quite portable, sandwich.

At the conclusion of the meal the Babester sighed contentedly, and suggested that we take a walk through our little swatch of earthly paradise. About a decade ago I gave away my two beloved milk cows (on the condition that they would not be slaughtered), and replanted most of their former pasture with hardwood trees. I did, however, leave a large swath that curves down to the pond, free of trees, and each spring I toss wildflower seeds hither, thither and yon, amongst the grass. Some seeds get eaten by the birds, but many make it to the ground, germinate, grow and propagate themselves. Through the middle of this flower-bedecked meadow, a narrow, well-trodden footpath leads down to the water's edge.

As always, the Babester and I held hands on our walk. After a quarter of a century we still love each other very much. I won't exaggerate and say that we're 'in' love because, frankly, the shine has worn off these two old cooking pots, if you get my metaphor. We've been dented and scratched by what life has thrown at us, and by what we've thrown at each other. One time we almost got a divorce – even though that's against my personal beliefs, and against the teachings of Jesus as well, unless one or the other of us had been unfaithful (which neither of us had been). My point is, why would either of us throw away a given quantity in hopes of finding a better replacement? I know all of Gabe's faults and foibles, and I'm sure that if he thought long and hard, he might come up with an imperfection to pin on me.

We'd had an early supper, and the late spring sun was still high in the sky, illuminating all the early blooming flowers along our way. The air temperature was about seventy degrees Fahrenheit (which I hear is a heatwave in the UK). Meadowlarks were singing, bluebirds were carolling, indigo finches were warbling, the Babester was humming – except for the Second Coming of Jesus, it could not have been a more perfect evening.

I leaned my horsey head on the Babester's shoulder. 'I love you, Pookey Bear.'

'I love you more, Sweetums.'

After reaching the pond we sat on a woven willow reed bench. There we snuggled in the cooling air and watched the swallows swooping for emerging mosquitoes. Neither Gabe nor I are particularly bothered by these nasty insects, nonetheless we'd slathered each other with a repellent before leaving the back porch.

Suddenly two hours had passed, and the sun was setting to the accompaniment of whippoorwills. Where had the time gone?

'Gabe,' I said, 'have you ever seen a sunset as beautiful as this one?'

My husband, who was sitting beside me, squeezed my shoulders lovingly, but when he spoke, it sounded like he was sitting on either side of me.

'No, hon,' he said in this strange stereo voice. 'Never.'

I got abruptly, if somewhat unsteadily, to my feet. 'Darling, I need to go back to the house. I'm not feeling very well.'

'Oh?' *Oh, oh, oh.* My husband's voice came at me as if broadcast through multiple speakers.

'I'm feeling – uh – weird.'

'Weird, like how?'

'Like I'm in a movie or something.'

'Yeah? Well, whatever you're feeling, I've got you, babe.' Gabe put a strong arm around me and told me to just put one foot in front of the other. He'd see that I got home and to bed safely, and if need be, he'd call Jacob Livingood, our village doctor who actually makes house calls.

'That's good,' I said, 'because I'm suddenly hungry. Hey, we forgot to have dessert.'

'That we did, babe.'

'We still have some of that chocolate fudge cake that your sister brought over. And an untouched quart of premium vanilla bean ice cream.'

'A winning combination,' Gabe said. 'And I'll heat up that jar of extra fudge sauce that Cheryl left.'

'Yummy for my tummy,' I said and giggled.

'You're a funny girl,' the Babester said.

I giggled again. Me? Funny? I was about as humorous as a cod liver oil milkshake. Now *that* was sort of funny – no, that was just bizarre. Who was this giggling septuagenarian whom my sexy husband had referred to as a 'girl'? She definitely wasn't funny. Bossy, maybe. Opinionated, definitely.

No, the funny thing was that despite having eaten so much for supper, by the time we got back to the house I was so ravenous that I forgot all about my earlier sense of being out of sorts. All I wanted to do was consume chocolate cake with hot fudge sauce, topped with premium vanilla bean ice cream. Fortunately, there was an ample supply of all three.

Finally, satiated with food, my still handsome hunk of a husband led me tenderly back to our boudoir and . . . well, the rest of it is simply none of your business.

TWO

My name is Magdalena Portulacca Yoder Rosen, although because I was a Yoder for most of my life, that's what most folks call me. Gabe is all right with that, because he knows what is on our marriage certificate, and he realizes that he doesn't own me. His full name is Gabriel Joshua Rosen. Ours is a mixed marriage.

Gabe is a non-believing Jew (and yes, there can even be atheist Jews), and I am a Conservative Mennonite woman of Amish descent. The Amish don't use electricity, they don't own and drive cars or tractors, they don't believe in education beyond the eighth grade, they have their own language, they dress a particular way, baptize only adults, and they don't believe in violence.

If someone in their community violates these strictures, they will be reprimanded and be required to repent in front of the community. If they refuse to do so, or persist in their behaviour, then they will be shunned. Shunning is meant as a way to keep the community cohesive, but in my opinion, it is a cruel custom. When someone is shunned, it is as if that person is dead. No one – not even their parents – is allowed to acknowledge the sinner's existence, until that person has repented. As a result, many shunned Amish move away and join other faiths, particularly the Conservative Mennonite Church, its closest relative.

It often happens that family members of the shunned person will begin to question key religious points of the Amish faith, or miss their relative so keenly, that they will break away from the Amish Church also. As a result, the Amish suffer a twenty percent attrition rate. However, their very high birth rate more than offsets this loss by a wide margin. All four of my grandparents were Amish, but they left that denomination when my grandfather, Melvin Yoder, bought a car when he was thirty-five. By then he and my grandmother had eight children. My grandmother decided to leave with my father when he was shunned, as did his parents, her parents, all of their siblings, along with their spouses and their parents – all told, two hundred and seventeen people eventually left the Amish fold and became Conservative Mennonites the day my grandfather refused to repent for buying a car.

At any rate, I *do* drive a car, live in a house with electricity, and we even have a television in the bedroom sitting area, where my husband spends many happy hours watching bright young men getting concussed (even though they wear helmets), and slapping each other's buttocks. I don't dress in a discernible costume as do the Amish, but I dress conservatively: skirts and blouses with elbow-length sleeves, or dresses with similar sleeves. The skirts fall to below my knees. The Holy Bible states that a women's hair is her crowning glory, so mine has never been cut. I wear it braided and the braids are wrapped around my horsey head every morning and held in place with enough hairpins to hold together the Hoover Dam.

My parents died when I was barely out of nappies, around age twenty. My younger sister and I inherited a two-hundred-year-old farmhouse, and a herd of dairy cows in the mountains of south-western Pennsylvania, four miles outside the quaint little village of Hernia. Dairy cows take a lot of work, so I put my horsey head to work and came up with the brilliant (if I say so myself) idea of selling the cows and turning the farmhouse into a full-board inn.

I named my inn the PennDutch, and styled it to cater to tourists wishing to have an authentic Pennsylvania Dutch experience. My cook was an Amish woman, and her recipes were her own. My décor was simple, because most Amish don't decorate, except with wall calendars. The guest rooms, which were all upstairs, were not air-conditioned, and the only heat they received was radiant heat through the floor from a large wood-burning stove in the parlour. In other words, my establishment was to be a quasi-authentic Pennsylvania Dutch inn.

Then I had another crazy thought, one that turned out to be really lucrative. The impetus for this came from listening to friends recount their tales of trips to Europe. It is as follows: tourists will pay big bucks to endure great discomfort, just as long as they get to view it as a cultural experience. Think about it. Visit just about any cheap chain motel in America, and the rooms will be large, with private baths, an easy chair, a closet with hangers, an ironing board, a coffee maker, quite possibly a small fridge and sometimes a microwave. And of *course* there will be a flat-screen television that receives dozens upon dozens of channels.

Are you having hot flashes? Then crank down the air conditioning. Are you cold-natured, even in the summer? Turn on the heater. Well, it's a good thing that you're in America then, isn't it?

By contrast, the rooms in some European hotels are so small, that you have to plop your suitcase on the bed so that you can open it in order to retrieve a fresh set of sturdy Christian underwear. By then you need to use the loo, so out comes a robe, because you will have to toddle down a dimly lit hallway to use a common toilet. In that horrid little closet, you try to line the seat, but instead of a roll, all you find are little squares of waxed paper, more suitable for hot cross buns than your own. And don't even think about controlling the climate in your room; air conditioning is almost unheard of, and if you complain that it's too cold in October, the manager will tell you that no one, *but no one*, gets heat until November.

But look at the bright side! You're in Europe, seeing European things. So, I reasoned, why not come to the PennDutch, pay exorbitant prices, have a pseudo-authentic Amish experience, and be just as miserable without the jet lag of flying to Paris or London. Even if one was the romantic type, whose wish was to visit Rome in order to get her rear end pinched (not an Amish desire), I could arrange to have them sit on my neighbour Janet's beehive. For a fifty-dollar fee of course. A mere two hundred dollars got one the privilege of mucking out the horse stalls and cow barn. For three hundred dollars one got the privilege of raking out the chicken house and putting down fresh straw. Collecting the eggs cost five bucks apiece. Weeding and hoeing in the vegetable patch was an activity guests would vie for, as it is backbreaking work. The base price was two hundred dollars a day for a single row. On hot days the price went up. And of course guests had to clean their own rooms and communal baths, for an extra fee – or they didn't get to eat. And they would want to eat, that was guaranteed, because the four Amish food groups are lard, sugar, starch and more starch.

Why would any sane person put up with this . . . uh – one might call it nonsense? Because there are people in this world with money to burn, and once word got out about my quirky establishment's existence, my little farm became the *in* inn place – pun intended. The filthy rich and the very famous from all over the world just had to say that they too had endured abuse at my hands, so to speak. To have stayed at the PennDutch Inn was like having gained access to an exclusive club from which the hoi polloi were excluded.

Then the unthinkable happened; someone was murdered in my inn. A normal person might guess that this would put a damper on business, but au contraire. Who knew that there are folks out there that request rooms where murders have happened? And there were plenty of murders. Death seemed to follow me like that fictional woman from Cabot's Cove. I started receiving letters and emails telling me that I was possessed by the Devil, and that *I* was the Grim Reaper. However, my best friend Agnes, who is a nominal Christian at best, came up with a theory that I like much better. Perhaps our omniscient God, knowing that these victims would soon be murdered, had directed them to the PennDutch to die, because He also knew that I was capable of solving their murders.

Frankly, I got too good at solving murders. Some have implied I was suspiciously good solving them. I took umbrage with those sentiments, as it implies that I had a hand in causing these deaths. What's important for you to know is that my reputation for solving murders was renowned throughout the State of Pennsylvania, and even grudgingly accepted as fact by Sheriff Stodgewiggle (he who should have retired many elections ago). That's really all there is to say about me, except maybe that I'm as sweet as brown sugar pie, and I eschew gossip, unless its victims really deserve it, like the three guests who were about to arrive at the PennDutch Inn that particular spring day.

THREE

Christine Landis was the first guest to arrive. She flew into Pittsburgh from her base in Chicago, and then hired a Lexus for the hour-and-a-half trip from the airport to the PennDutch Inn. When she drove up my front driveway, I was busy talking to my tulips.

'You've outdone yourselves this year, girls and boys,' I said. 'I'm so proud of you.'

'Thank you, Mama,' they said, in one voice. 'But we couldn't have done it without your expert care.'

'That's quite true, dears. I amended your soil, supplied fertilizer, and watered as needed, but the Good Lord supplied all of your sunshine – there's no arguing that. Still, I just hate it when folks claim to have *black* thumbs. All they have to do is follow the instructions that come along with each specific plant purchase. It's like cooking, or baking a cake. All one has to do is follow the recipe. Right?'

My tulips had the temerity to twitter. 'Then why are you such a terrible cook, Mama?'

'Hush, dears! Just for that I'm going to cut an armload of you to take inside.'

'Murderess,' my babies cried. 'You'll be committing tulipcide!'

That's when I hear a car door slam, and I looked up and saw the most beautiful woman whom I have ever had the pleasure of gazing upon. Believe me, I don't have a lesbian bone in my body, but if I did, this divine creation could just be the one to sway me in that direction. Dancing is, of course, a sin, but the thought of doing the satin sheet samba with this new arrival was not all repugnant. Au contraire . . . well, I shall stop there, lest I convict myself unnecessarily. However, please permit this short description. She was quite tall, perhaps five foot eight, with an hourglass figure. Her hair was very dark brown, bordering on black, but her flawless skin was milky white. Her face and long limbs exhibited perfect proportion. Her scoop-neck minidress matched her large green eyes. It's been said that I can be critical, but honestly, I couldn't find a thing wrong with her. She didn't have a mole, wart, or even a freckle on her that I could see, and those lips – they were bow-shaped for heaven's sake!

'Get behind me, Satan,' I muttered as I moved to greet her.

Miss Gorgeous grimaced, revealing teeth that either cost a fortune, or else were yet just another proof of how unfair the Dear Lord can be when he deals out our physical attributes. I'm not hopelessly uninformed; I have heard about genetics. But I've known many a handsome couple who've produced some real losers in the looks department, and vice-versa, so I'm pretty sure that the Almighty is still having fun trying out new recipes. Although to what end, I'm not sure. For your information, on a scale of one to ten, I rated this first guest a twenty, and myself a two. At least that's how we stacked up against each other by comparison.

'Hey,' she barked. 'Am I at the right place?'

'Of course, dear,' I said, as I offered her my bony hand, replete with liver spots and raised veins. She did not respond in kind. I may as well have proffered her a dead rat.

'Is this dump the PennDutch Inn?' she snapped.

'Why I never,' I said. 'And who might you be? The Queen of England?'

'No, but as a matter of fact, I happen to be—'

'That was a rhetorical question, dear. The queen would never be so rude.'

'Yeah? Well, how would a doddering old gardener like you know?'

By this time the woman who had just minutes before appeared flawless to me, and who had brought the Devil whispering at my heels, now held no attraction. She might as well have been a tree stump.

'As a matter of fact, dear, I happen to be Magdalena Portulacca Yoder Rosen, owner of the PennDutch Inn. And this is a replica of a genuine Amish farmhouse. Along with the original, which was destroyed by a tornado, the PennDutch has hosted presidents, senators and just about every film star that you could mention. For your information, my hand has always shaken theirs – except for that one rock musician, who always wore a glove, and just one glove, mind you.

'But thank you for not shaking my hand, as I never did like the custom. It is quite absurd, when you think about it. In the olden days, it was a way of showing other folks that one was unarmed. But back then, nobody knew that one was always armed with germs. Much better, I say, to put our two hands together when we greet, like the Thais do, and dip our head in respect to one another. What say you, dear?'

'I say you stop calling me "dear",' the Lexus driver snarled. 'We're not related.'

'Thank the Good Lord for that, dear,' I said calmly.

'Well,' she huffed, 'I may as well state my business, if this is as good as it's going to get. But you better not have lied in your email.'

There is a wrought-iron garden bench, painted white, set in front of those same flame-red tulips that I'd been fixing to murder (their words, not mine). Without further ado I plopped my patooty down with a sigh.

'Identify yourself, please,' I said. 'It helps me keep track of my lies – I mean my fabrications, or prevarications, or misspoken words, or alternative truths. You get the gist.'

'I suppose you think that was funny,' she said, tapping the red sole of a shoe that had a four-inch heel. 'Well, I don't.'

'Actually, I was just being truthful,' I said. 'I seldom out and out lie, because that would be a sin, but I do shade the truth from time to time, depending on the circumstances. By the way, the commandment in the Bible, which is one of the "Big Ten", has to do with not bearing false witness against your neighbour. So don't worry, I won't be dreaming up any lies about you to tell to the Schmucker brothers. In fact, just to show you what a good Christian I am, I'm going to give you a free piece of advice.'

The antagonistic guest had crossed her arms under her bosom and was pushing up her breasts. Those hapless twins were in danger of spilling out of that low-cut neckline, and precipitating a crisis of faith in me, despite how I now felt about the woman.

'Look lady,' I said. 'You still haven't told me your name, but you are either Kathleen Dooley or Christine Landis. Both of you are CEOs of grocery store chains, and both of you have requested that I introduce you to the Schmucker brothers—

'Now don't interrupt me,' I said, waving my garden scissors at the tulips. 'Your lives have been spared today.'

Christine Landis took two steps back on her Christian Louboutin shoes. 'Was that a threat?' she hissed.

'I was speaking to my flowers, *dear*. Now, I was about to say that the Schmucker brothers will not do business with any woman who shows up dressed like a trollop.'

'Like *what*?'

'You know, like a slattern. A slut. To start with, your baby-feeding station should be covered. Your thighs as well. Just to be on the safe side, even your knees. And I hope that you brought some actual shoes, because those things are liable to stab a road apple, or a goat raisin, and I'm not having you bringing the fruits of the farm back into my house.'

'*Road apples* and *goat raisins?* I thought the Schmucker Brothers Sausages were made from pork.'

'You're a city girl, right?'

'Yes. So what?'

'That means you are Christine Landis from Chicago. Well, Miss Landis, a road apple is a lump of horse poop, and goat raisin is poop from a goat. The Schmuckers, being Amish, travel by horse and buggy, and the goat belongs to Solomon Schmucker's youngest son, Benjamin.'

'Ha. So you're telling me that you know the Schmucker brothers personally.'

'I told you that in my email answering your query.'

'Yes, but you're not Amish. I can tell, because you're wearing a flowered dress.'

'My, how observant you are, dear. I know the three Schmucker brothers, and their eleven sisters, because they're my second cousins. My grandfather Melvin Yoder was an Amish man who became Mennonite, but his grandmother was a Schmucker.'

'*Fourteen* Schmucker children?'

I nodded, pleased that she was astonished. 'The Amish have large families. Anyway, like I said, they'll gently turn you away if you show up dressed like the Whore of Babylon. But never fear, my dear, your Auntie Magdalena's here – at a price, of course.'

'You're not my auntie – you're just Looney Tunes. But what's the price?'

'That you start acting like a *mensch*.'

'*You* know the word *mensch*?'

'My husband is Jewish. Now, here's my plan.'

'Miss Yoder,' Christine said in a surprisingly pleasant voice, 'may I join you on that bench? My feet are killing me in these heels.'

'By all means, have a seat. Now, my plan. I'll loan you one of my dresses. To account for your shapely parts, it will have to be one of my maternity dresses – did you know that I gave birth when I was almost fifty? Thank heavens I'm the sentimental type and couldn't bear to give all my *shmattas* away. And you can be glad that the one I saved is not the one that I gave birth in, lying right there on the floor of Yoder's Corner Market, with only Sam Yoder – who is another cousin, by the way – to assist me. But back to your outfit. I'm sure that my sturdy, sensible brogans will be too large for your unreasonably dainty feet, but my daughter keeps a pair of sneakers here for when she comes to visit. They look about right. If they're too big, we can stuff some rags in the toes, and if they're a mite too tight, then just keep your toes curled. The pain shouldn't last more than an hour or two after you take them off.'

Christine jumped to her feet. 'You *are* nuts, Miss Yoder. You're the scariest woman whom I've ever met. I might actually start to like you.'

I jumped to my feet. 'Oh, please, take that back, lest you lead me into sin. Besides, I positively don't like you. I think that you're rude, and you're crude, and I don't understand how you ever got to be head of a large chain of grocery stores.'

'Why, by stabbing people in the back, of course.' She made stabbing motions with her left hand. 'But first I had to play nice, just to get a foot in the door. I had to put up with a lot of road apples and goat raisins on account of my looks, when all I ever wanted was to look like you.'

'Which is *what*, exactly?' I said archly.

'You know, plain.'

'Bless my heart,' I said.

'Yes, it must be awful, but think of *me*? Think what it's like to look like me?'

'I'd cover all my mirrors,' I said.

'Now who's being rude? And you with that funny cap on your head. I thought that you were supposed to be nice.'

'I merely meant that it must be awfully hard for you not to feel vain. If I were you, I'd stay away from mirrors on that account.'

'Ha,' Christine snorted. 'One can't feel vain about something that's God-given. My extreme beauty is my gift to share with the world. They say that "if you have it, then flaunt it". I believe that just by allowing others to gaze upon perfection, I am encouraging them to run to their nearest qualified plastic surgeon and correct what's holding them back from succeeding in life. Take you, for instance, Miss Yoder, I've been studying that sweet potato on your face that passes for a nose. Yes, it would be quite the challenge for the most skilled surgeon, but if you had it carved down to a more manageable size, a couple of years from now you could be standing in front of a proper inn, and not a dump.'

I smiled pleasantly. 'Miss Landis, you are meaner than a bag full of cut snakes. Now follow me, dear, and I'll show you to your room in my dump.'

'Where's the valet?'

'That would be you, dear.'

'Say *what*? You expect me to carry my own luggage?'

'I'm old and have long, twig-like limbs. They could snap in half, and then the bottom halves, along with my hands, would be "gyring and gimbaling in the wabe".'

'You're psychotic, Miss Yoder.'

'I'm still working on it; at the moment I'm merely neurotic. Now, I have six rooms to offer you. Room number six has a view of Stucky Ridge and the famous Lover's Leap. Legend has it that a Lenape Indian maiden waited there for her lover to return from battle for a month, before throwing herself off. That was three hundred years ago. On full moons she is often spotted standing at the edge of the cliff, as if scanning the horizon for signs of her lover's approach.'

'Pfft,' Christine said. 'Only crazy and ignorant people believe in ghosts.'

'Well, then I advise you not to sit on the rocking chair in the parlour.'

'Why?'

'Because it is permanently occupied by an Apparition-American.'

'A what?'

'They object to being called ghosts, Miss Landis. They have

feelings just like us, and they are still Americans. They tend to be folks with unresolved issues who have resisted passing over.'

'The second after I make a deal with the Schmucker brothers, I'm calling the men in white to come take you away in their padded van. But in the meantime, run inside and fetch me a luggage cart.'

'No can do, Your Majesty. All the guest rooms are upstairs, and we have no elevator. We used to have a lift, but it was never very reliable. Shortly after it stopped working altogether, we started noticing a very unpleasant smell, which persisted for a full year. Then quite by accident, we discovered that one of our Japanese guests had been murdered and jammed into the space between the top of the elevator, and the ceiling of the shaft. We were decidedly unamused. Did you know that we have had eight murders here at the inn? Well, I'm sure you did, because it's on my website. For most of my guests these days, that's the main attraction. Fancy that.

'Of course, you didn't come here for a ghost tour,' I said, 'or because you have a morbid fascination with murder; you came to see my cousins about their big sausages. I have arranged for you to tour their entire operation, from the growing pens to the packaging plant, where you will be meeting with Peter Schmucker. He's the brother with the most business acumen.'

Christine Landis held her dainty hands up and covered her petite ears. 'I would rather be murdered in my sleep tonight than to have to put up with your incessant babble for another day.'

'Funny,' I said, 'but my husband says that to me all the time. So, are you going to grab a bag and come in, or do you plan to sleep in your car? Full disclosure, there's been a pack of coyotes yipping around here at night, and one of them is showing signs of being rabid.'

No sooner did I close my mouth on the last word, than the front door opened and out stepped my handsome hunk of a husband. Gabe, the Babester Rosen, had just returned from a week up in Pittsburgh, helping our son-in-law Michael put up siding on his new house. As a result, the Babester was tanned, and of course he, as always, was trim and fit. At seventy-five he still had most of his hair, but it had turned from black to silver. In his light blue shirt, and cream-colored slacks, he cut quite a figure standing on the front porch, one which still made my heart skip a beat, after two and a half decades.

'Who is that dreamboat?' Christine whispered.

'He's my lover,' I said.

'You're lying,' she said.

'Pookey Bear, come here,' I called.

'Okey dokey, Sugar Dumpling,' Gabe said.

My husband knew that he'd been pressed into performing. We never, ever use terms of endearment around strangers – or most of our friends for that matter.

'How did an old bag of bones end up with him?' she whispered.

'Maybe I've got the *it* factor,' I said in a loud nasal voice.

'You sure do, hon,' Gabe said. 'You're *it* for me.' Then laughing, he scooped me up in his strong, tanned arms, while Christine Landis watched open-mouthed.

FOUR

Kathleen Dooley was my next guest to arrive. I was upstairs showing a disgusted Christine Landis to her room at the time.

'Remember, Miss Landis,' I said, 'there is no electricity up here, as this floor is authentically Amish. At dusk you'll be given an oil lamp, but if you want to charge your devices, you'll have to do that either in the dining room, or else in the parlour.'

'This place is a hellhole,' she said.

'I'll thank you to not swear,' I said, and clattered downstairs and out the front door.

Kathleen Dooley had driven a hybrid rental car. My first impression was that she was the antithesis of Christine Landis. Miss Dooley was short, with a round face and apple cheeks, framed by a mop of curly blonde ringlets. A stub of nose just barely managed to support a pair of enormous plastic, black-rimmed glasses. In summary, the theme of Miss Dooley's face was 'circles'.

When she saw me, Kathleen Dooley practically tumbled from her car with excitement. Then she bounded towards me like a Labrador puppy.

'Miss Yodder?'

'It's actually, Yoder,' I said. 'But with enthusiasm like yours, you may call me anything – just not late to dinner.'

Miss Dooley howled with laughter at my lame joke. What would she do, I wondered, when I trotted out some good material?

'Miss Yodeller then, it is,' she said and giggled.

I grimaced. 'How about you use my married name, and call me Mrs Rosen.'

'Mrs Raisin! I love that. Do you bake much, Mrs Raisin?'

'Uhm, do you have a hearing problem, Miss Dolly?'

My serious question elicited a torrent of laughter. 'Nah, I just like to kid around with strangers – kinda puts everyone at ease. But I'll stop now if you want. Hey, nifty looking place you have here. Are you an authentic Conservative Mennonite woman, or is that a costume that you're wearing?'

'I'm as authentic as they come,' I said.

'Cool.'

'Are *you* an authentic Bostonian, and is that accent really yours?'

Kathleen Dooley laughed delightedly. 'It's really mine, of course. Who needs the letter "r" we say. And you know, the Brits obviously agree with us. They've tossed that poor letter right out of the English language – well, unless it is used at the front of a word. But I'm afraid that's the only nice thing that I can say about a British accent.'

'You take that back, dear,' I said hotly. 'There are *many* British accents, and some of them are even tolerable. Prince William speaks lovely English, as do the BBC News presenters.'

'Oh, I'm so sorry, Miss Yoder, I didn't mean to offend you. It was something my mother always said. Maybe because she was a direct descendant of one of the Boston Tea Party men.'

'All is forgiven,' I said. 'Just so you know, I am an avid Anglophile, a defender of all things British – except for Marmite. I will not put up with anything negative said about my beloved "second country". I would move there in a heartbeat, if it were not for the fact that they have put a moratorium on accepting "raving lunatics" – that's what their consulate in Philadelphia said in answer to my query. If only I had known that the ambassador and his wife were really my guests that awful weekend two years ago, when there was a double homicide, and not just Mr and Mrs Smith from Washington, DC.'

Kathleen Dooley beamed. 'Oh Miss Yoder, you are the joy of joys! Your zany whackadoodle nature is going to make staying here an awesome experience. May I give you a giant bear hug?'

Without waiting for an answer she ploughed into me. Had it not been for my shoes, each the size of a train caboose, she would have bowled me over. Warm bags of dough encased me – perhaps I should say her arms encased me, lest I sound judgemental. Nonetheless, I who despise handshaking for its intimacy (not to mention the transference of microbes), was at my wits' end to find myself wrapped tightly in sweaty flesh that belonged to someone other than my husband. And so tightly did those arms encircle my waist and solar plexus that I could hardly breathe, which meant I could hardly speak. So what is a Magdalena without speech, I ask? She might as well be dead.

Miss Dooley finally bothered to glance up. 'Goodness gracious me,' she said cheerily. 'Look at you! You're all blue in the face.'

'Air,' I gasped. 'Air!'

'Hair? Yes, it's my real hair, and my real hair colour,' Miss Dooley said. 'Born blonde, stayed blonde, and hope to die blonde – that's with an "I" and not a "Y".' She giggled, but mercifully released me.

'Miss Dooley, dear,' I said quietly, 'please don't you ever touch me again.'

'Oh, no!' she said, with a slight whine in her voice. 'You're not one of those, are you?'

'I'm not sure what you mean, but I probably am. I'm not one for exchanging atoms with strangers. Your embrace involved more bare flesh than I was subjected to on my first wedding night.'

Kathleen Dooley stepped back, but not out of pity or disgust, as some have shown. To the contrary, she wanted to get a photo of this Mennonite anomaly.

'Isn't that somewhat unusual for a woman of your faith?' she asked excitedly.

'Indeed it is,' I said. 'But I wasn't some hussy like someone . . . well, never you mind.'

'No, no,' Kathleen Dooley said, 'you can't do that to me! Whose name were you about to say?'

'Nope. I can't say. I'm a good Christian woman who doesn't gossip. But keep your eyes peeled the next couple of days. You might run into her, and it might even be on my impossibly steep stairs. Speaking of which, do you have a lot of luggage?'

'Tons,' Miss Dooley said, and giggled. 'I suffer from the "can't decides". And since I can't decide which clothes to wear, I save time by bringing virtually all of them. Of course, I left the winter things at home, which is why I didn't say "literally" all of them.'

'Noted, and appreciated,' I said. 'I hate it when people misuse "literally". So three cheers for you. The bad news is that you're going to have to act as your own Sherpa. Your room is up some wickedly steep stairs, which sound like a groaning old man, because we have no elevator.'

'No problem,' she said. 'I climbed Mount Kilimanjaro last year, and I had to carry my boyfriend's pack as well as my own.'

I have a sizable proboscis and can sometimes actually sniff out a liar. It didn't seem possible that this dumpling of a woman could climb Stucky Ridge, which rises barely a thousand feet above our valley. How she managed to lug even her arms up nineteen-thousand-foot-plus Kilimanjaro, much less the rest of her and two back packs, seemed beyond the realm of possibility. Nonetheless, I didn't pick up the scent of falsehood emanating from her, so I let it go.

'I'm giving you room number six, since my first guest passed on it when she saw that the wall colour didn't suit her skin tone. Anyway, room number six is the one with the view of Stucky Ridge and Lover's Leap. Full story upon request. However, to see the Ridge you will have to stand on a chair, with one foot on the windowsill, and lean out as far as you can. You will find a rope, which is pre-tied to your bedstead, and printed instructions. I suggest that you tie the other end of the rope around your, uh . . . hmm . . . middle portion. Don't worry too much about falling; the garden shed, which is directly below, has three mattresses piled on its roof to prevent one from breaking too many bones.'

Kathleen beamed and rubbed her hands together. 'Oh, goody. This sounds like so much fun. You know, I was a tightrope-walker when I was in my early twenties.'

'Get out of town and back,' I said, not sounding at all like a normal Mennonite woman. I have many guests, with their very different backgrounds to blame for my uncharacteristic way of speaking.

'Well, you see,' she said, 'I had a difficult home life, so I dealt with it by running away and joining a circus. I have always been short' – she giggled – 'but back then in my teens I was skinny as well. Not slim like you, Miss Yoder – I mean really skinny. So first I trained to be a contortionist. I was pretty good too; I got to the point where I could bend my body backwards and wrap my legs around my neck, and then start knitting with my toes.'

'Get behind me Satan,' I hissed. 'Stop right there.'

'Well, that's exactly what I had to do to stay ahead of the competition. But then the circus hired a sister act from China that was even better than me. These women played ping pong with their knees over their shoulders, and then finished their act with one sister – blindfolded, mind you – shooting a kumquat off another sister's head with a bow and arrow.'

'I will pray for them as well. Do you remember their names?'

'Miss Yoder, you're a hoot, you know that? As I was about to tell you, the circus had an opening for someone to be shot out of their cannon. The last woman landed wrong and broke her neck. So I volunteered, but I didn't get the job right away. First I had to bulk up – with muscle, that is. One can't be as pliable as a wet noodle when they come shooting out of a cannon at seventy miles per hour. So I started a weight-lifting program – which the circus strongman oversaw – and I ate tons of meat for protein. Meanwhile I was back to scooping poop and praying that someone else wouldn't come along to fill the human cannonball slot. But guess what?'

'You accidentally hit your head with the poop scooper, came to your senses, and decided that being shot out of a cannon was not the life for you.'

Kathleen Dooley's china-blue eyes bored through the giant lenses of her spectacles. 'What are you? A mind reader?'

'No, I'm just not as stupid as I look, dear. You're obviously a brilliant woman, or you wouldn't have been able to start your own company at age twenty-two, and make it the success that it is today.'

'How perceptive of you, Miss Yoder. So, although the circus provided us with an adequate diet, it didn't supply the variety that some of us desired. Therefore, if we were holed up in a place for two days or longer, we would drive into town and shop for food that we kept in the small refrigerators in our trailers. I generally bought already cooked or prepared meats like cold cuts. But breakfast was my favourite meal, and although the circus provided it, they never served sausage, which I love, only bacon. So I started buying sausages and frying them myself, and eating in. And I ate, and I ate, and soon I had enough pounds on me to become cannon fodder.'

'Congratulations, dear. Now may we go inside?'

'Oh, not just yet; I'm not done with the story. So anyway, because my natural blonde hair was cut in a pageboy style, and I had round rosy cheeks, someone suggested to the circus owner that I looked like your typical Dutch girl. Do you think so?'

'I have no idea.'

'Well, that didn't stop the owner from billing me as the Flying Dutch Girl. And I was a big hit, I'm telling you. I became famous in at least three states. But there was just one problem: I couldn't stop eating sausages for breakfast – I mean it got to the point that I ate myself right out of a job.'

'I'm sorry,' I said. Chalk up another white lie in my column of less regrettable sins.

'Oh, don't be,' Kathleen Dooley said. 'My wheels are always turning.'

'Oh, do tell,' I said, with all the enthusiasm with which I would beg my preacher to deliver a second, hour-long, sermon.

'Well, it's this,' Kathleen Dooley said. 'It occurred to me that I wasn't the only sausage-loving fanatic – although truth be told, I can't stand to look a sausage in the face now.' She giggled. 'Not that they even have faces. Anyway, I haven't touched one for years. But that didn't stop me from coming up with the idea of getting into the sausage-making business. Of course, the problem was that I didn't have any money—'

I held up a large but shapely hand. 'Really Miss Dooley, I don't need to know every detail about your life.'

'But you're such a good listener, Miss Yoder. Do you know how rare it is to find someone like you? Your children are very lucky to have you for their mother.'

'My *children*?'

'Oh come now, Miss Yoder, don't play coy with me. You're famous – or infamous. Whatever. Your charming inn, and you, have made tabloid headlines more times than Madonna. Anyway, I'm going to be your new best friend.'

'No, you're not,' I said. 'Agnes Miller has always been my best friend, and we're going to die on the same day. We pinkie swore that when we were ten, even though swearing was against our religion.'

'Then I'll be your second-best friend,' she said.

'When the cow jumps over the moon, dear, and the dish runs away with the spoon.'

Kathleen Dooley giggled. 'I get it. You're the dish, and I'm the spoon, and we're going to run away together. Is that it?'

'In a hog's ear, dear.'

The deluded woman was not in the least offended. 'That is such a cute, and oh such an appropriate, expression, coming from a farmer like you!'

'But I'm not a farmer! I'm an innkeeper, and you're a—'

That's when the Good Lord shut my mouth by sending yet a third guest barrelling up my driveway in a sleek black rental car. Since my driveway is gravel, these pesky rock chips sprayed onto my lawn the length of the road. Boy, did that raise my hackles.

'OK, if we can move this along, I'll upgrade you to room number three,' I said in desperation. 'It's the only room with an *en suite*. You are your own porter, dear, and don't complain. You may be short, but you could probably tote King Kong up my impossibly steep stairs with those ham hock arms of yours – no offense intended, or taken, I'm sure, given that you think the world of me.'

'But Miss Yoder—'

'Now run along, dear, unless you would like to see me scold this latest arrival.'

'You bet I would!'

'All right, but stand back, because this could get ugly.'

By then the guest was standing right in front of me and holding out a business card. I glanced at the card but didn't take it. I only flirt with germs; I don't care to get intimately acquainted with them. Who knew where that card had been, or what diseases its owner possessed? I didn't know anything about the owner except that he wanted to meet the Schmucker brothers. In fact, he was adamant about it, and willing to pay my exorbitant prices.

'Is that your real name?' I asked as politely as possible.

Ducky Limehouse sighed as he took back the card. 'Actually, it's Drake, ma'am. But I've gone by Ducky for as long as I can remember. You may call me by whichever name you wish.'

'I will stick with Mr Limehouse for now. Welcome to the PennDutch Inn. You will be in room number four. The shared bathroom is across the hall. We don't have a porter, so that is you, I'm afraid, and after you've settled in, report back to me in the kitchen for yard duty.'

'Yard duty, ma'am?'

'Someone has to rake up all the gravel that you scattered into my lawn while driving up here like a maniac.'

'I'm very sorry, ma'am. Where might I find a rake?'

I sized the man up before answering. Ducky Limehouse was a young man, possibly in his early thirties, who looked like your stereotypical Englishman. Lest you ask me what your typical English male looks like, just watch any English film, any English television series, and you will find yourself exclaiming, 'There, that man! That's what I mean. That's what an Englishman looks like, and that's exactly what I meant.' That's what Ducky looked like, maybe even more so because he wore a bowler.

However, he did not sound like an English male. He didn't speak with any of the myriad of English accents. This young man originally hailed from our Deep South. Plus, it wasn't just his accent that gave his origins away; he was far too polite by today's standards – setting aside his driving, of course.

I favoured the young man with a motherly smile. 'I will provide the rake in due course,' I said. 'But first I would like to ask you a few questions.'

'Certainly, ma'am.'

'Your license plate would have me believe that you are from the State of Maryland, but your accent tells me that you are from – let me guess – Charleston, South Carolina?'

Ducky recoiled slightly. 'Whoa, you *are* good! How could you tell?'

'I have an ear for regional accents,' I said, 'even if I do say so myself. Just so you know, you needn't attach a "ma'am" to every verbal exchange with me.'

'Yes, ma'am,' Ducky said.

'Oy vey,' I said. 'It's going to be a long week.'

No sooner were those words uttered than the fourth guest drove up in what looked like a hearse. What's more, the tall, slender man who stepped out was dressed in black and was as pale as if he'd spent his entire life in a sealed tomb. He'd pre-registered online, so that I knew his age to be eighty-one, which explained his snow-white hair. Even from some distance I could see that the irises of his icy blue eyes were rimmed with black. They reminded me of a husky dog I had once owned.

I willed myself to be non-judgemental, and approached him with a crooked smile. He in turn seemed to approach me shyly.

'Welcome to the PennDutch,' I said. 'You must be Terence Tazewell.'

'Please, call me Terry,' he said. 'Also, I hope that you overlook my means of transportation. When I flew into the Bedford executive airport, they were out of rental cars, so this was all they could come up with.'

'You have your own plane?' I asked.

'Yes, ma'am.'

'Well, as long as I'm being nosy,' I said, 'how did you come up with the name of Guzzle 'n Gorge for your chain of restaurants?' The name of his business had been on his registration form.

'That was easy,' Terry said. 'I simply observed how much food others ate when I went out to eat with my Evelyn. The serving sizes these days are what would feed a family of four when I was growing up. And then in addition to this amount of food, folks guzzle down sugary drinks from enormous containers – all this before ordering dessert.

'So, I figured why not parody this bizarre behaviour so that people would stop lying to themselves. They are *not* watching their weight. The fact that a salad comes with the mountain of fat and carbs they consume, means nothing.'

'Yes,' I said, 'but having your patrons eat their meals from plastic troughs, and guzzle their drinks from hoses – isn't that demeaning?'

'Nah.'

'Well, I heard that your waiters dress in bib overalls and straw hats, and make the customers squeal before they take their orders. Is that true? If so, surely that's demeaning.'

'Again, no,' Terry said. 'Our customers obviously love it. I started with one restaurant in South Bend, Indiana, and today we have one hundred and forty-four restaurants nationwide.'

'So you're here now hoping to work out an exclusive deal with the Schmucker brothers, whereby you get to serve their pork sausages to your hoggy patrons?' I mused aloud.

'That's exactly what I'm going to do,' Terry Tazewell said.

'Somehow I don't think so,' Kathleen Dooley said quietly. I'd forgotten that she was even standing there.

'Ignore her, dear,' I said to Terry Tazewell. 'You will all have a chance to make your pitch. Now just one or two housekeeping details. You wrote on your registration form that you're a vegetarian.'

'That's right,' Terry Tazewell said. 'I read somewhere that they put everything but the squeal into a sausage. I also revere life too much to consume something that once was aware of its surroundings.'

'Hmm,' I said. 'Yet you have no compunction about serving these animals, whose life force you revere, to your patrons?'

'Aren't we all hypocrites in one way or another, Miss Yoder?' he said.

'Speak for yourself, dear,' I said. 'Most of our menus derive from traditional Amish recipes, and the Amish recognize four food groups: sugar, lard, starch and more starch. However, for a mere surcharge of one hundred dollars a meal, our cook will attempt to prepare victuals that have never come into contact with the remains of a living, breathing creature.'

'A hundred dollars extra for vegetarian?' Terry said. 'Well, in that case, I'll happily go carnivore for a week. If it was good enough for old granddad, then it's good enough for me. He, he, he.'

'That's the spirit,' I said.

'Is there anything else that I should know?' Terry asked.

'Just that you'll be staying in room number one. It's the only room in which a murder has never been committed.'

Terry smiled. 'Yet,' he said.

FIVE

Since my kinswoman Freni Hostetler's death ten years ago, I've been employing a Central Conference Mennonite cook. Her faith permits her the use of an automobile. In many respects she is quite modern, although she too believes that the Bible is the word of God and that baptizing infants is illogical. Like me she believes that violence against a fellow human being is strictly forbidden.

Thank heavens that Anna Weaver is not only a skilled cook, but she can think fast on her feet. She'd been prepared to cook vegetarian meals, per Terry's registration information, but now she didn't have to make that accommodation. She didn't even blink when I informed her of the menu change. If anything, she seemed a bit relieved.

At any rate, with dinner in the capable hands of Anna, I was free to bathe and dress for dinner, undisturbed in the master suite of our remodelled facsimile of a genuine, historic Pennsylvania farmhouse. At least part of it stood on the original foundation of the house built by my five times great-grandfather Jacob 'the strong' Yoder. It wasn't my fault that a tornado blew the original house away with me in it, and that I landed with my face planted in a cow patty. Following the tornado, the men in my little village of Hernia reached out to me by gathering up as much salvageable wood as possible, and reconstructed a remarkable replica of the two-hundred-and-thirty-year-old house. About my face, they were able to do nothing.

'Gabe,' I said, as I dressed for dinner, 'what do you think of our guests?'

'May I take the Fifth Amendment?'

'So you don't incriminate yourself? That can only mean that you couldn't take your eyes off Christine Landis's baby-feeders. That's what they're meant for, darling – feeding babies – and she doesn't even have one. So get your mind out of the gutter. Didn't you find her personality abrasive?'

'I'm afraid that my poor male mind didn't get around to that,' my husband said.

'Oh my word! What am I going to do with you? You're seventy-five, for crying out loud. Aren't you supposed to start slowing down in that department?'

The Babester shrugged. 'But I hope that you realize that from the day I first saw you, you have always been my *numero uno.*'

'Ditto, dear, but how would you like it if I implied that I found Ducky Limehouse to be the cat's pyjamas?'

'I'd say that you needed to have your eyes checked. Also, that you've been lying to me about your age, since that expression is from the 1920s. And if you were to rob the cradle, it would be someone like Toy Graham, whom you've been drooling over ever since he moved to Hernia. Too bad for you that he's gay.'

I grabbed a pillow off the bed and threw it at my husband. 'Even if Toy was as straight as a yardstick, I would never, ever consider cheating on you with Toy, and you know it.'

'Likewise,' the Babester said. 'I would never, ever consider cheating on you with Toy, either.'

I threw another pillow at Gabe, and he threw it back. Then I threw two pillows, and he threw three pillows, and then I tackled him (he was a real pushover). Before we knew it, we found ourselves in a situation in which we were going to have to put our dinner clothes on a second time, so we decided to put it to good use. By the time we'd both showered, dressed, and I'd fixed my hair again, all four guests were waiting anxiously in the dining room.

'You said that dinner was at six o'clock sharp,' Christine Landis snapped, 'and here it is already half past.'

I smiled sweetly at the gorgeous woman from Chicago, who was now dressed in a low-cut red number. Her assets were threatening to tumble out at any moment, and if they did, the Babester's eyeballs would tumble out of his head and roll around on the floor. If that happened, I wouldn't be averse to stepping on them – accidentally, of course.

'Miss Landis,' I said archly, 'I also said that you need to find something to wear other than your "come-hither" frocks.'

'I thought that was only to visit the Amish,' she said in a whiny voice.

'Well, I'm amending that rule to include anytime you're near my husband,' I said.

'Come on, Mags,' Gabe said, from the other end of the table, 'she's a grown woman; she should be able to dress the way that she wants.'

'That's right, Mags,' Christine Landis said.

Oh, did that ever hike my hackles. It hiked them right up into my armpits. Only Gabe, my best friend Agnes, and my sister Susannah, are allowed to call me Mags. Close friends, and long-term acquaintances may call me Magdalena, but everyone else needs to use a surname. And I still don't understand how it is that doctors and dentists are allowed to call me by my given name. On my next visit to Dr Lowenstein, I wouldn't dream of addressing him as "Michael".

'Look, toots,' I said to Christine, 'unless you've shared my marital bed, slept in my hand-me-down crib, or pinkie swore with me in the first grade, you have no right to call me Mags. You got that?'

My tone of voice must have conveyed my seriousness, because she nodded.

'Well then,' I said, 'you, my dear Miss Landis, will sit at my right, and Mr Limehouse will sit at your right. Mr Tazewell, you will sit at my left, and Miss Dooley, you will sit at his left. Shall we be seated?'

After a bit of whining, snorting and chair scooting, I continued. 'Let us all fold our hands, and bow our heads, while we thank the Good Lord for the food we are about to receive.'

'I most certainly will not!' Miss Landis said.

My eyes popped open. 'What? Are you an atheist? Or an Episcopalian?'

'I am an *adult*, that's what I am. I will not be told when, or how, I should pray.'

Mr Limehouse cleared his throat quietly. 'I would have to agree, ma'am. I am an Episcopalian, by the way, and I always say grace before meals. But I do it voluntarily.'

'That may be, dear, but this is a traditional Mennonite inn, so you are supposed to be following *my* customs.'

'She means she wants you to follow her orders,' Gabe said with a chuckle. Perhaps he *meant* to defuse the tension in the room, but it didn't matter, because he had only added to it. Case in point: my folded hands nearly shattered.

'How about I say grace?' Kathleen Dooley piped up.

'Excellent suggestion,' Gabe said, and winked at me.

Without further ado Kathleen began. 'Rub-a-dub-dub. Thanks for the grub. Yay God!'

Christine snickered, Ducky laughed, and even Gabe, my Jewish husband, smiled. Well, that did it; their rude behaviour had just pushed one button too many. This bunch was in for a bit of religious instruction.

Every married woman knows that her husband only starts to listen after she's spoken her fifth word. God, of course, is not a man, but He is *male*, as the Bible states over and over again. I'm not saying that God waits until the sixth word of our prayers until He starts to listen, but it has occurred to me, that the very first Mennonites might have believed that to be the case. My theory is based on the fact that our prayers tend to meander on and on, until the food gets cold, the children have started to fight, and the elderly have fallen asleep. Along about the time that Great Grandpa slides underneath the dinner table, the person praying might wrap things up by saying, '. . . and Lord, we just ask you to heal Uncle Edwin's gout, and also bless this food to the nourishment of our bodies, and bless the hands who prepared it.'

Thus it was that I launched into the mother of all prayers. In it I thanked the Good Lord for all the wonders of nature, listing every National Park and its attractions. I prayed that God would heal the sick, and mentioned the names of everyone on the prayer list from my church, as well as other people in the village who were doing poorly. And you can bet that national and world events were a no-brainer. Of course, I would have been remiss if I hadn't prayed for everyone at the table, including myself, and that's who I started with when I circled back to home.

'Lord, I just ask for the wisdom to deal with these – uh – irreverent children of yours. Fill their hearts with the peace that I have found in this, the twilight of my life. I especially lift up in prayer my dear husband Gabe, who still has not been saved, and when he dies will burn forever in a lake of fire – your words, Lord, not mine. And I ask your blessings on the enigmatic young man from Charleston with his charming accent, and that Kathleen Dooley, wow, what a firecracker! Watch out for her, Lord. She's either led one heck of a life, or else she's an even better liar than I am. I also ask that you bless Terry Tazewell, even though he mocks the corpulent with his feeding troughs – although actually, Lord, we have become a nation of shamefully obese people who are perfect candidates for diabetes. Now, about Christine Landis. Lord, thou didst bestow upon her an uncommon amount of beauty, but Lord she doth comport herself like a trollop. Like a hoochy mama, as my sons would say. But thanks for the food. Amen.'

I was going to give God a better thank you, but by then everyone, except Ducky, was yapping at me. It was a wonder that I heard the gentle tapping at the swinging door that opened to the kitchen. The tapper, by the way, was on the dining room side.

'Can it!' I called sternly. 'We have an intruder!'

There are friends and neighbours, and then there are special people who have permission to knock on one's door, perhaps holler 'yoo-hoo', but need not wait for a response before entering. Such a person was Toy Graham, our town's chief of police for twenty-five years. By now Toy is like the much younger brother I never had, but I will admit that when he first arrived in Hernia, population 2,387 and two-thirds (Bonnie Stehly is six months pregnant), I developed a crush on him. And who wouldn't have? Toy is the most handsome man that God ever created. Fortunately for me, the Good Lord also created him gay, so shortly after he came out of the closet, I was able to rid myself of my lascivious thoughts. And also fortunately for me, I had not shared those thoughts with anyone except for Agnes Miller, my very best friend, and since she also shared those thoughts, our mutual secret was safe. Although – come to think of it now – I'm married, and Agnes isn't. Oh well, what's done is done.

In any event, there Toy stood, by the door, in all his handsomeness regarding us with an amused smile on his face. The first person to notice him, other than myself, was Christine Landis.

'Oh, hello,' she called, and gave her shoulders a little shake, which set her bosom to quivering like twin Jell-O moulds.

'He's not your type, dear,' I hissed.

'Every man's my type,' she hissed back.

'He's gay,' I mouthed.

'You're lying,' she hissed.

'Hey,' I said, 'no fair hissing without an "s". Only bigshot writers like Harlan Coben get to do that.'

'Mags,' Gabe said, with unnecessary sharpness, 'perhaps you'd like to make introductions.'

I smiled at my husband, but with my mouth only. 'Certainly, dear. Everyone, this is our chief of police, Captain Toy Graham. Captain, the lady seated at Gabe's right is the lovely Miss Kathleen Dooley. Beside her is the successful restaurateur, Terry Tazewell. At Gabe's left is the handsome Mr Duckworth Limehouse – from Charleston. And that leaves Miss Christine Landis who was ogling you just a moment ago.'

'Mags!' Gabe said again.

'Good evening, ladies and gentlemen,' Toy said. 'Please, go right on with your dinner; I'm here to see Mrs Rosen.'

'Mrs Rosen?' Christine Landis whispered across the table. 'Who is she?'

'She is me,' I said. 'By the way, whispering will profit you naught in this house. I can hear a fly fart at fifty paces.'

'More like a hundred and fifty,' Toy said. 'Magdalena – I mean, Miss Yoder . . . dang, I mean Mrs Rosen – has the keenest hearing north of the Mason-Dixon Line.'

'Look, Toy,' Gabe said, 'it's all right if you call Magdalena Miss Yoder in front of guests. That's how they know her through their emails, and it doesn't hurt my feelings any. I'm a big boy.'

'A very *big* boy,' Christine Landis said.

'*My* very big boy,' I said. 'We haven't started eating yet. Cook hasn't even brought the dishes in from the kitchen, so why don't you join us? We're having pot roast with potatoes, carrots and onions for us carnivores. In addition, we have baby spring peas, as well as a mixed green salad with oil and vinegar dressing, and two kinds of freshly baked homemade rolls. Also, for dessert we're having shoo-fly pie, made from a recipe that's been in my family for two hundred years. Oh, and that hallmark of every Mennonite home, a Jell-O salad.'

'Thank you kindly,' Toy said. 'I accept your invitation, but then after dinner I need to see you privately.'

All eyes turned to Gabe.

'It's perfectly fine with me,' my husband said. 'I trust my wife.'

Toy chuckled. 'And I'm happily married. My husband Jimmy

just happens to be in Harrisburg for a couple of days. He's arguing a case before the Pennsylvania Supreme Court.'

'How's that going, by the way?' Gabe said.

Not waiting for Toy to answer, Christine Landis piped up rudely. 'Sheriff, do you know the Schmucker brothers personally?'

Toy shrugged his shoulders helplessly, not knowing who to answer first.

'Go ahead,' Gabe said. 'Answer her question.'

'Well, for starters, I'm not the sheriff, that position is occupied by Sheriff Stodgewiggle in Bedford, our county seat. I'm a police officer.'

'You are the *chief* of police,' I said.

Christine Landis shot me the evil eye. 'OK, but do you know the Schmucker brothers? That's all I wanted to know. Heavens to Betsy, I wasn't trying to get your badge number.'

'Yes,' Toy said calmly. 'Hernia is a close-knit village, and I reckon that everyone in Hernia knows at least one of the Schmucker brothers. They didn't always used to make sausages; for years they ran a smithy on Main Street where the Amish got their horses shod. Anyway, I know them, but not as well as your hostess, who is kin to them.'

'So she says,' Christine Landis quipped.

I prayed that the Good Lord would forgive the thoughts that were running through my head. If put into action, those thoughts would start five hundred years' worth of ancestors spinning in their graves, causing earthquakes both in America and in Switzerland.

'Mags, ring the bell,' Gabe said helpfully.

So I did, and immediately Anna pushed open the swinging door, and entered carrying a huge platter of sliced pot roast surrounded by cooked vegetables. I'm quite sure that she had been eavesdropping, but I would have done the same thing if I had been in her place.

'Ha!' Christine Landis said accusingly. 'The so-called Pennsylvania Dutch have servants. That poor twig of a girl looks like she's about to snap in half under the weight of that platter.'

'I ain't no regular servant neither,' Anna said, placing the platter, which was admittedly rather heavy, directly in front of me. 'I'm what these rich folks call an indentured servant. My pappy back in Portsmouth, England couldn't pay his taxes, so the Crown sent me to the colonies to work off his debt. My employers take turns whipping me – twice on weekdays, and three times on Sundays.'

Everyone laughed except for Christine Landis. She shot me the evil eye, as if it was my fault that Anna Weaver had a mind of her own and wasn't afraid to speak it at the tender age of twenty-seven.

'Anna is a real pistol,' I said when the laughter had died down. 'Some day you might even be able to catch her act at open mic nights at the Crooked Goose over in Pittsburgh. Now run along, Anna, dear, and bring all the other goodies in – except for the pie, of course.'

'Yes, ma'am,' Anna said. 'But I'll shoo all the flies away from the shoo-fly pie, except for those flies whose wings you've torn off. They're in too much pain—'

'Run along, Anna,' I said. '*Vamoose*, dear.'

Out of the corner of my eye I could see Christine Landis smirking.

SIX

As soon as Toy swallowed his last bite of shoo-fly pie, he asked if we could talk in the parlour. Privately. I try to be a good Christian woman, but I will be the first to admit that I often miss the mark. That said, as I left the dining room, I looked behind me and smirked at Christine Landis. Unfortunately, that meant that I also saw Gabe's chastising look. Overall, it seems that my Jewish husband is a better Christian than I am.

Of course, once in the parlour we had to greet Granny Yoder. She's actually my great-grandmother, and she's an Apparition-American, which is now the preferred nomenclature for ghosts. Most people can neither hear nor see her, but both Toy and I are able to do so. Gabe cannot. Our son, Jacob, can. Granny refuses to acknowledge that she has passed, which is why she remains earthbound in the rocking chair in which she died. Apparition-Americans contradict my religious belief, but hey, we're all bundles of contradiction, aren't we?

'Magdalena,' Toy said, with sudden urgency, 'it's about Agnes.'

'Agnes Miller? My best friend since we shared a bassinet? My sister from a different mister?'

'The one and the same,' Toy said sombrely.

'She didn't choke on a ham sandwich, did she?'

'She had Schmucker Brothers Breakfast Sausages for lunch.'

'She didn't!' I said.

'That branch of the Miller family has always been two eggs short of a dozen,' Granny said. 'Your friend Agnes would buy a lame horse to pull her buggy to church if you weren't there to stop her.'

'Granny, for your information, my friend Agnes rides to church in a horseless carriage. No flesh and blood horses, lame or otherwise, are involved.'

'Does it go faster than fifteen miles per hour?' Granny asked. 'Your great-granddaddy had a horseless carriage and talked me into getting into it. But just once. When that cursed thing got to going twenty miles per hour, I thought my hair was going to rip right off my head. I'm telling you, Magdalena, those things are of the Devil.'

'You've been heard, Granny. Now Toy and I are going to get down to business.' I turned my attention back to the handsome police chief. 'Is there more to your story?' I asked.

Toy nodded. 'You know Erma Burkholder, the widow who lives behind her. Well, old Erma gets kind of lonely and spends some of her time spying on her neighbours. It wouldn't be so bad, I guess, if she did it surreptitiously, but Erma uses a huge pair of black binoculars, and does her snooping right at her property line. Sometimes she even steps over it. Neighbours on all sides have complained.'

'I know,' I said. 'Poor Agnes wants to sit on her back patio in her pyjamas reading the morning paper, but feels like she's being watched, like she's an animal in a zoo exhibit.'

Granny grunted. 'A woman should wear a *gown*, and over it a robe.'

'And some women should stay out of other people's conversations, dear,' I said.

'Why, Magdalena Portulacca Yoder! If your mother was alive, she would show you the business side of a hairbrush for talking like that to your last living ancestor.'

'Well, that's just the thing, Granny, you're not living, are you? I'd think you were just a figment of my imagination – or perhaps a mental illness of some sort – if it weren't for the gentleman sitting next to me here, who also happens to see and hear you.'

'What gentleman? I don't see anyone.'

'Huh?'

'Gotcha,' Granny said, and cackled.

'Let's just ignore her,' I said to Toy. 'I assume that you didn't come out here to tell me in person that Agnes's big faux pas was to eat breakfast at lunch.'

Toy smiled weakly. 'Right. It is worse. After lunch Agnes was sitting on her patio playing solitaire—'

'Playing cards is a sin,' Granny said.

'Face cards are forbidden,' I said. 'Other cards are allowed. Go on.'

'Anyway, so Agnes looks up and spies those big black binoculars pointed her way, and guess what she did?'

I gasped. 'She didn't!'

'No,' Toy said, reading my simple mind. 'It didn't involve fingers. *Guess.*'

'She stuck out her tongue,' I said.

'Oh, you Mennonites, and your kind and cloistered ways. She got up and mooned the woman.'

'Uhm – she did?'

'Magdalena, you don't know what that means, do you?'

'Should I?'

'Now you should. Your very best friend, who was wearing pyjamas with an elastic waistband, pulled the bottoms down, along with her underwear, and exposed her naked buttocks to Erma Burkholder. The act of doing that is called mooning.'

I was shocked to the core. Having raised three children, one would think that I would have heard that word before, but I'm quite certain that I hadn't. Not only did such an act shock and repulse me, but for a nanosecond, I had a vision in my mind of what Agnes's bare buttocks might have looked like, and then the term 'moon' suddenly made sense. On top of that, for a full second – or three – I thought that it was an entirely appropriate response that served that nosey Erma Burkholder right.

'Oy vey,' I moaned, using one of my husband's Yiddish expressions. 'What did you say to Erma?'

'I lied to her, that's what. Actually, first I asked her if she'd been standing on Agnes's lawn. And I stared directly into her beady brown eyes when I asked her that.'

'And?' I said.

'"Maybe just a foot or two", she said. Then I took great pleasure in telling her that was officially trespassing, but I lied when I said that by viewing Agnes's bare bottom through her binoculars, she had engaged in an official act of Interpersonal Pornography, Section two, Article eleven, and as a consequence I would have to confiscate her binoculars.'

'Then what?' I said.

'Quit interrupting the poor boy,' Granny said. 'You're like a child with a bedtime story.'

Toy flashed Granny a grateful smile which, frankly, irritated me a mite. 'Then I lied even further and told Erma Burkholder that under the above act she was compelled to keep what she'd done and seen to herself. If she gossiped, she could be subject to prosecution for disseminating information about a lewd and obscene act as per Article twelve. What amazes me is that I think that she bought it!'

'Oh, Toy,' I said, wringing my once beautiful hands, 'what have I done? You took an oath to serve the public with honesty and integrity, but your exposure to me has turned you into a liar.'

'Oh, get over yourself,' Granny snapped. 'At least now the boy can run for president.'

'You're wrong, Granny,' I retorted. 'A president should speak the truth at all times – no matter what.'

'Fiddlesticks,' Granny said. 'No one wants a *really* honest president, just like no woman really wants a *really* honest husband.'

'I do!' I said. 'I want a *really* honest husband, and I have one. So there!'

'Pshaw,' Granny said. 'You try asking that man of yours what he really thinks of that *shmatta* you're wearing, and see if you like his response.'

I was trying to wrap my head around the fact that my great-grandmother, who was Amish when she passed away, and had never met a Jewish person, had managed to add the word *shmatta* to her lexicon, when the door to the parlour was flung open. In waltzed the gorgeous Christine Landis from Chicago.

'Oh,' she said, 'I didn't realize anyone was in here.'

'How odd,' I said, 'given that you heard me tell the chief to meet me here. This is village business, and it's private.'

'Well, I didn't realize that you were going to hog this room that long,' Christine Landis said and plopped her patooty down on a chair opposite me. She glanced around. 'And anyway, you're already letting someone else attend your meeting. Why does she get to be here, and not me?'

The wee hairs on the nape of my neck stood up. 'Who else is in here?'

'Is this supposed to be humorous?' Christine Landis said. 'How do you think that old lady in the rocking chair feels being the butt of your lame joke?'

'She's one of us!' Toy and I shouted simultaneously.

'Oh, spare me,' Granny said.

'You'll never believe this, Miss Landis,' I said, 'but that old lady in the rocking chair is not an old lady at all.'

'Boogers,' Granny said. 'I ain't a horse.'

'She's an Apparition-American,' Toy said.

'I didn't fall off a turnip truck,' Christine Landis snapped.

'I've never heard that expression,' Granny said.

'That's because they didn't have turnip trucks when you were alive,' I said. 'Granny, ask this woman to come sit on your lap. That'll prove what you are.'

'You're a sick bunch,' Christine Landis said, and popped to her perfect feet.

'Hold your horses, girlie,' Granny said. 'I dare you to come over here and sit on my lap. If you can sit on my lap, without having your bottom touch the chair, then Magdalena will not charge you anything for your stay here. Isn't that right, Magdalena?'

'Absolutely,' I said.

'You heard that, Sheriff Toy,' Christine Landis said and winked.

'It's Chief Graham,' Toy said, with surprising gruffness. Clearly her womanly wiles were not going to go very far with him.

I held my breath, and leaned forward to watch. Miss Landis put on a show of wiggling her posterior as she slowly lowered herself down onto what she supposed was Granny's lap. When her buttocks hit the hard wooden surface of the rocking chair, there was a brief moment of reckoning, and a look of puzzlement crossed her face, to be quickly replaced by one of horror.

The scream that subsequently escaped her throat put my hens off laying for three days, and revived an old rumour that cougars still roamed the mountains of south-western Pennsylvania. Within a few seconds Gabe and the other three guests came thundering into the parlour, which meant that they'd been lurking nearby, probably even eavesdropping.

'What happened?' Gabe demanded.

'Miss Landis can see and hear Granny.'

'I'll be a monkey's uncle,' Gabe said. 'Man, I wish I had that ability.'

'It's a hologram, you faker!' Christine Landis shrieked.

'I don't get it,' Ducky Limehouse said. 'What hologram? Where?'

'There, you idiot!' screeched Christine Landis. 'In that rocking chair.'

'I don't see anything either,' Kathleen Dooley said.

'Then go sit in it,' Christine Landis hissed. 'And you, Doody, watch what happens. Maybe the old lady will reappear then.'

'My name is Ducky, ma'am.'

'Whatever. Will one of you just go and sit in that stupid chair, for goodness' sake.'

'Look, girlie,' Granny said, sounding rather peeved, 'I haven't disappeared, have I? So how can I reappear?'

Christine Landis closed her eyes and moaned. 'This isn't happening,' she said. 'I didn't eat any Schmucker Brothers Breakfast Sausages today. Not a one. Even when I couldn't help myself and ate two, I didn't have this reaction.'

'What is she talking about?' I said.

'Never mind, babe,' my husband said. 'Miss Landis,' he said, addressing the other two, 'is freaking out because she is a very rare and special person, one who has the ability to both see and hear my wife's great-grandmother.'

Christine Landis snorted. 'These wackos refer to ghosts as Apparition-Americans.'

Kathleen Dooley chuckled. 'Are we to believe that this particular Apparition-American is at this moment sitting in that rocking chair?'

'Indeed, my great-granny is doing just that.'

'Hmm. Well, then maybe two is company, as they say.' Without further ado Kathleen Dooley walked over and plopped her plump patooty atop Granny's lap. In an effort to dislodge the unwanted guest, Granny immediately attempted to squirm. Occasionally Granny is successful in breaching the wall that separates the living from the dead when it comes to touch, but that was not the case this particular evening. However, Granny was not about to give up easily.

'Maybe Doody should sit on my lap,' she suggested. 'After all, he *is* more my type. Or how about the tall, pale one who looks like a mortician?'

'There! Did you hear that?' shouted Christine Landis, pointing to Ducky Limehouse. 'The old lady called you Doody.'

Ducky Limehouse glared at Christine Landis. 'I'm from Charleston, South Carolina, one of America's oldest cities. Most of the residences south of Broad Street were built by enslaved Africans and their descendants, and have been inhabited by generations of people. My city abounds with ghost stories, and I choose not to believe them, because frankly, ghosts make me very uncomfortable.' He strode from the room.

'Doody Face,' Granny said. 'Boogers on that boy.'

Christine Landis laughed with glee. 'This is one heck of an interactive hologram. If you ask me, this is a better financial investment than sausages. No, don't get me wrong, they're both good, and I've got the money for the sausages, I'm just saying . . . well, enough said.'

'It's not a darn hologram,' the Babester growled. 'It really is my wife's great-grandmother. Search the place; you won't find any hidden electronics, other than these two ugly lamps.'

'Why, I never,' I huffed. '*Ugly*, did you say? You told me that you liked them, dear.'

'Yeah,' Gabe said, 'but that was before I learned that your ex-husband was the one who picked them out at the Pottery Barn in Pittsburgh.'

'I can't believe this, Gabe! You're still jealous of a dead man?'

'Ahem. Folks, let's all take a moment to step back and breathe,' Toy said, trying bravely to step into the fray and take things down a notch, but nobody likes a buttinsky.

'Oh, shut up,' said Christine Landis.

'Put a lid on it,' Gabe said, but I wasn't sure to whom he addressed his remark.

'Well, I'm out of here,' I said, and stalked out of the room, head held high.

After grabbing my pocketbook off a hook by the back door, I headed out to the back parking lot and my car. The cool night air was invigorating and smelled of lilacs. It should have been a balm for my soul, but the stressful afternoon and evening required more. Strange as it might seem, I had a yen for one of the Schmucker Brothers Dinner Sausages. Whenever I ate one of those, I always feel so peaceful afterwards. Mellow, Gabe called it.

Unfortunately, I didn't have time to fry up a sausage just then, for I needed to drive the four miles into the village of Hernia itself, and pay an impromptu visit to my best buddy, Agnes Miller. Between the two of us, I was always the one who came the closest to crossing over the line when it came to socially unacceptable, and/or quasi-illegal, behaviour.

SEVEN

Agnes *does* lock her doors. She is one of the few residents of Hernia to do so, however. She started this practice after she caught Tommy Kauffman, the fourteen-year-old paper boy, in her bathroom while she was having a good soak in her claw-foot tub. Just how long Tommy had been watching my friend is disputable, but Agnes was about to climb out of her bath because the water had gotten cold. Poor Agnes was so startled that she lunged for a towel at the foot of the tub, slipped, and not only broke a well-padded arm, but chipped an incisor.

At any rate, after Agnes failed to answer her front door, I trotted around to the back, and there I found her still in her pyjamas, and catching fireflies. She didn't seem at all surprised to see me.

'Remember the story of Peter Pan and Tinker Bell?' she trilled.

'I'm pretty sure that wasn't in my Bible,' I said.

'Honestly, Mags, you were exceptionally deprived as a child. Anyway, Tinker Bell was a little fairy, and that's what these are – fairies. You might think that they're fireflies, but at night, when no one is looking, they shed their bug shells, and display their fairy bodies.'

'Let's just suppose that story is true.' I said. 'What do you plan to do with a jar full of fairies?'

'Why, I'll have the world's first fairy colony, of course.'

'Or maybe you'll have a jar full of bugs,' I said, 'since you said, yourself, that they only turn into fairies when no one is looking.'

'Aw, Mags, don't be a downer, and spoil my fun.'

'Agnes, I need you to get serious for a minute. I came to talk to you about the incident with Erma Burkholder.'

'You mean my *Moon over Miami* moment?' she said.

'I suppose that's a worldly reference, so it's beyond my ken,' I said. 'But I'm guessing that the answer is "yes". In any case, at the time, what you did may have scratched that itch to get back at Erma, but it could really have backfired on you – pardon the pun.'

Agnes giggled. 'No pardon for you, missy. Wissy. Tissy. Kabissy.'

'Agnes, are you drunk? You haven't been consorting with the Methodists again, have you?'

'How dare you even suggest such a thing, Mags? You know that I can't stand the taste of alcohol. And I wasn't consorting with the Methodists that time; I had one date with Willy Potter when we were both sixteen.'

'Well, you're not acting like yourself,' I said. 'Usually, you're the most level-headed person I know. Seriously, you almost always make more sense than Gabe when the going gets tough, and I need a bit of sound advice. But I don't know who you are today.'

'Well, I haven't shaved my armpits lately, so you can call me Shaggy Aggie if you like.'

'Ach! You see what I mean? You're lucky that Toy found a way to get Erma to keep mum about what you did. Otherwise, your reputation as an upstanding citizen in this community, and a good Christian woman, would undoubtedly suffer.'

'Mags, I'm seventy-four. I, and other women my age – and yours – refer to ourselves as crones. Do you think that I give a rat's patooty what people think about me?'

I was stunned by her remark, which might have explained my physical reflexes. I'm quite sure that I did not present a pretty sight.

'Mags,' my friend said, 'your mouth is open so wide that I could easily shove a baked potato down your throat if I so choose. Chill out. I love you dearly, but you're the biggest drama queen that I know.'

'I am not!' I said hotly. 'Wait. What does that mean – a drama *queen*?'

'It means,' Agnes said, 'that you turn everything into a crisis, every molehill into a mountain. You don't even wait to see if there might be a simple solution to a problem, before going off half-cocked.'

'Oh yeah?' I said. 'What's your simple solution for repairing your relationship with Erma Burkholder?'

'Easy peasy,' Agnes said with a giggle. 'I'll send her a huge bouquet of flowers, and a note saying that I hope she enjoyed getting to know me better than before.'

'Agnes! That will just make things worse.'

'Oh, get off your high horse, Mags. Or else stay on your high horse and ride it back to the PennDutch. You're bringing me down on what was a very magical evening.'

'I'll gladly leave,' I snarled.

And so I did. But I returned the next morning at first light. Not only did I want to apologize to my best friend in person, but I wanted to give her a big hug. Even though I am decidedly not a touchy-feely person, the older I get the more I understand that every time that I see one of my friends, it could very well be for the last time. Heaven forfend that my last memory of Agnes was one in which she sent me away because I was ruining her evening.

When I arrived at Agnes's house, I realized that I'd been silly to get there so early. Agnes has never been a 'morning person', and since she retired eight years ago she has been known to sleep in to noon. If I dared to wake her before nine, it would be off with my head. In case she had something planned that she hadn't bothered to share with me (the chances were one in a billion), I parked my car in Agnes's driveway, directly behind her car, so that she couldn't move it very far unless she gunned the engine and was able to bash a hole in the rear wall of her garage. I didn't do this to be mean; I simply didn't want her to slip away without giving me a chance to apologize in person.

As Agnes lived a mere three blocks from the police station, I decided to fill my time by paying Chief Toy a visit. It was another lovely spring day, perfect weather for a short walk. For the first block the only other living creatures I saw were butterflies, and several red-breasted robins hopping about in search of worms.

Then on the second block I had an interesting encounter with Shirley Valentino, who had a heavy canvas bag slung over her left shoulder. Shirley is our village's mail carrier, and a recent immigrant from Philadelphia. She had come to visit her sick aunt in Bedford (twelve miles away). Shirley had taken a side trip to visit our charming village and had fallen deeply in love with us, and we with her. Her bubbly personality charmed every person she encountered, whether young or old. Even the Henderson's cat warmed to her immediately, and Mikey hated everyone, most especially women.

'Good morning, Shirley!' I trilled.

'Aunt Persephone?'

'No, dear, it's me, Magdalena Yoder. I'm the mayor of this charming village.'

Shirley made circles with her thumbs and forefingers which she held up to her eyes. I supposed they were to mimic spectacles.

'Your Honorship, it *is* you! What brings you to town so early in the morning? Wait! Don't tell me; you're still looking for that lost dog of yours. A piddle, right? I mean, a puddle.' She giggled. 'Nope. Not that, either, but I almost got it right. It's a poodle!'

I eschew gossip, which I listen to only on special occasions. Plus, I have little tolerance for old biddies who jump to false conclusions, make snap judgements, and then pass on those assumptions. I get especially irritated when I hear disparaging remarks made about someone with regard to their religion, ethnicity, or race. But that said, it was plain as the liver spots on my hands that Shirley Valentino was as drunk as a Presbyterian high schooler at the after-prom.

I held two fingers in front of the woman's face. 'Shirley, dear, how many fingers do you see?'

'Whoa! I *thee* only two. Do you want to borrow *thome* of mine?'

Yup. I was right. Our village mail carrier had consumed a liquid breakfast. That went a long way to explaining why it took a month for my cousin in Indiana to get a letter, whereas a pen pal in Australia received hers in less than half the time. When I sent a letter to Flora in Indiana, I placed it in my mailbox beside my driveway for Shirley to pick up along her route. However, I mailed my pal Ruby her letter directly from the post office, where it was handled only by Henny, the postmistress.

'Well, now,' I said calmly, in response to her generous offer for more fingers, 'I could use an extra thumb. Do you have one of those you could spare?'

Shirley studied her hands carefully for a minute. 'Nah. I thought I might. I mean, there was a lot of everything – but I just *thee* two. Although I could give you one of the two little *fingerth*. I don't remember using them for much.'

I pointed to my nose. 'God gave you those two wee fingers to help you breathe. Think about it.'

It took her a minute, but she got my drift. 'Aw, you're *tho withe*, Madeline Yother.'

'That's Magdalena Yoder, dear, and you're so drunk you couldn't walk a straight line if your life depended on it.'

'Don't be *thilly, dear*. I'm not in the *leath* bit drunk. I'm just feeling all *looth* and happy.'

'Oh yeah?' I said. 'What does *looth* even mean?'

'Looth? Now you're toying with me, Morgana. Surely you've had a looth tooth at some point in your long life. *Thince* I'm a lady, and a newcomer to your village, I'm not even going to mention what I heard about you being a looth woman – you know, that bit about you being an *adultereth* and all.'

'I was an *inadvertent* adulteress!' I wailed. 'I didn't know that Aaron Miller was married. Isn't that story ever going to stop being repeated in this town?'

'But *ith* a good *thory*,' Shirley said. She began to sway, and her eyes started to roll back in her head. 'Here,' she said, thrusting the mailbag at me, 'you *finith* my route. I'm going home. I wanna take a nap.'

'But I can't take this mail bag; it's government property!'

'Well, I'm too tired to handle government *pooperty* right now. Ha! Did you hear what I *thed*, Magdalena? I *thed* a naughty word. And you a Mennonite! Are you *thcandalized*?'

I shouldered the bag, which was surprisingly heavy. 'No, I'm not scandalized. I've raised two sons. At least you got my name right this time. Do you mind if I smell your breath?'

Shirley's irises resumed their normal position. 'No, but you have to buy me dinner *firtht*,' she said. Then she howled with laughter. She laughed so hard that she tripped over her own feet. '*Woopthie daithy*,' she said, as I helped get her back on her feet.

'Do you need me to take you home?' I said.

'And tuck me in bed?'

'Well . . .'

'You can read me a *thtory, thweetheart*.'

'Just go home and sleep it off, dear,' I said, trying my best to hang on to my last shred of Christian charity. Then I let go. 'Tsk, tsk,' I said under my breath. Surely one gets some credit for only quietly passing judgement, don't you think? It's not like I condemned her behaviour publicly by throwing rotten tomatoes at her. (This happened to me when word of my illegal marriage to Aaron leaked out.)

But really, what was this younger generation coming to? Did they not read their Bibles anymore? Proverbs 20:1 states quite succinctly that 'wine is a mocker'. At an hour when the good Christian folks of Hernia (and even our two resident Jews) were drinking their morning coffee and tea, this normally buoyant millennial was falling down drunk. What's more, Shirley Valentino was a public servant! Yes, Miss Valentino applied for her job, but I shuddered to think of the day when we might have elected officials – maybe even in the highest offices in the land – who lived by their own moral code and might really have committed adultery.

I stood and watched Hernia's first female mail carrier weave her way back down the sidewalk in the direction from which she'd come – sans her mailbag, of course. If I hadn't been such a judgemental old woman, I would have gone with her, and at the very least seen her safely to her door. Instead, I whispered a prayer for her safety, and as soon as she turned right on Tulip Street, I turned and pointed my long Yoder nose back in the direction I had begun walking.

I am a very tolerant woman, mind you, but I just can't stand to see folks ignoring the safety of others by texting while they walk. These rude people should be pelted with popcorn. If they don't look up from their screens, then I say bring out the big guns, and lob a caramel popcorn ball at their phone, while loudly hissing without an 'S' (although you'll have to contact a *New York Times* bestselling author for instructions on how to do this).

That said, while I walked quickly toward the police station, to make up for lost time, I texted Gabe back at the PennDutch. In essence I told him that I wouldn't make it back in time to serve our guests breakfast, but that he was certainly capable of that task. In the event that our cook didn't show up to cook their promised 'farmhouse spread', he should carry some cereal boxes and milk out to the front porch, and then charge them extra for the privilege of taking their morning meal 'al fresco'.

I was so focused on what I was doing that I didn't even hear the 'clop, clop, clop' of the approaching horse, but I did hear it neigh when Jacob Schmucker pulled back hard on the reins, causing the animal to rear up. A moment later its descending hooves came close to shortening my signature proboscis.

'*Ach du leiber!*' Jacob said. 'You are wanting to kill yourself, yah?'

I gulped for air. 'No. I – uh – I apologize. Jacob, I hate it when other people do this very same thing. I don't know what came over me. Maybe it was—'

'Miss Yoder, I cannot talk now. I am on my way to get the midwife for Rebecca.'

'That's right,' I said. 'I knew her time was close. Well, tell her that I'm praying for her.'

'Yah, thank you. Und pray for a boy.'

'I will pray,' I said.

He gave the reins a gentle slap across the horse's back and off it went at a fast trot. How odd, I thought, that he should still be praying for the gender of the baby, rather than just the safety of the mother and her offspring. Surely the Good Lord had decided the baby's sex a long time ago. I seriously doubted that there would be any last-minute structural changes if I asked God to give the child a penis and testes. On the other hand, scripture does state that faith the size of a mustard seed can move a mountain, so who am I to say that the Almighty couldn't – or wouldn't – do a little remodelling at the finish line?

I kept my word and prayed, but I did so *before* crossing the street, and then immediately after reaching the other side. Also, I restricted my prayer to asking God to give a healthy infant to Rebecca and Jacob Schmucker. This was, after all, their third attempt to start a family. On their first two tries Rebecca had delivered full-term babies that were stillborn.

After my prayer – which took less than thirty seconds – I entered the police station. Amelia Morris, who was Chief Toy Graham's part-time secretary, as well as mine, was sitting at her desk reading a gossip magazine. This particular rag didn't even pretend to have serious articles. The headlines on the front page screamed: KENTUCKY WOMAN FALLS INTO POND AND GIVES BIRTH TO ONE HUNDRED FROG CHILDREN!

Usually I cough or clap my hands when I want Amelia's limited attention, but that particular day, I was quite happy for her to discover the fate of the Kentucky frog children. The fact that her lips were moving at a furious pace, however, meant that I had to slip into the next room quickly, if I wanted to go unnoticed.

'Magdalena!' Chief Toy said happily, as I entered the room. 'I was just thinking about you.'

'Were they good thoughts?'

'Of course. Sit down and have a doughnut.'

'Don't mind if I do,' I said, as I plonked my patooty in one of the two chairs facing his desk and dropped the mail bag on the other. Toy gladly lives into the stereotype of the doughnut eating police officer. On the plus side, the doughnuts in his office are the ones I prefer: yeast doughnuts that are glazed. On the downside, Toy's husband brings them in from Bedford the evening before, when he returns from work. Still, a day-old pastry beats nothing.

'Coffee?' Toy asked.

'Who made it this morning?'

'I did,' he said.

'Then the answer is yes.'

'So that would be three sugars and bring the cow, yes?'

'You know me too well.'

Toy opened the mini refrigerator behind his desk and brought out a carton of half and half. As he fixed my coffee in a super-size mug, I told him about my conversation with Agnes, and my weird encounter with Shirley, the mail carrier.

'You don't intend to fill in for her today, do you?' he said.

'Even on a good day I wouldn't want to walk that far. My next stop is the post office. Anyway, you said that you were thinking about me. That means you were about to ask me for a favour. Am I right?'

Toy grinned and pushed the box of doughnuts in my direction. 'Here, help yourself to as many of these as you want.'

EIGHT

After digesting what Toy had to say, along with four glazed doughnuts, I dropped the mail bag off at the post office. Then I pressed the pedal to the metal, in order to pick up my guests for their visit to the sausage source at the appointed time. The three Schmucker brothers were in the catbird's seat. They'd already entertained several offers to do business with major distributors and were a handshake away from sealing a deal.

For what it's worth, the Schmucker brothers were exceptionally pious men, even by Amish standards, and would only have dealings with the outside world via an intermediary – a blood relative who had one very large foot planted firmly in the modern world, but who respected the old ways. This meant that the many offers that they received to buy their business were referred to me, and the burden of sifting through them, and selecting the most promising offers, was placed on my scrawny shoulders.

However, as both a friend and relative of the Schmucker family, I had opened my big yap, and convinced them that the more options they had, the better the chances were that they found a good fit. So, I arranged for one *last* meeting with clients, only this time there would be four interested parties. One of the parties wasn't even a potential buyer, but I chose him purely because I could – because I liked his name. Being the wealthy owner of a famous inn has its perks, you know.

Anyway, while the Schmucker brothers were fine with this arrangement, not all of my guests were. This was apparent before we even got into the car.

'I'm calling shotgun,' Ducky Limehouse said. That meant he wished to ride up front with me.

'Well, dear,' I said, 'I don't think that's such a good idea, because someone might think that you're my gigolo.'

There was a period of shocked silence, followed by all four guests exchanging glances. Finally, Christine Landis spoke up.

'I didn't think you'd even know that word, Miss Yoder.'

'You'd be surprised what I know, dear,' I said to her. 'Why don't you sit up front?'

I made the offer to Christine Landis solely because she was such an unpleasant person. All I wanted was to get this show on the road, so to speak, and get these guests out of my hair. After this morning I was going to butt out helping my friends with their business ventures. In fact, I might even listen to the Babester's pleas, and just shut down the PennDutch altogether. A month-long sail to the Antipodes (Australia and New Zealand) via Hawaii, Tahiti, Morea and Bora Bora might just be the ticket to celebrate our twenty-fifth wedding anniversary.

Christine Landis smiled. 'Miss Yoder, I think that Miss Dooley should have the honour.'

'I'm cool with that,' Kathleen Dooley said.

I smiled sweetly at everyone. 'Now, who would like to volunteer to sit in the middle back seat?'

'I'll do it,' Christine Landis said without a second's hesitation.

It's at times like that I thank the Lord that I still have my natural teeth. Otherwise, I might have swallowed my dentures, or at least bruised my chin when it hit the driveway.

'Then it's settled, dears. Hop in. Time's a-wastin'.'

To my further astonishment, they seated themselves without further ado, and even buckled their seatbelts without having to be reminded more than twice. As the Schmucker brothers' slaughtering house and meat processing plant was a fifteen-minute drive from my establishment, I decided to fill them in on a few details, and then give them an opportunity to ask questions.

'Folks,' I said, 'there is nothing in this world that smells worse than a hog farm,' I said.

'Pardon me, ma'am,' Ducky Limehouse said in his charming Deep South accent, 'but I beg to differ. My Granddaddy Limehouse used to employ a gardener who ate Limburger cheese sandwiches for lunch. When I was around five or six, I asked him if I could have a taste. All he had to do was hold that sandwich up to my nose, and I thought that I would pass out. I reckon that Limburger cheese smells a sight worse than any hog farm.'

Kathleen Dooley chuckled. 'It's *Brevibacterium linens* that produces that smell. That's what is partly responsible for foot and body odour in humans.'

'Ugh,' Terry Tazewell said. 'I never could stand to eat the stuff.'

'Enough about cheese,' I snapped. 'My point is that the place smells awful, and if you've elected to take the entire tour, from where the hogs are raised to cellophane-wrapped package, one needs to have a pretty strong stomach.'

'I'll be fine, I'm sure,' Christine Landis said from behind me. Her voice was soft and sweet. She was altogether a changed woman from the day before. It would behove me to discover her secret, for it has been suggested by more than one person that my edges could use a little smoothing. That, of course, is confidential information.

'I will be fine as frog's hair,' Ducky Limehouse said resolutely.

'How interesting,' I said, 'given that frogs don't have any hair.'

'Oh yes, ma'am, they do,' Ducky said. 'It's just so fine that you can't see it. It's a Southern expression, by the way.'

'No kidding.'

'But if one is feeling really fine,' Ducky said, 'then one is "fine as frog's hair split three ways".'

'How quaint,' Kathleen Dooley said.

'And another thing,' I said. 'The Amish prefer not to have their pictures taken.'

'Why not?' Terry Tazewell said.

'The reason that they don't want their pictures taken is based on the Third Commandment. Do any of you remember what that says?' After a telling silence, I continued. 'It says that we are not to create any likeness of anything on earth.'

'But doesn't that mean a carved likeness?' Kathleen Dooley asked.

'Well, first it says a carved image, and then it says *any* likeness. Admittedly, it's a bit confusing, since in One Kings, chapter six, verse twenty-nine there is a description of carved angels and palm trees decorating the inside of Solomon's temple. At any rate, the Amish believe that a photograph is a forbidden image. Even the dolls that their children play with don't have faces.'

'No way!' Kathleen Dooley said. 'Where do they buy these dolls?'

'They're homemade,' I said.

'Do you think that they would sell me one of these dolls?' Christine asked softly.

'Will wonders never cease?' I said under my breath. 'Ask them nicely,' I said aloud, 'and they might.'

'Miss Yoder,' Terry Tazewell said, 'you keep calling these animals hogs, but I thought pork sausages came from pigs.'

'They do – sort of. In the United States a hog is a large pig, weighing over one hundred and twenty pounds, and ready for slaughter.'

'And hence the name of the children's story,' Ducky Limehouse said.

'Excuse me, dear?'

'Well,' he said, 'it's not called the *Three Little Hogs*, is it?'

Kathleen Dooley laughed. 'Can you imagine a mother playing with her baby's toes and saying, "this little hog went to market"?'

Then they all laughed briefly but didn't actually speak again for the remainder of the drive out to the three Schmucker brothers' farms, which were laid out in a row along a narrow dirt road. The first farm, managed by Solomon and his children, was where the animals were bred and raised. If you ask me, there is nothing that smells worse than pig manure, so I prayed that our visit there would be brief. The second farm was managed by the expectant father, Jacob, with the help of eight cousins. It was where the hogs were slaughtered, and was euphemistically known as the 'processing' plant. Believe me when I say this: Jacob's operation stunk even worse than Solomon's farm. The third location was the packaging plant, which was overseen by the youngest brother, Peter. At all three the brothers also farmed corn, which was their hogs' primary diet.

Except for Ducky, who was a tourist, the other guests were competitors, so I wasn't surprised by their silence during the drive. Frankly, I was so grateful for it that I whispered a prayer of thanksgiving. But I shouldn't even have whispered.

'Are you all right?' Kathleen Dooley asked as we turned up the lane to Solomon Schmucker's hog farm.

'I'm quite all right. Why do you ask?'

'Because your lips were quivering, and I thought I heard you trying to catch your breath.'

I rolled my eyes. 'Be a dear and reach into the glove box for some face masks. Take one, and then pass them back.'

'I'll pass them back,' she said, 'but I'm sure I won't need one.

In the circus we had multiple jobs, and one of mine was cleaning up after the elephants. Nothing bothers me.'

Before I turned off the car, so that the doors would unlock, I donned a double layer of masks. A glance at the back seat informed me that not one of my guests had followed my advice. Oh, well, tough cookies then.

When I turned off the engine my guests piled out, eager to be the first to meet Solomon Schmucker, the oldest of the three brothers. I slid out of the car quickly and locked it behind me. Not thirty seconds later they were pulling on the handles of my already locked car with one hand, with their free hand holding the top of their shirt or blouse up over their nose.

'Put your masks on, you silly geese. Then hurry up and follow me. Solomon is waiting for us up by the pens. I'm sure he has a lot of interesting information to share about this particular breed, and what makes it so delectable. Why, it smells just yummy from here.'

I glanced behind me to see that Ducky was striding back down the road, *away* from the hog farm, as fast as his legs could carry him. Even though the other three had donned their masks, they still hadn't advanced any. Someone slightly more critical than I might even comment on the fact that they were staggering about like a trio of drunken penguins. I knew that they had really wanted to speak to all the brothers to pitch their offers, and they were counting on me to make a meeting with Peter, at the end, happen. But what was I to do, I ask you? Lasso them and drag them behind me, as I marched up to greet my waiting friend and kinsman? I think not.

Instead, I trotted back to my car, opened all the doors, and got back behind the wheel.

'OK, guys, hop back in. Visiting hours are over.'

'What?' Terry Tazewell said. 'We can't leave now. We haven't even gotten the chance to say one word to Mr Schmucker!'

'Au contraire, dear,' I said. 'You had your chance, and you blew it.'

'Can't you at least run up there and explain the situation for us?' Kathleen Dooley begged.

'*Nooo*, dear,' I said. 'I don't have a dog in this hunt.'

'What is that supposed to mean?' she said.

'It means,' Terry Tazewell said, 'that this isn't her affair.'

'Right you are, sir,' I said. 'Now buckle up,' I barked.

With that we were off. I drove at a good clip, but even then, it wasn't until I was about a quarter of a mile down the road that I caught up with Ducky Limehouse. That young man had really been booking it. What's more, he wasn't even out of breath.

'Care for a ride, stranger?' I said, pulling up alongside him.

'Yes, ma'am. I'll go anywhere but to a hog farm.'

'Climb in, son.'

After I got back up to speed, I broke the bad news. 'Sorry, Mr Limehouse, but we're headed to farm number two. This is where they slaughter the hogs. If you folks thought the stench at the growing pens was unbearable, wait until you get a whiff of this place. That's because you will smell not only their excrement, but their blood, offal, and their fear.'

'Ma'am?' Ducky said. 'Did you say fear?'

'Oh yes, young man,' I said. 'The animals at the head of the line know what's about to happen to them when they face the butcher's knife. Then they relay this information to the others behind them. This phenomenon has been known to cause the whole herd to panic, producing hormones that causes their meat to have an "off" flavour.'

'Ahem, Miss Yoder,' Terry Tazewell said, 'but that sounds like a load of manure.'

'Oh, really?' I said archly. 'Who would know more about live-stock, you or me? Did you know that swine – that's pigs and hogs – are omnivores? That means that they'll literally eat just about anything, vegetable or protein. In fact, the wife of the Amish man whom you just met, Solomon, was eaten by some hogs.'

'Ugh. No way,' Christine Landis said. She sounded on the verge of tears.

'Definitely *way*,' I said. 'She was feeding the hogs one afternoon when a thunderstorm came up and she was struck by lightning. That's the theory, at any rate. Her husband was working at the slaughter – I mean processing – plant the next farm over, so he heard the strike, but assumed that his wife was safely inside the house. At any rate, when he returned home she wasn't there, but he did find a few bits of her clothing and part of one boot in the hog pen.'

'Do you expect us to believe that the pigs actually ate the woman?' Ducky Limehouse asked.

'Indeed, I do,' I said.

'Well, I hope her husband killed every last one of them,' Terry Tazewell said.

'Eventually,' I said. 'But you can't fault the hogs; that's how God made them.'

'Stupid, disgusting creatures,' Christine said. She spoke emphatically for the first time that morning.

'No,' I said, 'swine are not stupid. To the contrary, they are uncommonly intelligent creatures. People who have studied pigs say that they are even more intelligent than dogs, and possibly as smart as a three-year-old child.'

'Come on, Miss Yoder,' Terry Tazewell said. 'That's a bunch of bologna, pardon the pun.'

Mr Tazewell's cavalier attitude got me hot under my starched, if somewhat prudish collar. 'You say that, sir, because you've never owned a pig. Do any of you own dogs?'

'I own a standard poodle named Baklava,' Terry Tazewell said.

'Well, I dare say that if Baklava tasted like bacon, you might be tempted to fry her up for breakfast.'

Everyone gasped, including me. Oh dear, I had gone too far. But it wasn't so much my fault, as it was the fact that the Devil had set me up with Terry Tazewell's bologna comment. I'm only human after all, and every now and then I do yield to temptation.

'Get behind me, Satan,' I said firmly.

'I beg your pardon?' Terry Tazewell said. 'Did you just call me Satan?'

Ducky Limehouse snickered. 'No, sir, she did not. She's what we call a "Bible-beater" in the South. That means she takes the Bible literally, and most probably visualizes the Prince of Darkness actually sitting behind her now. Oops, I guess that would put him right in my lap.'

'How exciting for you,' Terry Tazewell said. 'What does old Beelzebub feel like? I bet he feels hot to the touch. Is he burning your thighs?' He guffawed, which I thought was extremely rude.

'Speaking of unusual experiences,' Kathleen Dooley said, 'when I worked in the circus, I once sat in a gorilla's lap. It wasn't a real gorilla, of course, but a very large man in a gorilla costume, dressed up like King Kong. I was supposed to be Ann Darrow. Unfortunately, that act was short lived, because Big Jim, who played the gorilla, ran off with Walter after just three performances. The owner of the circus never could find someone as big as Jim again, except for Hairy Mary, and she refused to play an animal.'

'How interesting,' I said pleasantly.

'Miss Yoder,' Kathleen Dooley said, 'was that supposed to be sarcasm?'

'Absolutely not, dear. How could it be? I read an article that said that women were incapable of sarcasm. Believe me, I'm just grateful that you changed the subject. I am used to my family members mocking my staunch religious faith, but they do so lovingly, and know when to quit.'

'Miss Yoder,' Christine Landis said, 'you are a bundle of contradictions.'

'Thank you, dear. I'll take that as a compliment. Now folks, you have a decision to make. Do you wish to skip both the slaughterhouse *and* the packaging plant, and proceed directly to the office, or are they both still on our agenda?'

'*What?*' Ducky Limehouse said. 'Do you mean to say that we could skip the horror show and proceed directly to "Go"?'

'What is a "Go", Mr Limehouse, anyway? I said that we could proceed directly to the office.'

'He was making a Monopoly reference, you twit,' Christine Landis said.

'Oh no,' Kathleen Dooley said. 'She's back. The witch from Chicago came out of hibernation.'

'Straight to the office,' Ducky Limehouse said emphatically. 'No one here is interested in the packaging plant.'

'Now you wait just one cotton-picking minute, *dah*ling,' Christine Landis said. It was clear that she was mocking his Southern accent. '*I'm* interested in the processing and packaging plants. The Schmucker Brothers hand-produced brand sells for a premium in the deli section of my stores. I'd like to see how it's done. Donald Duck here is merely a tourist, and as you might say, Miss Yoder, has no dog in the hunt. So, I say that we take a vote – but only amongst us three business owners.'

A glance in my rear-view mirror informed me that Ducky Limehouse was not amused. His face had reddened, and a vein the size of the Chunnel had popped up along his right temple. It was up to me to intercede before the poor man died of an aneurism. The last thing that I needed was to have an Apparition-American as a permanent passenger in my car, particularly one who'd been literally killed by a Yankee. It's a sad fact that the Civil War is still being fought after one hundred and fifty years, but my automobile was not going to be a memorial to a lost cause.

'There is no need to vote!' I cried. 'We are going to the processing plant next, then the packaging plant, and that is that. I brought enough masks for you to double up – you can even wear three. I find that when I start getting queasy, reciting scripture verses always helps. For instance, you could try recalling some of the lesser-known passages, say from Second Chronicles. Wasn't that Donald Trump's favourite book of the Bible?'

'Miss Yoder,' Ducky Limehouse said, 'sarcasm does not become you.'

'*What?* I'm being quite serious, dear. What is wrong with my suggestion?'

The sound of four sighs in an enclosed space can be compared to that of a toilet flushing.

'Well?' I said. 'Who is going to elucidate me?'

'Miss Yoder,' Kathleen Dooley said hesitantly, 'what makes you think that any one of us can recite scripture verses? We weren't raised like you.'

'More's the pity,' I said sadly. 'At any rate, if you think now that you won't be able to handle this stop, just stay in the car and breathe through your mouth. But this is going to happen, whether you like it or not.'

NINE

As it turned out, the two women and the octogenarian all found the process of turning pig carcasses into sausages so fascinating, that I had to pull them away from the processing plant and bundle them into the car to get them to the packaging place. The odd thing was that when we got back to the car after visiting the packaging plant, Ducky Limehouse was nowhere to be found, even though there really wasn't anywhere for him to disappear to. The surrounding cornfields had only just been planted, and the road that connected all three Amish farms was as straight as my long Yoder nose. The only living thing that I could see on it was an orange cat.

I confess that it did occur to me that the Rapture had happened during the time we learned how sausages were made. That is not to say that I dwelt on this matter, but I did think it for just a second or two. But I have been assured of my salvation because I gave my heart to Jesus when I was a child of seven. Therefore, deep down I know that I will be whisked up into the clouds when the Rapture happens. I'm pretty sure that the three Schmucker brothers have also been saved (although the Amish don't bank on their salvation). As for my guests, I didn't have the foggiest idea where they stood with God – but surely at least one of them was headed up, and not down, at the End of Times. I just wouldn't have picked Ducky Limehouse as harp-plucking material, but then who am I to judge?

At any rate, I quickly ruled out the Rapture as fearful thinking, the product of slippage in my prayer life. So, I resolved to resume praying a full hour every day, and after that I tooted my horns – well, not *my* horns, but my car's horns. My vehicle has been especially outfitted with two horns; one emits a deep, loud tone, and the other has a very high, soft pitch. There are times, you see, when loud tone is needed to alert another driver that they are about to crash into your car. However, there are other occasions, like when you are stopped at a green light, and the person in front of you is not moving, when it is OK to give that person a 'heads-up'. That's when a soft, high note is the perfect thing.

All that said, I gave Ducky Limehouse both 'barrels', alternating between tones. If only I'd installed three more horns, I could have played him the birthday song.

'Look!' Kathleen Dooley shouted in my ear. 'There he is, rounding the corner of that shed.'

'That shed is an outhouse,' I said.

'A what?'

'A toilet with no plumbing,' I said. 'I used to have a six-seater at the PennDutch. Actually, it's still there, but it's non-functional these days. You should check it out this afternoon.'

'Imagine that,' Kathleen Dooley said. 'An outdoor restroom with six separate cubicles.'

'Au contraire, Miss Dooley,' I said. 'This is a long wooden plank with six round holes cut into it. Between each hole there is a wooden panel that reaches to the ceiling, but they are certainly not enclosed.'

'Eew, gross,' Christine Landis said. 'That's barbarian.'

'It's not barbarian,' I snapped. 'Going to the bathroom is a natural function, and males and females use the outhouse at separate times.'

'But why so many holes?' Kathleen Dooley asked.

'Ah, a reasonable question,' I said. 'That's because Amish families tend to be quite large, so that they could have extra hands to help them work the land. My great-grandparents, who were Amish, had sixteen children.'

'How selfish of them to procreate at that rate,' Christine Landis said.

Just then Ducky Limehouse popped open the back door and jumped in. 'Sorry guys,' he said. 'Nature called.'

'How many holes did that one have?' Kathleen Dooley asked pleasantly.

'I beg your pardon, ma'am?' Ducky Limehouse said.

'She means,' Christine Landis hissed, 'how many over-sexed Amish get to do their business side by side in that miserable-looking shed?'

I am not a violent woman. Jesus taught us to turn the other cheek. But if I *were* a violent woman, I might have reached into the back seat and slapped one of Christine's perfect cheeks, turned her face, and then slapped her other one.

'There's only one seat in that outhouse, of course,' Ducky Limehouse said. 'Don't be crude. The Amish are a very conservative people.'

'That says how much you know, doofus,' Christine Landis said. 'Witch!'

'Children,' I shouted. 'Play time is over; we're going home.'

'But we haven't been to the office,' Kathleen Dooley said calmly. 'Don't we get a chance to pitch our business propositions?'

'Actually, you don't,' I said.

The ensuing cacophony caused me to clamp my hands over my ears. It was only by the grace of God that I had yet to commence driving, or we might have ended up in the ditch, and given my heavy foot (can I help that it is so large?), we might all have been killed.

'Children!' I hollered. 'Order in my car. Whoever says the next word without my permission gets to walk home. Just so you know, cell phone reception out here is very iffy, and good luck on getting a cab, because Hernia doesn't have any.'

There followed a minute of silence which I savoured. Then came the coughing, sniffing, lip-smacking, foot-shuffling and raised hands that eventually got shoved in my face. None of that bothered me; I enjoyed knowing they were squirming with frustration. When I put a stop to their foolishness it wasn't because I gave in to them, but because I wanted to be the one who spoke first.

'I know what you all are thinking,' I said, 'but you are wrong. You have already unknowingly made your pitches to the Schmucker brothers. You see, they are only interested in partnering with a company that is interested enough in the product to see how it is made – that they use the finest cuts from the hog, and the purest spices. The previous guests that I brought refused to even step out of my car, once they got a whiff of the farm. They didn't expect you to want to see the slaughtering house, and anyway, the Amish normally slaughter their hogs in the autumn and winter. But all three of you passed the test by showing up at the processing plant.'

'That's excellent news,' Terry Tazewell said.

'No, it's not!' Christine Landis snarled. 'We can't all be winners. Aren't they going to be interviewing us individually?'

I looked at her beautiful, but sullen, face in the rear-view mirror.

'They already did. At the processing plant. Those Amish men may have just been Jacob's cousins, because he's at home with his wife who's having a baby, but believe me, you were on trial. Those men paid close attention to the questions that you asked. They observed your comportment, and how you interacted with each other, with me, and how you treated them. They also made note of how everyone dressed.'

'Why, that's absurd!' she raged. 'It's my right to show some cleavage. This is America; this isn't Saudi Arabia.'

'They didn't say anything to me about you specifically,' I said, 'but you didn't respect their religious sensitivities. And I did warn you.'

'So?' she said. 'When do we hear their verdict?'

I shrugged. 'Perhaps in a day or two.'

'That long?' Kathleen Dooley asked, sounding a mite put out. She at least had worn a shirt dress with elbow length sleeves that could be buttoned to the throat. Her hemline also reached below her knees.

'Well, we had an appointment,' Christine Landis said. 'At least *I* did. What kind of man puts babies before business?'

'A good husband,' I said. 'Clearly that's something you've never had, bless your heart, as they say in the South where Mr Limehouse comes from.'

'You seem to know a lot about my part of the country, Miss Yoder,' Ducky Limehouse said. At least he was agreeable, but then again, he didn't have a dog in the hunt.

'That's because a dear friend of my lives in Charleston. Her name is Abigail Timberlake, and she owns an antiques shop on King Street called the Den of Antiquity. Have you heard of it?'

'Heard of it,' Ducky Limehouse exclaimed excitedly. 'Abby is a dear friend of mine as well.'

'Shut the front door!' I said.

'Will you two stop your yakking, and get back to what's important,' Christine Landis said irritably.

'Look, toots,' I said. 'I've had it up to the top of my impossibly big head with your nasty attitude. If you keep this up, I might have to give the Schmucker brothers my two cents' worth of opinion.'

'You wouldn't dare!' Christine Landis shrieked.

'Don't push your luck, sister. At this point, I'm trying as hard as I can to remain neutral – but it's getting very difficult. I suggest you revert to your post-breakfast state of civility. I think that we would all agree that we liked you much better then.'

'Harrumph,' she said.

'Well, you at least get points for saying the actual word. People only ever say it in fiction in America, and now in real life you've uttered this peculiar word. I'll take that as half an apology.'

'I don't need to apologize to you for anything,' Christine snapped.

'Tut-tut,' I said, 'your fate now hangs in the balance.'

'You think so?' Christine Landis sneered. 'Perhaps your braids are pulled too tightly back into that abysmal pile atop your boulder-sized head. You've stupidly shown me the way to the Schmucker brothers' farms. As soon as you drop me off at your faux farm-house, I'm going to jump into my decent automobile, and drive myself right back there.'

I prayed for patience, but as it's my least answered prayer, I didn't wait for it to be answered. Instead, I smiled.

'That's a wonderful idea, dear,' I said. 'OK folks, once more, buckle up, and off we go.'

Then, because I had a metaphorical bee in my pile of braids, and a perennially heavy foot, I pressed the pedal to the metal and made the trip back to the PennDutch in record time. I'll say this, Christine Landis was not talking through her hat when she said she'd be heading right back to the Schmucker brothers. I'm not as agile as I was at her age, but I'm no slow poke. Still, I didn't expect her to get to her car and start it before I'd even planted both feet on my driveway. Then I remembered that Chief Toy had asked me to do him a favour, so I hauled my gigantic feet back into my car.

'My husband will take care of lunch for you,' I called out to the others. 'And I think that he has some sightseeing planned, if you're up to it. Frank Lloyd Wright's house, Falling Waters, is an easy drive, and it's a "must see".' Then I drove the easy four miles back into the village of Hernia to execute the favour I'd promised Chief Toy.

One might assume that ours is a pretty monolithic population, but let me assure you that it is far from the truth. We are, however, a very religious town, in that we have a ridiculous number of churches per capita. Given the number of church steeples in Hernia, an unskilled parachutist would do well to steer well away from us. At any rate, while it is true that most of our citizens are Mennonites, their membership is almost equally split between just two churches. But we also have a Lutheran church, a Baptist church, a Methodist church, and even a church with sixty-six words in its name, where the parishioners handle poisonous snakes as part of their worship experience. Although I refuse to call it a church, we have a wholly heathen, surely satanic, cancerous cult that bills itself as the Church of Melvin, and I'll touch on that later, after I get all of my inoculations up to date. As we only have two Episcopalians, and three Jews, they have to travel further afield to get their religious needs met. But we do have one very liberal, la-dee-da church that does have a woman pastor and is open to having a non-celibate gay pastor, and that is the Presbyterian Church (USA). Except for me, that's what our village's wealthiest citizens call their spiritual home.

Bill and Linda Steele are lifelong members of the Presbyterian Church (USA) and would appear to have a lot of dough. They live in a massive 'new build' on the east side of town, which can only be described as ridiculously gauche, and I'm not a judgmental woman, mind you. Their mansion resembles a Hollywood version of a Southern plantation house, replete with massive white columns. Both Linda and husband Bill drive Porsches, and trade them in every year for the most recent model.

Both of them are native Herniaites, which explains their presence in our humble village, even after they obtained their wealth. Also – mind you, I eschew gossip and gossipers – it's been said that they *continue* to live here because anywhere else they might choose to live, they'd be in danger of 'soiling their nest'. That is to say that they are both real estate developers, and there are numerous places throughout the county where one sees denuded patches of forest and bulldozed farmland, all in the name of 'development', and most of them have Bill and Linda Steele's Development Cooperation signs on them.

Fortunately, this couple is two decades younger than me, so that I hold nothing personal against them, except that I just can't stand them. Please allow me to clarify that statement. What I meant was that we never crossed paths in school, so they never rubbed me the wrong way, and when I say that I can't stand them – well, they *are* raping the land for the almighty dollar, and it does get me pretty hot under the collar. But I do pray about this very wrong, very unchristian attitude of mine, so that puts me one step ahead of Chief Toy. That, in a nutshell, is why he asked me to drive out and talk to the Steeles, so that he didn't have to. Apparently, they had requested yet another audience with Chief Toy, but it wasn't going to happen. However, as Mayor of Hernia, Pennsylvania, and Chief Toy's boss, I was to be his proxy.

However, when I drove up to the massive wrought iron gates and punched in the code which Toy had supplied, nothing happened. I tried again.

'We asked to see Chief Toy Graham,' said a deep male voice. Bill Steele, by the way, sings bass in his church's choir.

'Yes,' I said. 'I know that you wanted Chief Graham, but—'

'Magdalena, go away,' Linda Steele said. 'We don't want to talk to you.'

I let out a long, protracted sigh. Toy was going to owe me big time for this.

'The truth is, dear, Chief Toy doesn't want to talk to you. He thinks that subject has been exhausted; that's why he sent me.'

'*Exhausted?*' Bill boomed in his basso profundo voice.

If I hadn't still been buckled in, I'd have jumped and hit my head on the ceiling of my car. I've been called hard-headed many times before, but the repeated knocks on my noggin over the years have started to leave my grey matter a mite scrambled.

'Look, dear,' I said, when I'd recovered enough to speak, 'it's either me or my shadow. You've already decided not to sue Brian Epps, your late son's best friend. It seems to me—'

'Oh, quit your blathering and get your bony butt in here,' Linda said.

The gates swung open. I drove up the circular drive and parked directly in front of the bank of marble steps that led to the massive front doors. When I pushed a buzzer, a smaller door set inside one of the large doors was opened by Linda Steele. She was wearing so much diamond jewellery that I had to squint in order to protect my retinas until my vision could adjust.

'Baines, our butler, quit without giving notice last month,' she said. 'Left like a thief in the night, without even saying "tootles". Since he lived in another wing of the house, we didn't hear him packing, much less leaving. When he didn't show up with my morning cup of tea, I went looking and found a note on his bed. Which he'd made, of course – hospital corners and all. But the wardrobe was empty, as well as the dresser drawers. Do you know how hard it is to find a good British butler out here in the boondocks?'

'Oh, it's ever so hard,' I said, with only a slight eye-roll. 'What did the note say?'

'Baines said that the food we provided him caused chronic constipation, and that if he was going to die, it would be on English soil.'

'One can die from constipation?'

'Yes, you twit, if it leads to bowel obstruction and worse. Again, quit your blathering and come all the way in.'

I stepped into a foyer that soared so high that one could easily imagine angels in the upper reaches plucking at their harps. Unfortunately, my attention kept returning to her jewels. She was wearing a diamond choker which, had the likes of it been around the neck of Marie Antoinette when the guillotine blade fell, would have prevented her execution. In addition to that, another diamond necklace covered her chest, and draped down into her deep cleavage, like the aftermath of an ice storm that had been bulldozed into a ravine. From her stretched earlobes dangled chandelier style earrings that crashed against her choker with the slightest movement of her head. On her slender wrists she wore diamond encrusted cuffs, and the diamond in her engagement ring was so huge, and heavy, that she had to support her left hand with a cane. (*That* part may not have been true.)

I may be a simple Conservative Mennonite woman who doesn't own a single bracelet, necklace, or a pair of earrings, but I have learned from well-groomed guests in the know, that when it comes to wearing jewellery, less is more. And never wear diamonds during the day. Of course, some rules are just silly. I, for one, wear white two weeks *before* Memorial Day, and two weeks *after* Labor Day, just to show the world that I am my own person. Nevertheless, even a country bumpkin like me can recognize vulgarity, and the temptation to point it out was too strong for me to resist.

'Linda, dear,' I cooed, 'what a lovely collection of cubic zirconium you're wearing. Wherever did you purchase it?'

Linda beamed and patted her chest. 'From the Lifelike Fakes catalogue. You wouldn't believe how reasonable—'

'They're not fakes!' Bill bellowed, as he stormed into the foyer. 'Every single one of those stones is a flawless diamond.'

Linda coloured as deeply as a maple leaf after a hard frost.

'I'm *sure* they are – quite something,' I said, trying to be conciliatory. 'Now dears, might we commence to what I can only assume is your sumptuous drawing room for our conversation. And a spot of tea would be nice, along with a biscuit or two.'

Linda led me to a drawing room that would have made the British royal family weep with envy, and bade me sit on a chair, that was certainly far more comfortable than anything that I had seen in pictures of either Buckingham, or Windsor, Castles. Then the two of them promptly sat.

'You can forget about the tea,' Bill snapped. 'That would have been Baines' bailiwick. Absentee butlers don't serve tea.'

Linda sighed. 'It would have been Earl Grey, and the biscuits were always quite good.'

'Yes, a good man, Baines, despite him stealing away like a thief in the night,' Bill mused. 'Seldom stole silverware, and only rarely broke into the main safe and lifted cash.'

'A decent sort of chap then,' I said drily. 'Now, what is it that you two wanted to see Chief Toy about? Remember, I'm his duly appointed representative.'

'Well then, if that's how it must be,' Bill said, 'even though it will never bring back the life of our son Jason, nor alter the fact that his best friend Brian will spend at least ten years in prison for driving drunk when the accident happened, we want you to know that we still believe Brian's story.'

I took a deep breath, wishing that I had a biscuit to cram into my mouth so that I could delay my response. Fortunately, Linda tag-teamed her husband.

'You see, Miss Yoder, we've known Brian his entire life. His parents go to our church and move in our circle. They're *our* sort of people – if you know what I mean.'

'Vulgarly rich?' I said.

'Now, now,' Bill Steele said. 'Let's not forget that King Solomon was very rich, and he was also very wise.'

'Indeed,' Linda Steele said. 'At any rate, Brian was a good

Christian and never told a lie. Surely you would agree with that, Miss Yoder, that good Christians don't lie?'

'Unless they're politicians – of all political stripes,' I hastened to add.

Linda frowned. 'Oh, no, you're not one of *those* people, are you?'

'Just on alternate Tuesdays,' I said. 'Please continue with your case. It's my lunchtime, and without biscuits or treats of some kind, I could get crabby.'

'What my wife was trying to say,' Bill barked, 'is that we believe Brian. This means that without a doubt an Amish farm wagon was out on Augsburger Road at two a.m., and that it did not have the two flashing red lights attached at the rear, as required by state law. Brian swerved to avoid hitting the wagon, and that's when he hit the telephone pole.' He stopped to wipe tears from his eyes. 'We know that Brian's story didn't hold up in court, because so-called Amish experts – such as you, Miss Yoder – swore that no Amish person would be about at that hour of the night, unless it was a family emergency, and if they were out, they would be driving a buggy, not a farm wagon. But Brian wasn't lying, and he wasn't hallucinating either.'

'And he's a good Christian boy,' Linda repeated. 'He's a Presbyterian.'

'And listen, Miss Yoder,' Bill added, 'we presume that the Amish are good Christians as well. We have no intention of suing anyone; all we want is justice for Brian, who was swerving to *prevent* an accident. He didn't lose control of the car because he was drunk.'

I'll say this for the Steeles, they certainly were loyal supporters of their son's best friend. On the face of it, I'd have to agree with Toy's conclusion, and the jury's, that Brian was responsible for Jason's death because he'd been driving drunk. But it was clear to me that the Steeles believed Brian's account. On the other hand, something was definitely fishy in Halifax, to coin an expression. Someone, quite possibly me, was going to have to prove the existence of an unmarked farm wagon.

'Well,' I said at last, 'as much as it pains me to say so, I think that your concerns have merit.'

'*You do?*' they asked in unison. Linda's voice was a squeak, and Bill's scraped the bottom of the bass barrel.

I nodded. 'I have two sons, and even though neither of them are Presbyterians, I have taught them to be honest – uh, well, my husband did. I, as you might have heard, have a tendency to embroider stories, but to good effect.'

Linda smiled gratefully. 'Everyone in Hernia knows that you have impressive embroidery skills.'

I felt my cheeks redden, so I changed the subject. 'Where in England was your butler from. I mean, did he have family to return to? Loved ones to look after him?'

'Oh yes, his husband Hank of twenty-four years. They have a home in Bognor Regis, which Baines claimed is the sunniest town in England.'

'Baines was gay?' I asked.

'Of course,' Linda said. 'He was English.'

'Don't be ridiculous,' I said. 'Not all English people are gay!'

'Oscar Wilde was,' she said, as if that proved her point.

There is no use arguing with Presbyterians, because they generalize so much, therefore I said my goodbyes as quickly as possible.

Gabe proved to be a wonderful host, and tour guide, in my absence. He'd seen to it that everyone was properly fed – with our cook's help, of course – and then he took them all to see the Frank Lloyd Wright masterpiece, Falling Waters.

Even the rest of the evening transpired without an undue amount of drama. I kept reminding myself that Christine Landis was one of God's children, just like the rest of us, and that I only had tonight to put up with her tongue, which was sharper than a two-edged sword. Tomorrow I'd get a call from one of my Amish cousins (there is an old-fashioned call box out by the highway), informing me of their selection, if any. If they decided to choose Miss Landis, then I had a motel or two in nearby Bedford already lined up for her if she needed to stay longer to sort out business details. Satisfied that everything was under control when I crawled into bed that night beside my Pookey Bear, I was at peace with the world. In a manner of speaking.

TEN

I once thought that I heard a panther scream (there are rumours of them still roaming these mountains), but the sound I heard that time was merely one of our guests achieving marital bliss. I have heard many six-year-old girls scream, and six-year-old boys, for that matter. However, none of those ear-piercing sounds have come close to comparing to the sound that woke me from a deep sleep at around three o'clock the next morning.

I could tell that it came from upstairs, so without even donning slippers and a robe, I gathered my long cotton night-gown in clenched fists, and raced up my impossibly steep stairs. Fortunately for me, the stairway light had already been switched on, otherwise I would have broken my foolish neck. When I reached the top, I didn't have to go far, because lying on his back, halfway out of his room, room number one, was Terry Tazewell. Even an amateur sleuth such as myself could diagnose the cause of this man's death: his jugular vein had been sliced. I shan't go into any details, except to say thank heavens that the hallway wasn't carpeted, or it would have cost me a pretty penny to get it cleaned.

It was also obvious who had been screaming, because she was still at it. Therefore, I had no choice but to clamp one of my large, yet shapely, hands over Kathleen Dooley's mouth.

'Let's take a little walk,' I said gently in her ear, and then with my other arm around her shoulder, I steered her back to her room. I was very much aware that the other guests were also at the scene of the crime, their mouths agape, and they trooped in after us. Momentarily Gabe thundered up the stairs, and I could hear him talking on the phone out in the hallway.

'Ducky, dear,' I said, 'please close the door.'

'Yes, ma'am. Shall I lock it?'

'Yes,' I said. 'My husband will knock if he wants to come in.'

'Miss Yoder, you're a twit,' Christine Landis said. 'Why did you bring us into this bedroom? Why not take us downstairs, where we could make a run for it? Now we're sitting ducks – and one of us is literally a sitting Ducky.' She laughed hysterically.

I don't mind sharing that this remark infuriated me. 'For your information, sister, I didn't take *you* anywhere. You followed Kathleen and me into this room. I happened to choose not to go downstairs, because blood has pooled across the width of the hallway, and I didn't want Kathleen to have to step through it to reach the stairs. Are you satisfied? Well, even if you're not, just shut up!'

Both Ducky and Kathleen applauded my tirade, which informed me that the latter had recovered enough for me to ask her a few questions. I am not a touchy-feely sort of person, so I had long since dropped my arm from Kathleen's shoulder, but I was still holding one of her plump little hands in mine.

'Tell me, dear,' I said, 'what were you doing up at this time of the night?'

'I was looking for the toilet,' she said. 'All I have is this little pencil-size flashlight, and the battery is dying, and well, I didn't think to use my phone. Anyway, I was really groggy, you see – I'd taken a pill – and I forgot which direction to turn once I got outside my door. All of a sudden I felt something wet under my feet, and then that's when I looked down. Then I found the wall switch.'

'Why wasn't the hall light even on?' Christine Landis demanded. 'Are you *that* cheap?'

I bit my lower lip before answering. 'Because you signed on for the full Amish experience. Their houses don't have electricity, remember? At least I supplied you with flashlights.'

'Yeah, dinky little ones,' Ducky Limehouse said.

'Well, they're meant to be keepsakes,' I retorted. 'They have the name of my inn printed on them. But enough of that. Did any of you hear anything unusual tonight?'

'I'm a sound sleeper,' Christine Landis said. 'I don't need to take pills. I don't take any medications. Never have, never plan to.'

'Never say never,' I said. 'Once you turn sixty, then it's patch, patch, patch.'

'Ha!' she scoffed. 'That's only if you've ruined your body with chemicals, which is what medications are.'

'Well, in that case, I hope that you give thanks to God every day for giving you a perfect body.'

'Was that supposed to be sarcastic?' she snarled.

'Don't be silly,' Ducky Limehouse said. 'Women aren't capable of sarcasm; Miss Yoder read that in a book somewhere.'

'If it's in black and white, then it must be right,' I said. 'So how about you, Ducky, did you hear anything unusual this morning, other than the perfect Christine Landis snoring?'

'*What?*' Christine snapped. 'I don't snore!'

'That's why I had to take a pill,' Kathleen Dooley said.

'You do sound like a chainsaw,' Ducky Limehouse said, 'but it reminded me of home.'

'You came in loud and clear through the ceiling,' I said. 'I had to turn our white noise machine to a higher setting. It's a wonder that I could hear Miss Dooley scream.' That might have been a wee bit of an exaggeration, but it wasn't an out and out lie.

'Harrumph,' Christine Landis said, or something approximating that.

Thank Heavens I heard Toy's voice in the hallway then. He must have been returning from a night call of some kind to be so close, and for that I was grateful.

'Stay here,' I told the others, as I slipped out, and then closed the door behind me.

Toy was looking at the corpse when I stepped into the hallway, but he looked up and drew a finger across his own neck. 'This is a first, isn't it?'

'Yes,' I said. 'The first in Hernia that I know of. God willing it's the last of its kind.'

'It's barbaric,' Gabe said.

'Taking a human life is always barbaric, dear,' I said.

My beloved gave me the evil eye. He is not a pacifist. He believes that there is such a thing as justified war. He even vacillates on the death penalty – which surprises me, considering that he's Jewish and calls himself a liberal.

'Life is precious,' Toy intoned, which sounded like something that he'd heard at one of his Episcopalian funerals. 'Anyway, I've already called the coroner. She'll be here within the hour. Then we can move the cor— I mean the victim.'

'Which coroner did you call?' I asked.

'Beth Gordon, of course. We only have the one.'

'Ferret Face,' I mumbled.

'Magdalena!' Gabe said.

I hung my head in simulated shame. I would have to repent of my name-calling later when I was genuinely sorry. The truth is that if one created a Halloween mask that looked exactly like a ferret's face, and then held it up to Beth Gordon's face, one would think that they were seeing double. That is hardly an exaggeration. Now, normally I would not stoop to name-calling, or judging a person by their appearance, but Beth Gordon is even meaner than a bag full of cut snakes. Maybe throw some poisonous spiders into the mix. Beth Gordon makes Christine Landis seem like a pussycat by comparison. And by that, I mean a teensy-weensy kitten that's curled up inside one of my otherwise, almost empty, bra cups, fast asleep.

'That's OK, Magdalena,' Toy said, 'no one likes that woman. She is, however, good at her job, and willing to work for a salary that any other qualified medical doctor would laugh at. We're lucky to have her.'

'Does Magdalena even have to be here when Beth arrives?' Gabe asked.

Toy shook his head slowly. 'Nope. Not at all. Not if you think you can entertain the guests until she returns? Make them coffee, or a light breakfast. Heck, I could use a strong cup of jo now too.'

'Can do,' Gabe said.

'Where are the guests, anyway?' Toy asked.

'All in room number three. But I have to warn you: Christine Landis is not a happy camper at being sequestered. She thinks that her human rights are being violated. That woman is a—' I stopped myself, before my tongue could speak more evil.

'Then off you go, Mags,' my dear, considerate husband said kindly.

'Uh – like where? Do I take some bedding, and go sleep in the barn?'

'Didn't you and Agnes used to do that when you were kids?' he suggested helpfully. 'You've talked about having sleepovers in the hayloft.'

'Yeah,' I said, 'when I was ten.'

'I had a thought,' Toy said. 'How about you give Agnes a call? You can stay with her.'

'Wait a minute. You want me to wake her up at this obscene hour. You know she'll throw a hissy fit, and then when I get there—'

It was too late. Gabe already had her on the phone. And on speaker.

'Who died?' Agnes asked calmly.

'One of our guests was murdered.'

'And you have to call Ferret Face, so you need to get rid of Mags for a spell. Am I right?'

'You either have ESP, or you've bugged our house,' Gabe said. He wasn't joking.

'I just know my girl. The bed in the guest room already has clean sheets. I might fall back to sleep by the time she gets here, so I'm leaving the back door unlocked. If she needs to talk, tell her to bring something sweet and to put a pot of coffee on before waking me. Night.'

That was my cue, so I stepped back over the corpse, and made a beeline for the historical part of the village of Hernia. I knew my girl as well, so I didn't bother bringing anything sweet with me. She heard me drive up and met me at her front door with a giant mug of coffee with extra sugars and real cream, and there were cinnamon rolls defrosting in her microwave.

'Details, details,' she demanded as she sat me down at her kitchen table. 'But first, two rolls, or three?'

'Three.'

'And that's why we're friends,' she said.

'Well,' I said, 'I did read once that the reason one always seems to get so hungry when one travels, is because our ancestors, like a million years ago, never knew when they could count on their next meal as they travelled. But of course, that theory is a bunch of hogwash, since God created us only six thousand years ago.'

'Whatever,' Agnes said. Agnes belongs to a more liberal branch of the Mennonite church, but she's still supposed to be a Bible-believing Mennonite. Yet the older she gets, the shakier her faith becomes. One of these days she might topple right off the ladder of belief, and land in the lap of that liberal branch of the Presbyterian Church to which Linda and Bill Steele belong. Then only God can save her.

I thought it wise to change the subject, so I gave her all the details about the murder that I could. I also filled her in on each of my guests, and my visit to the Steeles.

'Hmm,' she said, sympathetically, 'you've definitely had your hands full. That Christine Landis sounds horrid. Mags, I don't know why you don't just sell the inn and move someplace nice and warm. And beautiful. Like Charleston, for example.'

'Charleston has hurricanes.'

'Then what about California?' Agnes said.

'Because then I'd lie awake all night expecting the next big earthquake. They say it's long overdue.'

'Well, you could still retire from inn-keeping,' Agnes said. 'Lord only knows that you don't need the money. And you certainly don't need to be getting involved with the Steeles.' She sighed. 'Oh, but I do miss Baines. Still, I'm sure Hank is awfully glad to have him back home, and he'll see Baines gets the proper medical care.'

'You knew Baines, the Steeles' butler?'

'*You* didn't? No, then why would you? Baines was an accomplished pianist, who played for the Pittsburgh Philharmonic Orchestra. He worked for the Steeles part time – mostly when they gave parties and wanted to impress their friends. Although he was a musical prodigy, Baines grew up in a circus family, and was trained as a tightrope walker. When he was seventeen, he had to run *away* from the circus to follow his passion. Imagine that: someone running away from the circus to find themselves!'

'Oy vey,' I said. 'My, how you do go on. So, Agnes, dear, I doubt if my guests are going to want to sleep upstairs another night, but we have to billet them somewhere, given that they are all persons of interest in this murder, and—'

'You want to stash them in my two extra bedrooms,' Agnes said sharply. 'You just said they were persons of interest. That means one of them could be the killer.'

'But if two guests stayed here, there's about a thirty percent chance that one of them might *not* be the killer! You have to maintain a positive outlook on life, Agnes.'

'When pigs fly, Mags. You have that suite of rooms behind your house that you built for Freni. Put your guests in there.'

'Agnes, you know that my cook, Anna Weaver, lives there, now that Freni has passed.'

Agnes picked up a fourth cinnamon roll, and then wisely put it down. She gave up on dieting long ago, but she still wants to be able to *walk* into a nursing home when the time comes.

'So? Send Anna here for a few days, and house your murder suspects in Freni's grandmother suite.'

'They aren't suspects yet, dear,' I reminded my friend. 'Currently they are merely persons of interest.'

'Oh, bull-hockey! You know, Mags, as well as I do, that one of them did it. And I can tell you right now that it wasn't that horrid woman from Chicago.'

'Is this your psychic powers at work again? Should I start calling you Madam Agnes?'

Agnes laughed. 'Yeah, I like that. But really, I said that because she's too horrible to be a really bad character. The really dirty stuff is always done by the "goody two shoes" in books. That mean woman from Chicago is a red herring.'

I had just bit into my fourth cinnamon bun, and that fragment went flying across the room as I burst out laughing. I laughed for far too long, stopped, and then laughed some more. I finally stopped altogether when I noticed that Agnes's normally round and rosy face appeared pinched and white.

'Agnes,' I said quickly, 'I didn't mean to offend you. It's just that this isn't one of those cozy mysteries that you are so fond of reading; this is real life. There isn't some talented author behind the scenes trying to throw Toy and I off the track of catching Terry Tazewell's killer. But even if that were the case, there would always be the chance that mean Christine is just an act, and that usually she is a saint, and the much more cooperative Kathleen is actually a monster back home. A really clever author could do that – or make Ducky Limehouse the killer. Or even Gabe.' I paused dramatically. 'Or *you*! Now that would be a surprise.'

Agnes snorted coffee out of her nose, which made up for me spitting a cinnamon roll fragment across her kitchen. '*Me?* What possible motive would *I* have? But Mags, has it occurred to you that this wasn't a murder after all, but a suicide?'

A goose walked over my grave. '*Suicide?*'

ELEVEN

'Suicide? How would that even be possible in this case? Wouldn't he have to have a large, sharp knife? Like a butcher's knife? I certainly didn't make a thorough sweep of the area, but I didn't see one.'

'Well, it was just a thought,' Agnes said.

'Well, if you have any thoughts about how I should handle the Steeles, let me know. I realize that they're grieving, but wet birds don't fly at night, and the Amish don't drive at night. It's as simple as that to me.'

'Those are two truisms I can't argue with – well, I don't know about the first. It seems too general, and too flip. What about a night-flying bird that suddenly gets caught in the rain?'

'Anyway, I'll send Anna Weaver over – but not to cook for you. Just to stay here. I mean, she can bring back food from the inn for you, but that's all. I still need her to feed my guests.'

Agnes stuck her tongue out at me. It's something she's done to show her displeasure ever since we were three years old.

'If I didn't love you so much, Mags, I'd – I'd – well, I'd do something you wouldn't like.'

'Toodles, dear,' I said, and saw myself to the door.

And speaking of the devil, with a small 'd', of course, Anna Weaver was the first person I saw when I returned to the PennDutch. She was in the kitchen manning two large cast-iron skillets. In one she was frying bacon, and in the other she was scrambling eggs.

'Here, Miss Yoder,' she said in her bossy-pants manner, 'you take over the bacon. I don't want them eggs to scorch.'

'Yes, ma'am,' I said.

'And when it looks nice and crisp,' she said, 'take those tongs over yonder and lift them pieces out and lay them atop them paper towels. Nobody likes greasy bacon, except for you and Mr Yoder.'

'His name is Dr Rosen,' I said, not that it made any difference.

Anna Weaver marches to her own drumbeat, and one of the drumsticks was lost years ago. The woman is less than half my age, and has no education beyond the eighth grade, but she still manages to intimidate me.

'You Englishers and your strange ways,' she muttered.

To the Amish, anyone not of the faith, is referred to as an Englisher. That's because the majority of the people whom the Amish associate with speak English in their daily lives, whereas the Amish speak a dialect of Swiss German. At any rate, Anna was born and raised Amish, but left her people behind during her rumspringa. This is a grace period accorded all Amish youth in their late teens, when they are permitted to experience the ways of the outside world for a period of two years. The Amish baptize young adults, and they want to make sure that these candidates know what they're giving up, in order to formally enter into a covenant with such a strict faith.

Although it has been several decades since Anna ceased to be Amish, and she is shunned by her family, she still refuses to think of herself as an Englisher. A more stubborn woman I have never known. If it weren't for the fact that she was a double second cousin on my mother's side, and triple third cousin, once removed, on my father's side, I'd have half a mind to send her packing on some days. Still, she does look a lot like Mama did when she was young – more's the pity, though – and it helps keep me on the straight and narrow.

'*Cousin* Anna,' I said as I started plopping the bacon on the mound of paper towels, 'serve the Englishers, and then come back right away. We're going to have ourselves a little chat.'

'Chatter now, Miss Yoder,' she said insolently, as she scraped the eggs into a serving dish.

'*After*,' I said, through gritted teeth.

Anna grabbed the tongs from me, flung the bacon on a platter, and within seconds was out the swinging door to the dining room with both dishes. I could hear her plonk the dishes on the buffet, and she was back before the door stopped swinging.

'What have I done now that you don't like? Or this time do you think that I killed the Englisher man upstairs? Because I know how to kill a pig, yah?'

I threw up my hands in exasperation. 'That hadn't even occurred to me!' Then the Devil grabbed my tongue and gave it a good hard tug. 'But come to think of it, you are very adept with knives, particularly the butcher's knife. Plus, there's the fact that you don't seem very fond of us Englishers, even though you decided to join our world.'

'Ach, Magdalena, you are not a real Englisher; you are only sort of an Englisher. Your grandparents were all Amish. Besides, who would not like to live in the world of the Englishers? It has electricity, and television, and Adele.'

'Is Adele that new coffeemaker that you can start from your phone?'

'Ach, Magdalena, you are so behind the times.'

'I'll grant you that. This time. Now listen up, dear, because I have a proposition.'

Anna's hands flew to her face. 'Shame on you, Magdalena. What kind of woman do you think I am? Attractive, yes, but to proposition me, there is no excuse!'

'Oh, hush up,' I said crossly. 'Not *that* kind of proposition. Besides, you're the spitting image of my mother. I want to make you an offer you can't refuse, that's what.'

'I refuse.'

'But you haven't heard the offer!' I shouted.

'Is everything all right in there?' Gabe yelled from the other side of the swinging door. 'If it is, we need more cinnamon toast.'

'And more coffee,' Christine Landis hollered.

'Ignore them,' I said sternly. 'I need you to move out of Cousin Freni's old quarters, and move in with Agnes. This is because the guests will need to be staying on for some time, and they can no longer stay upstairs, because that's a crime scene.'

'Yah, they are suspects!' Anna said smugly.

'No, no! They are still just persons of interest,' I said.

'Potatoes, potatoes,' she said, pronouncing both words alike. 'One of them is guilty. You will see.'

'Have it your way, dear. Now go take a fresh pot of coffee out there, while I make some more toast.'

'No.'

'I beg your pardon?'

'Miss Yoder, I will not move to Agnes's house unless I get a ten percent raise in pay.'

'What *chutzpah*!' I cried indignantly.

'Ach! Because you called me a name, I demand twenty percent.'

'Why I never,' I said, shaking my head. 'You are such an insolent woman, Anna Weaver. I have half a mind to fire you.'

Anna Weaver looked like the love child of Jay Leno and Jennifer Aniston. When she jutted out her chin, she could balance a glass of water on it, and walk across a room without spilling a drop. I say that merely as an objective observer, and not with a shred of meanness. I absolutely adore two of the three aforementioned parties, and I reiterate that Anna was the spitting image of Mama.

'Yah, Miss Yoder? If you fire me, then who will cook for these Englisher suspects, and of course you and Mr Yoder? You do not even know how to boil water without burning it.'

'For the last time his name is Dr Rosen, not Mr Yoder,' I screeched. 'And if I looked on the internet, I'm sure I could find plenty of instructions on water-boiling. I might even learn how to fry it!' Of course, I was being facetious. I learned how to boil water when I was in my teens, when Mama took to her bed during one of her many nervous breakdowns.

'Look, toots,' I said, wagging a long shapely finger at Anna, 'I can always hire another cook. But who is going to hire a cook who can't stand the Englishers? Why did you give up being Amish, if you have so much contempt for people of the outside world?'

The Amish are known for being a kind and gentle folk. Anna Weaver was clearly the exception. I already knew that, but I had never been so direct in asking her to explain herself.

'I wanted TV,' she said simply. 'And to drive a car. But no cell phone. Cell phones are like a halter for a horse that has blinders attached. The horse can see only straight ahead, never from side to side. The cell phone user is a prisoner of his phone, yah? He can see only it, never his companions, never anything around him. Just tap, tap, tap.'

At that point Gabe barged through the swinging door. 'What is going on in here?' he demanded. 'It sounded like the turkey farm down on Koenig Road.'

'Yah?' Anna said. 'That was your wife, Mr Yoder.'

I smiled sweetly at Gabe. 'Perhaps we did both get a wee bit carried away. But dear, sweet Anna has agreed to move in with Agnes for a twenty-five percent boost in her salary, so that our guests can move into Freni's old cottage. Wasn't that decent of her?'

'Anna, how wonderful!' Gabe said, and flashed her one of his beguiling smiles.

'Gabe, sweetheart, would you please make some more cinnamon toast while I carry the coffee out? I need to catch up with Toy.' I kissed him and snuck out with the coffee pot before he could answer.

The three remaining guests looked up from their food when I walked in and set the coffee pot on the sideboard, but they wisely said nothing. Since Toy wasn't with them, I poured him a cup of coffee, fixed it to his liking, and hiked up my impossibly steep stairs. In my absence, Terry Tazewell's body had been removed by the coroner, and a thick sheet of plastic had been used to cover a good deal of the hallway floor. I could see immediately that no attempt had been made to clean up what lay beneath it. That job would be either mine, or Gabe's, later on that day. Anna would certainly not agree to do it, not for any amount of increase in her salary.

'Toy?' I called. 'Are you up here?'

He popped his head out of the victim's room. 'Come in but be careful that you don't slip. What took you so long?'

I handed him the coffee. 'I made nice with Agnes first and arranged to have Anna sleep over there. That frees up Freni's old place for the guests. You're welcome for the coffee by the way.'

Toy took a couple of deep sips before answering. 'Thanks, this hits the spot. Although some bacon would be nice too. Don't think I can't smell it up here.'

'I'll see that you get some. Have you learned anything so far?'

'Just enough to be confused. Magdalena, to whom was this room registered?'

'The murder victim, of course: Terry Tazewell.'

'Hmm. Were he and Ducky Limehouse lovers?'

'*What?* Not under my roof!' I slapped my mouth gently when I considered how that sounded. Toy is, after all, a dear friend, and gay. 'What I mean, Toy, is that I sincerely hope that they weren't engaged in any rumpy-pumpy, as the Brits would say, because I find it so icky to think of anyone else doing it – other than, well, you know.'

'You and Gabe?'

I nodded.

Toy laughed. 'Magdalena, this is an inn – where adults stay the night. I dare say that there have been a great many rumps pumped here over the years. That's just a fact of life.'

'Nah, nah, nah, nah, nah, nah, nah, nah,' I said with my hands over my ears.

Toy gently clasped one of my hands in his and pried it from my horsey head. 'I asked the question because I found evidence that both men seem to have been using this room.'

'No way!'

'Yes way,' he said. 'The tag on the suitcase has Ducky Limehouse's name, and his address in Charleston.' Then he pointed to the bed. 'However, in the nightstand I found this set of car keys, with Terry Tazewell's name attached to it, as well as his wallet, and this copy of an email he sent you preregistering with you, concerning his stay. Wouldn't you say that's a bit odd?'

I frowned. 'I would, indeed. Perhaps Terry Tazewell and Ducky Limehouse switched rooms, in which case I would be very unhappy. Guests aren't supposed to do that. I need to be able to keep track of their whereabouts when they are under my roof, because I'm responsible for them.'

Toy smiled. 'I understand, but in this case, Terry Tazewell is even unhappier than you – well, maybe he was for a second. His relatives certainly will be.'

'You haven't notified them yet?'

'I'll do it right now, if you'll go downstairs and fetch me up a plate of bacon and cinnamon toast. Oh, and another cup of coffee will be nice.'

I bowed deeply. 'Yes, Chief Graham.'

When I returned the plate of bacon was three slices lighter and I was still munching on my second slice of cinnamon toast. It wasn't my fault, mind you. Murder is a major cause of stress, and that morning I dealt with stress by returning to my roots – that is, eating from three of four Amish food groups. Lard, sugar, starch and more starch.

I'd taken care to pile the plate high enough so that Toy didn't miss what I'd taken from it, but he nailed me on the coffee.

'I need my java,' he groused good-naturedly. 'I can't think without my drink.'

I saluted him. 'Yes, sir,' and down my tortuous stairs I went again. It's a wonder that no one has ever died from breaking their neck on those steps. When I returned, I found Toy lifting finger-prints from the bathroom fixtures.

'Is that to see if both men shared this room?' I asked.

'Yes,' Toy said without looking up.

I set the coffee on the bathroom counter. 'There's a quicker way to do this.' I went to the door of the room, faced the stairs, and hollered like I was calling my children in from the backyard for dinner.

'Ducky Limehouse! Come upstairs! You're wanted for questioning!'

TWELVE

Ducky Limehouse is both quick to respond, and light of foot. He leaped up my impossibly steep stairs like the ibex in a nature film I'd seen on Gabe's gargantuan TV. Ducky, unlike most ibexes, was wearing light blue cotton broadcloth pyjamas. When he reached me, he wasn't even breathing hard. Oh, to be that young and spry again.

'Yes, ma'am,' Ducky said. 'You called?'

'You bet your bippy I did. Were you and Terry Tazewell sharing a room?'

Ducky Limehouse blinked. Aha, I thought, guilty! In my experience, guilty people always blink while they consider which lie they're going to use for an answer.

I tapped the toe of one of my scuffed black brogans. Incidentally, I had changed out of my nightclothes into a fresh set of daytime clothes when I was at Agnes's house. I keep a spare set of clothes, and shoes, in the back of my car, which is something that every sensible person should do. Accidents do happen the older one gets. Along those lines, one would do well to stay away from the back end of a horse.

'You may as well confess,' I said, 'because we have incriminating evidence.'

'Indeed we do,' Toy said. He was holding *my* coffee, which I'd set on the bathroom vanity, and then he had the temerity to sip from it.

Meanwhile Ducky sucked air in between his brilliantly white teeth because he knew he had some explaining to do. 'OK, I confess – but it's not what you think. Here's what happened. I'm afraid of ghosts. I always have been. I know, I'm from Charleston, and the city is supposedly teeming with them, but that doesn't mean that I find them amusing. I find them terrifying.

'Long story short, I did not want to stay in a room in which someone was murdered. To me that was just plain creepy, and I didn't understand your cavalier attitude to assigning us those rooms without checking with us first. In fact, I distinctly remember requesting a "murder free" room.'

'I'm sorry,' I said. 'I wasn't thinking straight then. My mind was still in a kerfuffle, thanks to my encounter with the ever-so pleasant Christine Landis. Talking opposites, of course.'

'Anyway,' Ducky said, 'I was able to persuade Terry to switch rooms with me, and we were both tired. So, I'm guessing that one, or both of us, must have left some stuff behind.'

'You guessed correctly. But now answer me this: Terry Tazewell was half in, half out of your new room when he was so brutally murdered. We'll have to wait on the coroner's report to see if the perpetrator rendered him unconscious first, but even if that was the case, surely you would have heard *something*.'

Ducky Limehouse shook his head vigorously. 'No, ma'am. I don't sleep well when I am not in my own bed. I always travel with Xanax and pop a pill ten or fifteen minutes before turning in. Last night I took two pills, because I was afraid of waking up to find a stinking spectre standing at the foot of my bed. But then when I actually got in bed and felt all the lumps in that fifty-year-old mattress, I downed a third pill. For me it was "lights out" until I heard your shrill voice waking us all up at this ungodly hour.'

'Why I never!' I huffed. 'First of all, my granny does *not* stink! And second, that mattress is thirty-five years old, and not a day older. And thirdly, my voice is not shrill; it has been known to calm babies.'

'Maybe baby wolverines,' he muttered.

I stomped one of my boat-size feet. 'This is outrageous. Whatever happened to that sweet Ducky Limehouse from Charleston? It's like you've been possessed.'

Ducky stepped over to the nearest wall and slumped against it. He reminded me of my sons during their teenage years, when they were growing so fast that the boys' bones seemed unable to support their bodyweight.

'Look, I'm sorry, ma'am. I truly am. I don't know what came over me. My mama would be truly ashamed of me if she'd heard how I'd just spoken to you.'

Sincere apologies are always accepted by Yours Truly. 'That's quite all right, dear.'

'You're excused for now,' Toy said, and since he'd been slurping from my coffee all along, he drained it before continuing. 'But send Kathleen Dooley up. And another coffee for Miss Yoder. Heavy on both cream and sugar. If it didn't sound racist, I'd have said sticky and white, just like her.'

'But you *did* say that,' I protested. 'And I'm not sticky; I bathed this week.'

Toy smiled. 'I meant it affectionately.'

'Hmm, Toy Boy, I shall keep that in mind.'

Perhaps we bantered further, if so, I choose not to recall what was said. Friendly exchanges like this can easily go off the rails when one has been deprived of sleep, caffeine and carbs. What does stick out in my memory is that for a decidedly plump person, Kathleen Dooley appeared to be in remarkably good shape. Although she didn't leap up my impossibly steep stairs like an ibex – after all, she was carrying my coffee – she scaled this mini-Everest like a Tibetan pony. The 'clop, clop, clop,' of her feet never paused on the wicked ascent, and when she handed me the cup, I could see that not a drop had spilled over into the saucer.

'You're still quite an athlete,' I said. She was even dressed like one, in sweatpants and a sweatshirt.

'Walking up stairs isn't anything,' she said dismissively. 'Anyone healthy should be able to do that.'

'But you didn't spill a drop!'

'It's my old circus training. When you're walking the high wire, you can't afford to be wobbly.'

'For a long time, I wanted to be a trapeze artist,' I said.

'Get out of town and back!' Toy said. 'No way!'

'Way,' I said. 'Agnes's parents were the more liberal kind of Mennonites, and for her tenth birthday, they took us to see the Ringling Brothers Circus in Pittsburgh. When I saw the beautiful woman flying through the air, and then being caught by the handsome man, I thought that there couldn't be anything more wonderful than that. Not even Heaven. Of course, the costume that she was wearing was sinful. I'd have to wear a skirt that went below my knees, and then if I went flying through the air, the skirt would fly up over my face, and expose my sturdy Christian underwear. That would be even more sinful. Besides with my skirt over my head, I wouldn't be able to see the handsome man, so I would crash to the floor of the big tent and die.

Then I would go to Hell. So, as you might guess, that fantasy didn't last very long.'

'Or maybe you would have just floated down, buoyed by your skirt,' said Toy, trying to be helpful. 'Sort of like a parachute.'

'The clowns would have had a great time with that,' Kathleen Dooley said, and then clamped a hand over her mouth.

'I thought that was a wonderful story, Miss Yoder,' Ducky said. 'When I was little, my parents took me to the state fair in Columbia, and I saw all these fancy breeds of chickens. I decided then and there that I wanted to be a chicken farmer. I especially wanted to raise Wyandottes.'

'How fascinating,' I said. I meant it. In my opinion the Wyandotte breed of chicken is the most beautiful of all, and that happens to be what I have scratching about in my chicken yard.

'Those were Wyandotte eggs that you had for breakfast, dear,' I said proudly.

'Ahem,' Toy said, 'My, how we've digressed.'

'Well, it's your fault, Toy,' I said.

'*Me?*'

'Yes, you,' I said. 'You got me side-tracked, because you expressed such surprise that I wanted to be a trapeze artist. Anyway, Mr Limehouse, please go back downstairs, and feel free to ask the cook to make you some fresh Wyandotte eggs. Anna is not married, and she is very susceptible to flattery – but then aren't we all? My point, if you sense any reluctance from her to resume her cooking duties, then pour on some of your Southern charm.'

Ducky bowed slightly. Then, like an ibex leaping down a sheer mountainside, he disappeared from sight.

'Now then, Miss Dooley,' Toy said, as he consulted a small notepad, 'I understand that you had the room next door to Mr Tazewell – er, Limehouse.'

'Excuse me?' Kathleen Dooley said.

'So then you were not aware that the men switched rooms, Miss Dooley?' Toy said.

'No, sir,' Kathleen Dooley said. 'I was not aware of that fact. I was outside stargazing until quite late – out in one of the pastures out back. When I turned in everyone was in bed. You see, in coastal New Jersey where I live, there is so much light pollution. I had a hunch that the air would be clear out here in the sticks, so I brought my own telescope with me. Would you like to see it?'

'The *sticks*?' I hissed. Please note that the hissed word not only contained two 'S's, but it was italicized. Had a spitting cobra been lurking nearby, it would surely have been impressed.

Kathleen Dooley's hands flew to her face. 'Oh, I didn't mean to offend you, Miss Yoder. Please forgive me. I really like it out here. In fact, last night, before the unfortunate incident, I was contemplating buying a summer cottage here.'

Toy's face hardened. 'The *unfortunate incident* took a person's life.'

Kathleen Dooley's face reddened. 'Dear me, again I misspoke. Believe me when I say that I see every human being as precious. I'm pro-life, by the way.'

'Most living people are,' Toy said archly.

'No, I mean—'

'He knows what you mean, dear,' I said quickly in order to stave off a potential argument. 'Please go back downstairs and send Christine Landis up. Tell her to bring up some bacon if there is any. If there isn't any bacon left, then I'd like you to please tell the cook to fry up some more and have her bring it up herself.'

Kathleen Dooley turned to go, but then turned again. 'Wait a minute,' she said, speaking to Toy. 'I thought that you were the law. And if so, why is Miss Yoder allowed to give orders?'

'Because *mea est secundum imperium.*'

Kathleen Dooley's eyes widened. 'Because she's your second in command? Do you mean to say that Miss Yoder has had police training?'

Poor Toy. He looked like he'd been caught with his hand still in the cookie jar. How was he to know that Kathleen Dooley had taken Latin in school, much less paid attention? The only reason that Toy knew some Latin was that he had attended a Catholic high school in Charlotte for two years.

Toy brought out his biggest weapon – his smile. It's the kind of smile that makes you feel that he sees right through your exterior, and that he genuinely cares about you as an individual and respects your journey through life.

'Magdalena Yoder's experiences in crime-solving make her eminently more qualified to be my *secundum imperium* than any amount of formal police training. If you prefer, however, I can make the same request of you that she did.'

'No, I get the picture,' Kathleen Dooley said. However, she took her own sweet time getting back downstairs. Granted that the staircase was steep, and it had a sharp turn, and the steps were narrow – oh, and the handrail was a mite wonky, but she'd ascended it much faster carrying my coffee. Still, I had to give the woman props for maintaining a calm tone throughout our little exchange. At no time did she raise her voice, or employ sarcasm, or cause us any problems.

I wish I could say the same for the entrepreneur from Chicago. Apparently, Christine Landis was one of those hedonists, like my own Sweet Baboo, who believed that the nightclothes the Good Lord gave them at birth, could not be improved upon. Therefore, when she'd heard Kathleen Dooley screaming, she'd slipped on a diaphanous silk robe that tied in the front, and which left very little to the male imagination. I trusted Gabe and appreciated how hard he had tried to avert his eyes away from Christine's bodacious and telling assets, if you get my drift. The corpse had shown no interest in Christine's private parts, that I could tell. To my great embarrassment, Ducky obviously had. Thank heavens Toy was gay.

'Yes? What do you want now?' she snapped. 'I'm here to secure exclusive rights to Schmucker Brothers Sausages, not to murder some weirdo restaurateur who humiliates his patrons by making them eat from pig troughs.'

'Of course, that's exactly something the killer might say,' I said.

When a beautiful woman glares at you, it can be strangely alluring. 'Who's to say that you're not his killer? You own a kitchen full of knives, don't you?'

'Well – um, yes I do.'

She turned to Toy. 'So put the screws to her. Everywhere Miss Yoder goes, murder follows. That should be your first clue, Inspector.'

I put my hands on my hips, a decidedly un-Mennonite thing to do. Mama would have scolded me, to see me adopt such a 'proud' worldly stance.

'Look, toots,' I said, 'I follow murder, not the other way around.

Our chief of police here will be the first to acknowledge that I am quite good at solving them.' I glanced at Toy. 'Isn't that right?'

'Yes,' Toy said, 'but you have to admit that an uncanny number of murders happen here at your inn.'

'*Et tu*, Brutus,' I wailed. 'You just told Miss Dooley that I was your *secundum imperium.*'

'Huh?' scoffed Christine Landis. 'Just because you're his second in command, doesn't keep you from being a murder magnet, and this so-called Pennsylvania Dutch inn of yours from being murder central.'

They say that the best defensive is often a good offensive. Well, I can be very offensive when I put my mind to it. I slipped my hand into the pocket of my thick, modest robe, and withdrew my phone. Then I pretended to listen to a call.

'Uh-huh, OK,' I said to my phone. 'I'll tell her.' Then I looked at Christine Landis. 'That was the Sodom and Gomorrah costume shop calling for you, dear. They want Jezebel's see-through handkerchief back.'

'No problem,' Christine Landis said, and in a twinkling of an eye, the scrape of filmy fabric that she'd been wearing floated to the floor, leaving her in the altogether.

Toy and I both gasped. I, for one, gasped at her audacity, but also at the sight of such physical perfection. Why on earth did the Good Lord have to match up such beauty with such an ugly personality? I would have been happy to have been given even just ten percent of her looks. It just didn't seem fair, but then again who am I to judge the Lord? Maybe back in Biblical times, *I* was what passed for a good-looking woman, and that's what God was remembering when he created me. Perhaps women with hourglass figures, and perfect features, would have made grown men scream with fright, and run for the hills. OK, that was unlikely to have happened, but thinking of it gave me a small measure of comfort.

Toy came to his senses first. 'Miss Landis, I can either arrest you for public indecency, or you can repair to your room and get dressed.'

'Well, Toy Boy,' Christine Landis purred, 'if you arrest me, you'll have to get close enough to handcuff me, won't you?'

'That woman is evil,' I said.

'Pot calling the kettle black!' Christine Landis snapped. 'By now everyone in America knows that you're an adulteress. And don't give me that song and dance about you being an inadvertent adulteress either, because you didn't know he was a bigamist. Only a truly ignorant bimbo would be so stupid that she wouldn't think to do a background check on the man she was about to marry.'

I hate to admit it, but sometimes the truth really *does* hurt. Ignorant and bimbo would henceforth be added to the long list of names I'd either been called, or that I called myself.

'Ignore her,' Toy said. 'She's trying to distract us. Miss Landis, go back to your room and put on something decent. If not, you will spend the night in my lockup, where the accommodations are even sparser than they are here – no offense, Magdalena.'

Christine Landis ran her tongue seductively around her lips. 'I look forward to spending one-on-one time with you, Chief.'

'Go, get dressed,' Toy said gruffly.

'All right,' she huffed. 'You don't have to be mean about it.'

I waited until she'd disappeared into her room. 'I don't understand how a person like that managed to become CEO of a string of grocery stores throughout the Upper Midwest.'

Toy shrugged. 'Beats me as well. All I can think of is that we all have many sides to us, and we just haven't been shown her managerial side.' He cleared his throat. 'By the way, Magdalena, Miss Landis did make one salient point: I do need to interview Anna Weaver. So go take stock of all your kitchen knives. *Every* knife needs to be accounted for. Even the steak knives that you store with the dinnerware.

'Oh, and send the guests up, one by one, so that I can supervise them packing their belongings. After all, this entire floor is now a crime scene, and we wouldn't want one of them chucking a knife out of their bedroom window now, would we?'

'Is that so?' I said, perhaps a mite snarky, which is not my usual style, I assure you. 'What about Miss Hotsy Totsy, who this very minute could be tossing a guillotine out her window for all you know?'

Instead of getting angry, Toy's eyes twinkled. 'Magdalena, please, just go and do as I ask. *Please.*'

It is hard to make my seventy-four-year-old faded blue peepers twinkle, but I gave it the old college try. 'OK, Toy Boy, since you asked me nicely this time, instead of ordering me like you did the first time.'

THIRTEEN

Then I turned, and despite feet the size of tennis rackets, and stair steps as narrow as my mind, I was able to get to the dining room in a jiffy. Practice makes perfect, as they say. I'd been going up and down that wicked staircase since I was a toddler. (Correction: when I was a toddler, I *tumbled* down it countless times.)

Anyway, Kathleen Dooley and Ducky Limehouse were both relieved that they were being given new, more comfortable quarters. The building where Anna Weaver now lived, and which had been Freni Hostetler's retirement house, had two bedrooms, each containing two single beds. Ducky Limehouse immediately requested the room that had been vacant when Freni had died. I didn't have the heart to tell him that Freni's husband Mose had passed on in the room he selected. At any rate, what was I supposed to do? Put Ducky Limehouse up in the barn? Thank heavens Kathleen Dooley, although a somewhat eccentric woman, was at least gracious about doubling up with the most unlikable Christine Landis. Maybe Gabe or Toy could inform her of that. But speaking of Gabe, he'd already headed outside to milk our last remaining cow, a sweet little Jersey named Lady Latte.

My duty to my guests temporarily fulfilled, I headed into the kitchen. There I found Anna Weaver dutifully cleaning up after breakfast, but with a bit of an attitude. In fact, one might say that the scullery maid was scowling whilst she was scouring, were one given to tongue-twisters and alliteration. Although personally I eschew clever wordplay.

I knew better than to poke a hornet's nest while it still hummed, so I set about taking an inventory of all my knives. Most established kitchens contain a broad variety of knives, from the small paring knife up to the much larger butcher's knife, each blade designed for a specific use. Since mine was a very old kitchen, and no one in my family ever threw anything away, I probably had close to twenty cutting implements scattered around the room (all out of reach of small children, of course). There was absolutely no way I could make an accurate count of the knives from memory. Some of these utensils I hadn't even looked at closely in years, much less used. Their absence would mean nothing to me, except—

'*Gott im Himmel*,' I shrieked, which is as close as I've ever come to taking the Lord's name in vain. On the other hand, since God *is* in Heaven, perhaps that wasn't so bad after all.

Anna stopped scowling and dropped the cast-iron frying pan in the sink with a porcelain-cracking thud. A second later Gabe charged through the swinging door.

'Babe! Are you all right?'

'I'm fine dear; I've got this covered. Please go back to your milking. And thanks, by the way, for taking care of that.'

'Anna, dear,' I said as calmly as I could when the door closed behind him. 'Where is the bread knife?'

She shrugged. This razor-sharp knife is used exclusively for slicing our home-baked loaves into slices thin enough for the toaster.

'I couldn't find that one this morning,' she said. 'So I used store bought bread from the freezer. You didn't notice?'

Store bought bread is never as good as Anna's, but we always keep a couple of loaves in the deep chest freezer 'just in case'. In other words, they're there for emergencies.

'No, I didn't notice,' I said. 'I had other things on my mind, like a dead man in the upstairs hallway.'

'Huh,' Anna said. 'Well, you always said how much better you liked my bread than store bought. Maybe a thoughtful person would have noticed.'

I swallowed my irritation. One may be interested in knowing that irritation, like pride, contains very few calories.

'Anna, might I assume that you did a *thorough* search of the kitchen? Even the laundry room? You know how absent-minded you get when you start singing one of those endless Amish hymns from your childhood.'

'Maybe if you put a radio in the kitchen, then I don't have to sing,' Anna said, and folded her arms over her chest.

'Over my dead body,' I said, and copied her stance. 'With a radio comes that stuff they call rap music and listening to that will lead you straight to Hell.'

'That is silly, Miss Yoder.'

'Oh yeah? I would bet you dollars to doughnuts that the Devil plays rap on his radio, except that I'm not a betting woman, because that too will lead you straight to Hell.'

Anna started to say something, then thought better of it, uncrossed her arms, and put a hand over her mouth. I'll say this for the ex-Amish woman, she had chutzpah.

I decided to ignore her insolence. 'Well?' I demanded. 'Did you do a thorough search?'

'What do you think?' she said. 'I'm not a stupid teenager. I'm almost thirty.'

'Anna, dear, if your mother could hear you now, and see how you act—'

Anna's face clouded over. 'My mother doesn't speak to me. You know that. Because of the Ordnung – the rules – no Amish person is allowed to speak to me. Forever, unless I repent in front of the church. Because I stopped being Amish. Even my baby sister is forbidden to look at me.'

'Yes, I do know that, Anna, and I am so sorry that you have this burden. But now I have to concentrate again on the murder that happened here last night. Did you hear, or see, anyone walking outside your apartment, or the main house late last night?'

'Yes,' she said, without hesitation.

'Who?' I asked excitedly.

'My friend.'

'Your friend?'

'My girlfriend. She went into your house to get some milk.'

'Did you say *girlfriend*?'

'Do you have trouble hearing, Miss Yoder?'

'It's more of a comprehension problem, Anna. Are you saying that you are gay?'

'No. I am a lesbian, Miss Yoder. That is why I can never re-join the Amish community. What I really mean to say is that I do not *want* to re-join the Amish, because I refuse to say that who I am is a sin.'

Despite five hundred years of inbred reticence to hug another person other than one's parent or sibling, I opened my long, gangly arms wide and took a few tentative steps toward her. But much to my relief, Anna took as many steps back. It wasn't that I was afraid of catching 'lesbian germs', I just didn't want to give her the false impression that pats on the back would give her. We Mennonites can never seem to hug, without patting the recipient of our hugs, as if we were trying to burp a small baby after bottle-feeding time.

'Anna,' I said, 'not that it's any of my business – but it sort of is, because I own the cottage . . . Do you and your girlfriend do the mattress mambo in there?'

I may as well have asked my Jersey cow a trigonometry question.

'Huh?' she said.

'You know, the two-sheet tango.'

Anna's right index finger made circular motions beside her right temple.

'Don't be rude, dear,' I said. 'So now you're going to force me to come right out and say *that* word, which should only be whispered behind closed doors. Do the two of you have sex on *my* sheets, on *my* bed and in *my* personal guest cottage?'

'Sometimes,' Anna said, and neither blinked nor blushed.

'Why, you little hussy,' I hissed.

'It is not a sin, Miss Yoder. The Bible does not say woman shall not lie with woman.'

'But you're not even married!'

Anna shrugged. 'Why would I marry a woman that I do not love? Shirley Valentino is sexy, yah? But she has too many bad habits. Miss Yoder, you like to gossip; would you like to hear some of Shirley's bad habits?'

'I do *not* like to gossip!' I huffed. 'Wait just one pea-picking minute. Did you say that your girlfriend is our mail carrier? *That* Shirley Valentino?'

Anna rolled her eyes. 'Do you know another one in Hernia?'

Suddenly Anna's love life had taken on a new dimension. 'How did you meet Shirley?' I asked.

'Duh,' Anna said, in an explosion of breath. 'At the mailbox by the road. Where else did you think? At the Mattress Mambo Club?'

'Ha, ha,' I said, 'good one.' Then I realized how foolish I'd been to let my preoccupation with premarital sex lead my investigation so far astray. 'Anna, did you say that Shirley came in here in the wee hours this morning to fetch some milk?'

Anna twittered. 'I did not say *wee* hours. What are "wee" hours?'

'Very early. Small hours on the clock – like one, two, or three o'clock. Anna, strangers are not permitted to come in by themselves and wander around unaccompanied.'

'Shirley just went for milk because the milk in the cottage fridge ran out. She is very trustworthy; everyone in Hernia knows her. Besides, you do not lock your house.'

'That doesn't matter,' I said. 'This is still my house, and no one is allowed to come in without my permission. You do realize that this makes your girlfriend, Shirley Valentino, a suspect in the murder of Terry Tazewell?'

Anna rolled her eyes again. 'Do not be ridiculous, Miss Yoder. Shirley did not even know this man.'

'And you know that for a fact?'

'Maybe, maybe not,' she said. 'But Shirley is a good woman, even though she belches at the table, and snores louder than my papa. Shirley delivers the mail rain or shine, and always with a smile.'

'Let's put it this way, dear,' I said. 'Only two people, other than my husband and myself, had easy access to the kitchen knives last night. That is to say, those two people didn't have to creep down, and then back up, my impossibly steep stairs, which sound like a groaning old man.'

Anna's jaw dropped. 'So you think that maybe I killed the Englisher man?'

'Did you?' I asked.

Her chin scraped the floor. 'In my heart, Miss Yoder, that is where I kill people. Not in the flesh. In my heart I do not need a knife.'

'Did you kill Mr Tazewell, the murder victim, in your heart?'

'Yah,' she said, and her lower lip began to quiver. 'Yah, in my heart I killed this Englisher man because last night, after dinner, he came into the kitchen and put his hands on me.'

'*Where* on you?'

Anna cupped her left breast.

'Oh, Anna, why didn't you tell me?' I cried.

'Because it was business, yah? And I planned to get my own revenge on this Englisher man.'

'Revenge?' I said. 'Like what?'

'Hot chilli peppers in his breakfast omelette. Shirley got them for me from the supermarket in Bedford.'

I shook my head. 'So your girlfriend knew that this man assaulted you, and wanted to help you get back at him. Then she comes here in the middle of the night to get milk – *here*, where there are oodles of knives. Doesn't that seem crazy to you?'

Anna laughed. 'You are the crazy one, Miss Yoder. Everyone in Hernia loves Shirley. They say things like: what stranger can move into a village and become so popular so quickly? Only Shirley Valentino! Maybe if she did not have so many bad habits, then I would marry her.'

People's bad habits always intrigue me. Maybe that's because I have so many of my own. And who knows, it was theoretically possible that her habits would be germane to my investigation.

'What other bad habits does she have?' I asked. 'Besides belching and snoring?'

'She does not always shave. Under her arms, or her legs.'

'How very Amish of her,' I said.

Anna glared at me. 'Yah, but Shirley is an Englisher. Those are things she is supposed to do.'

'Not necessarily, dear,' I said. 'Anything else?'

'She insists that I shower every day. Not once a week, but *every* day! Even when it is cold outside. When I tell her that this will surely bring on sickness, she just laughs. Old wives' tails, she says. Magdalena, I try not to judge her, but when have you seen an old woman with a tail?'

'Only rarely,' I said. 'Any other truly awful habits you care to share?'

'Magdalena, are you mocking me?' Anna said.

'I was, and I apologize.'

'Very well. Yes, Shirley must touch everything three times. For example, if she wants to go outside, she must touch the doorknob twice before she can touch it again so that she can turn it. The same thing for the faucet, or for picking up a book. Magdalena, this makes her a very good lover.'

'TMI!'

'What does that mean?'

'Too much information – although, on second thought, I might pass that tidbit on to Gabe. Not that septuagenarians are interested in such matters anymore.' I tried to wink, but as usual, I must have looked as if I'd gotten cinders in both eyes.

Anna gasped. 'Miss Yoder, I did not know that you changed religions.'

'What on earth are you talking about, Anna?'

'Septuagen – you know, what you said.'

I smiled gently. 'It means someone in their seventies.'

'Then who were you talking about? Aren't you and the doctor both eighty?'

'Look, toots,' I said, 'if I had the power to arrest you on account of your *chutzpah*, I'd whip out the cuffs right now.'

'Not if I arrest you first,' Anna said with a glint in her eye. 'When I was on rumspringa I learned about this thing called citizen's arrest. You have a very bad temper, Miss Yoder. Maybe you got angry at the tall Englisher man, and it was *you* who took the bread knife.'

I threw up my hands. 'You're exasperating. I don't know why I even put up with you. Give me one good reason why I shouldn't fire you right now.'

Anna blinked, which was a point in her favour. 'Because, Miss Yoder, you are a kind Christian woman who always calms down and does the right thing after she flies off her handles.'

'Well, you better hope that I didn't fly too far off my handles this time, dear. Continue with your work in here, and then when you're done, go and strip the beds in the cottage and replace them with fresh sheets. In the meantime I'm going to have a little chat with our chief of police.' I turned to go.

'Miss Yoder, wait!'

'Yes?' I said hopefully. 'You wish to confess.'

'In a goat's ear,' Anna said.

'My, aren't we colourful? Is that an Amish expression that I'm unaware of?'

'It is an Anna expression. Goats have big ears, and they are good listeners that never tell secrets.'

'I'll keep that in mind when I have something I'm bursting to spill,' I said. 'What is it that you wanted?'

'Now that I told you all Shirley's bad habits, what do you think? Are they really so bad? Because if I can prove that she didn't kill this strange Englisher man who makes his customers eat like pigs, then I hope that you will approve of my marriage to Shirley Valentino. Trust me, Miss Yoder, she is the only woman who I will ever love. We will be two peas in the same pod, just like you and Mr Yoder.'

I sighed so hard that flour, spilled on the floor a decade earlier, and which had found its way into the corners of the kitchen, rose in little puffs. Unless one uses cotton swabs dipped in a water and vinegar solution, and gets down on their hands and knees on a regular basis, those corner bits are nearly impossible to keep entirely clean by Mennonite standards. I've become a little less obsessive (dare I say, rigid, in my thinking?) as I've gotten older, and one of my first outward manifestations of this is kitchen corners that, upon examination with a magnifying glass, are no longer spick and span.

'Anna, dear,' I said, 'first of all, you should have said "whom" instead of "who".'

'Huh?'

'Never mind. And secondly, my husband is Dr Rosen, *not* Mr Yoder, as you very well know. Also, given that my beliefs are based on scripture, I can't approve of your marriage to Shirley. But on the other hand, I can be happy that you have found someone who makes you very happy.'

Anna wagged a finger at me. '"Whom", Miss Yoder, *not* "who".'

'Whatever,' I said, as I rolled my eyes. It felt good. No wonder so many young people do it.

Anna laughed. 'Ha, ha! You look so silly. So uncool. But now that you are happy for us, I can invite my new bride to move into the cottage once this group of Englisher guests leave, yah?'

'*What?* You're married? You played me for a fool?'

Anna smiled broadly. 'Yah! Shirley is my wife.'

'*Oy veys mir!*' I cried in Yiddish, and fled the kitchen.

FOURTEEN

Toy was amused to learn that Anna and Shirley were wife and wife. However, he was extremely troubled when I immediately followed that bit of news by telling him that Shirley had had the run of the house during the night at what could have been the time of the murder. He was livid when I told him that the bread knife was missing.

'Magdalena,' he said sternly (always a gentleman, that's as livid as he gets), 'you should have called me immediately with that information.'

'Yes, well, I was trying to ferret out as much information as I could first.'

'About her love life?' he said.

'It's my cottage, and they're my sheets. And fornication is forbidden in my Bible.'

'Magdalena, I swear, sometimes I think that I don't even know who you are anymore. I thought that you had stopped being judgemental.'

'I had,' I said, close to tears. 'But just not in my house. I still have a right to judge in my own personal space, don't I? Or else what's America for?'

'Look,' Toy said, and I knew that he was struggling to keep his emotions under control, 'I'll handle things here, if you drive into town and talk to Shirley. Please, Magdalena, don't get side-tracked, and get into the same-sex marriage issue. Not this morning. Not unless you can bring me back a gallon of Starbucks coffee and a dozen Krispy Kreme glazed doughnuts that are still warm from the conveyor belt.'

'But we don't have a Krispy Kreme bakery anywhere near here,' I wailed.

'And another thing, Magdalena, you are to *talk* to Shirley, not to grill her like a Schmucker sausage. I let you assist me for three reasons: you have a fine track record in solving murder cases; you are the mayor of our little village; and you are incorrigibly nosy.

But if you hadn't insulted Officer Smith last month so badly that she quit, I would have an actual, trained person to assist me on this case.'

'Harrumph. All I said to her was that her handwriting looked worse than chicken scratching. Her annual report on your department looked like the proverbial homework that the dog supposedly ate, and then threw up. If you ask me, the day that they stopped teaching cursive writing in our schools, is a day when the barbarians at the gate celebrated. How are the future generations going to be able to read our historical manuscripts? Maybe their true meanings will be twisted, or lost altogether.'

'You have a point,' Toy said. 'But then again, can you read the Bible in its original Hebrew, Greek and Aramaic?'

'Don't be absurd,' I said, and thundered down my impossibly steep stairs.

I wasn't in the mood to be outfoxed for the second time that morning. I was also going to take a gallon of coffee for me, but I preferred warm cinnamon buns as they were more substantial than doughnuts. My needs were more easily met, so I pressed the pedal to the metal and sped into the city of Bedford, which is our county seat, and just twelve miles away. There, within minutes, I was able to zero in on both my carbs and my coffee, and by the time I parked in front of Shirley Valentino's house I was already partially refuelled.

One might reasonably suppose that Shirley would be out on her route, but when have I ever thought reasonably? Perhaps I just misspoke. What I mean is that I try to think outside the box as much as possible. Boxes like boundaries are meant to be ignored. There are only two occasions when something must absolutely stay inside a box as far as I'm concerned: one is when your cat goes to relieve itself, and the second time is a funeral.

My thinking was that if Shirley Valentino was indeed the murderer – she certainly had the opportunity – then she would probably be home now, trying to recover from the traumatic experience. I know that I would. Don't get me wrong! I could never take a human life. I apologize to the weeds that I pull up in my garden (a practice I learned from my daughter, Alison), but *if* I did commit murder, the energy it would take to force one's soul to leave their mortal husk would wipe me out, so to speak. It would leave me flat on my back for weeks.

Thus it was that I rang Shirley's doorbell, fully expecting her to be there, and so she was. In fact, she was fairly bouncing with what appeared to be happy energy. Could it be that I was dealing with a serial killer? Had a merry psychopath moved from Philadelphia to Hernia, to settle in our midst?

'Magdalena Yoder!' she exclaimed. 'How good to see you. Come in, come in. I've been expecting you – well, sooner or later.' She had a way of laughing that sounded like the sleigh bells some Amish attach to their horse-drawn sleighs in the winter. And yes, the Amish hereabouts actually use 'old-fashioned' sleighs when snow covers the roads.

The second I stepped over the threshold I smelled warm cinnamon buns. My nose twitched and my eyes watered.

'Have you been baking, dear?' I said.

'Oh yes,' Shirley said, 'I just took them out of the oven. Would you like one? And I also made a pot of homemade hot chocolate – from scratch. I can pour you a mug if you like.'

'You didn't scorch the milk, did you?' I asked. 'One has to stir it constantly, you know.'

'It's smooth as silk,' Shirley said, and the sleigh bells jingled again.

Now this was an offer I couldn't refuse, given that the cinnamon buns that I'd purchased earlier in Bedford were already cold. Plus, hot chocolate is always an improvement on coffee in my book. The only problem was that in order to partake of her sweet treats, I needed to make room.

'Shirley, dear, where is the ladies' room?'

The mail carrier laughed loudly. 'That's a good one, Miss Yoder! That implies that there might be a men's room as well. Anyway, it's straight down the hall. At the end. If you do miss it, you'll have walked through a wall and into my neighbour's yard.' At this point she was bent over with laughter.

That was fine with me. It meant she didn't see me carry my purse with me into her bathroom. I always find using other folk's toilets a dicey business at best. Of course I line their seats with toilet tissue – any sane person would do that. But beyond that, I never touch anything with my bare hands. That's what my purse is for. In it I carry multiple pairs of disposable gloves, of the sort that doctors wear when examining their patients.

To be completely germ-free, one needs to put the gloves on *before* entering the lavatory and remove them *after* exiting. I follow this regime even in public loos, but I have to sneak out of the stalls when no one is around. Otherwise I will garner dirty looks when folks spot me leaving the room without turning on the tap.

At any rate, you can bet your bippy that I made a thorough search of Shirley's modest bathroom for any clue that would support my theory that she might be a serial killer. Well, lo and behold, I actually found one! I didn't find my bread knife – that would have been so obvious as to have been unbelievable. But what I did discover immediately put her on my list of official suspects. Shirley Valentino's toilet tissue rolled the *wrong* direction! Every normal, rule-following person sees that their toilet tissue rolls in the same direction that my tissue does, and I don't need to tell *you* which direction that is – if *you* are a law-abiding person. So here was Shirley, our village mail carrier, employed by the United States Post Office, a branch of the Federal Government, secretly rebelling against bathroom convention. Add in the fact that she came into my house uninvited, in the dead of the night, which is a real crime. That is called 'breaking and entering'. To sum it up, here lived a woman who was capable of just about anything.

When I returned to the kitchen Shirley gave me the cutesy-face frown which I hate to see on a grown-up woman. 'Oh, Miss Yoder, is there something we've forgotten?'

'To say grace over my bun?'

She giggled. 'To flush the toilet, silly. Also, I didn't hear you running water in the sink.'

'*What?* You were listening for water sounds?'

'Miss Yoder. I can't very well have you returning to my kitchen with unclean hands now, can I?' She giggled again.

'Well,' I huffed, 'I did nothing that required me to wash my hands, or to flush your precious commode, with its paper rolled the wrong way. You, however, committed a crime this morning, by coming into my kitchen uninvited! The law calls that "breaking and entering".'

Instead of giggling, Shirley gulped. 'B-but you don't have security cameras.'

'Don't I? Plus, your wife's a tattle-tale.'

She swallowed hard again. 'You know that Anna and I are married?'

'Yes, dear,' I said. 'Anna squealed like a piglet that had been caught by its tail.'

'So you know *everything*,' Shirley said.

'That's what I just said, isn't it?'

'So you're fine with me living in that cute little cottage with my wife?'

I recoiled in horror at the thought. 'I most certainly am not!'

'Because we're gay?'

'Because you have no manners! You took milk from my refrigerator without asking; that is stealing, my dear.'

'You have got to be kidding,' she scoffed. 'I just borrowed a cup of cow juice because I wanted to make some hot chocolate. I was having trouble sleeping.'

'Did you return the milk?' I said.

'Miss Yoder, forgive me for saying this, but you're even wackier than Anna says that you are.'

'Anna thinks that I'm wacky?' My cheeks burned. Trust me, even the wackiest of people don't like being accused of this personality trait.

'She says that you're three pigeons shy of a hayloft,' Shirley said smugly.

'My, what an interesting Amish metaphor,' I said. 'Perhaps it lost something in translation. While you reheat my hot chocolate in the microwave, I'm going to look around here for knives.'

She had a set of six knives on the counter that were housed in a block of wood. However, there may have been others lying around in drawers, so I began opening them.

'Stop that!' Shirley yelled. 'You can't do that without a search warrant. In fact, you can't even get a warrant, because you're not even a proper policewoman, you're just a buttinsky mayor.'

'Oh yeah?' I said. 'Well, you're a very much misinformed, lazy mail carrier who should be working today. Or did you wear yourself out making that peanut butter and jelly sandwich at three o'clock this morning in my kitchen? Or maybe it was the extra effort you took to stick your grubby finger into the marmalade jar, lick it, and make that horrible face? At least you used a spoon on the raspberry jam, but then you licked it before putting it back into the jar for another teaspoonful. Is that how you behave at your mother's house, dear?'

Shirley Valentino was ashen-faced. 'It's not my fault that I was caught. Anna told me that there weren't any cameras!'

Now it was my turn to smile smugly. 'I'm not as stupid as I look, dear. What kind of full-board inn could I run if I didn't have security cameras, especially given our reputation as the murder capital of America? Of course I checked them after your wife told me about your unlawful visit.'

The microwave signalled that my beverage was hot so I removed it while Shirley nattered away. 'Well then, Miss Big Shot Yoder, your latest murder should be already solved, shouldn't it? Just review your security footage and quit hassling me, the brave and loyal government employee.'

'Would that we could, if I wasn't such a cheapskate. The last time foul play ensued upstairs at my inn, the perpetrator disabled the nanny-cam before committing his crime. As I am basically retired, and these guests were here as a special favour I was performing for the Schmucker brothers, I didn't see the need to lay out the money to have the upstairs system repaired for a "one-off".'

Miss Giggle Pants was capable of a good, *long*, belly laugh. I didn't mind all that much because it gave me time to eat my fresh cinnamon bun (which I reheated for ten seconds) and sip my hot chocolate.

I waited until she was quite through before I spoke. 'You owe me one,' I said.

'I beg your pardon,' she said.

'It is common knowledge that a good hard laugh has health benefits – both physically and spiritually. So, you're welcome, and now let me inspect your drawers. And I don't mean the kind of drawers that a girl with your upbringing probably showed the boys at recess.'

Shirley grinned and wagged a finger at me. 'Miss Yoder, that was a mean thing to say, but it was also a lucky guess. You might have shown your drawers, too, if you had a dad who was career military, and you had to attend a different grammar school every six months. I may be rough around the edges, but I'm no killer.'

I took a couple more sips of my beverage before it cooled too much. A hot drink should be *hot* (just shy of scalding), or else it's a waste of water, and whatever else one chooses to add. Case closed. That said, I feel sorry for Her Majesty, the Queen of England, who must invariably suffer through endless tepid cups of tea. There is no conceivable way palace servants could deliver a pot of anything remotely hot from the kitchen to wherever she is, given those miles of corridors.

At any rate, while I enjoyed the fast-cooling cocoa, I considered Shirley's declaration of innocence. Shirley had certainly had opportunity, but what could have been her motive? There was none that I could think of. As much as it makes me uncomfortable to think of two women doing the headboard *bossa nova*, that does not give one of them a motive for murder. But if they danced the actual *bossa nova*, well that would be a different matter, because dancing is a sin. I'm not saying that I would write the word 'dancing' in her motive column, but I wouldn't be so quick to dismiss her as a suspect.

'Shirley, dear,' I said at last, 'have you and Anna ever gone dancing?'

'No. But I fail to see how it is any of your business.'

'Well, then my investigation is concluded. Now, if you and Anna wish to live as wife and wife, you will have to live here in this charming house – the one with the bathroom tissue rolled the wrong way. But Anna may keep her job and continue to work as usual.'

'Thank you, Miss Yoder, I accept that. But I'll have you know that my tissue *is* rolled the correct way.'

'Millions of Americans disagree with you, dear,' I said kindly. 'You need to get out more. Also, thank you for the delicious snack – although the cinnamon bun could have used just a pinch more cinnamon, don't you agree?'

'I agree that your visit is over, Miss Yoder.' She headed towards the front door.

'But first, would you be a dear and wrap up a few of those cinnamon buns for the road? One never knows what lies around the bend, so travelling with victuals might actually be a lifesaving move – even if the buns do need a pinch of salt.'

'Salt?' Shirley hissed. 'I thought you said they lacked cinnamon.'

'Did I? Dear me, it's so easy to get confused when one is my age.'

'Out!' Shirley barked. 'Get out now. And don't be surprised if your mail is late tomorrow. It might even be accidentally dropped in some mud and stepped on first.'

Having said that she grabbed one of my long, gangly arms and attempted to pull me to the door. Fortunately for me, the Good Lord saw fit to create me with two long, gangly arms, and I was able to snatch another cinnamon bun off the kitchen counter with my free hand. To be perfectly honest, Shirley's buns were actually quite tasty.

FIFTEEN

It may come as a surprise to a few Englishers that there are some strikingly handsome Amish men. One just has to overlook their scraggly beards, and how odd they look without moustaches. The custom of the Amish men forgoing facial hair on their upper lips dates back to the early days of the sect, when military officers wore long, curled moustaches, which the Amish saw as a sign of vanity. Incidentally, only married Amish men are allowed to wear beards. Whether or not a widower reverts to the smooth face of a bachelor depends on the local Ordnung – or community rules.

When Peter was sixteen, and went on rumspringa, he disappeared into the canyons of New York City. He was gone five years, not the usual two, and when he emerged from the city of nearly eight and a half million sinners, he brought with him a wife. This woman, age thirty-five, was anything but Amish. She had a PhD in sociology, and a master's degree in English Literature. It is important to note here that Peter, like virtually all Amish, had only an eighth-grade education, and was by then a full decade younger than his spouse.

Everyone in the Amish community (and quite soon in many other Amish communities) was dumbfounded. And since the Amish were not the only ones to shop at my Cousin Sam's grocery store in the village of Hernia, most of the Englishers were also gossiping about this unlikely duo, and speculating on how long this marriage would last.

Now, according to the Ordnung, this wasn't a real marriage because Peter and Delilah had been wed in a Unitarian Church, not an Amish Church. In order for them to be married in an Amish Church, Peter had to make his confession of faith, now that he was an adult, and be baptized into the Amish Church (the Amish baptize only adults). For Delilah, the path was not going to be quite so straightforward.

Bishop Schrock (my third cousin, twice removed) decided that

Delilah first needed to spend a year living with an Amish family and learning their ways. This included learning to speak their particular dialect of Swiss German, dressing like them, and of course religious instruction. Delilah surprised everyone by taking to it like a kid to candy, and when the year of probation was over, both Peter and Delilah were baptized and formally received into the Amish Church and subsequently married.

Peter went to work full-time for his brothers at Schmucker Brothers Sausages, which was still just a local brand, where he'd been apprenticing for the year leading up to his marriage. Meanwhile Delilah kept house (no small task without electricity) and maintained a large vegetable garden. As Delilah was by now almost thirty-seven, the couple wasted no time trying to get pregnant. They tried until Delilah turned forty.

On Delilah's fortieth birthday, Peter came home from work to an empty house. On the kitchen table, in his wife's spidery hand-writing, was a 'Dear John' letter. In it, Delilah wrote that she had never loved Peter; she had always only seen him as a subject to study for a book that she intended to write: *My Life as an Amish Wife*. She instructed him to thank everyone who had played a part in her 'acculturation', especially her host family. She did not, however, thank Peter, whom she viewed as 'oversexed'. Furthermore, she wrote that Peter should make no attempt to contact her in New York City, because if he did, she would immediately file for a restraining order to be placed on him. All this was apparently delivered in one run-on sentence, more's the pity. One would think that a woman who claimed to have both a doctorate and a master's degree would have learned how to write.

But anyway, one would think that such a letter would not have seen the light of day in Hernia. That Peter, who'd spent a good deal of time in the outside world, would have immediately burned it. But au contraire. His heart broken, Peter shared the letter with his baby sister, who was his favourite sister, who then shared it with her favourite sister, who was so upset that she ran and told their mother, who told Peter's father. Peter's father immediately saddled a horse and galloped over to see Bishop Schrock, who was at that moment meeting with a group of church elders. In turn the elders were so outraged at being deceived by this Englisher, that they hurried home and unloaded on their wives.

The next morning these wives were in my Cousin Sam's Corner Market rehashing every delicious and salacious detail, whether true or not, and my cousin, who happens to speak their dialect, felt compelled to share this interesting bit of news (in translation, of course) with all his Englisher customers throughout the day. Of course, those Englishers had phones, so that by the third day, virtually every adult in the village of Hernia, and the three Amish Church districts in the area, learned that they had been nothing but a sociological experiment.

Today was merely the fourth day since Delilah Schmucker retreated back into the canyons of New York City to write her expose of Amish life from her warped perspective. Thus, I was shocked, when upon returning to the PennDutch Inn, to see Peter sitting on the kitchen steps. He'd parked his buggy to the left of the driveway, close to the barn, and his horse was grazing contently on a strip of unmown grass. Almost equally surprising was the fact that Peter was clean-shaven, since the Ordnung requires all married men to wear untrimmed beards.

Peter with, or without, a beard, is unmistakably recognizable, because he is – in the words of many Englisher girls – drop-dead gorgeous. If I were to be honest, I would have to agree. And if my aging libido were to rob the cradle, so to speak, I would also have to admit that seeing Peter close-up caused my candle to flicker when I thought the flame was on the verge of being snuffed out.

Peter looks remarkably like the bronzed young men with the chiselled features one might see on the cover of those trashy novels sometimes referred to as 'bodice rippers'. You might rightfully ask how a Mennonite woman, such as myself, would know about these sinful wastes of paper, not to mention the destruction of the rain-forest in Borneo, and the habitat of endangered orangutans. The answer is quite simple. A powerful senator's wife, who was a guest at the PennDutch, left behind three of these books in a room. Each of these books bore a salacious title and a picture of a buxom woman dressed in period clothing. Her enormous assets threatened to spill out, and over, her cinched corset. Standing behind her, his strong arms helping to keep her balanced on her tiny feet, was a Peter Schmucker doppelganger – same wavy black hair, broad forehead, chiselled cheekbones and strong jaw.

The Bible specifically says that we are not to judge, lest we be judged. Some folks might say that this verse applies solely to judging people. But surely there is nothing wrong in giving it an expanded interpretation. Besides, unless I actually read one of these supposedly trashy books, I might just write off this great senator's wife as having low-brow tastes. Taken to the extreme, I might even jump to the conclusion that she was a slut (bear in mind that jumping to conclusions is my main form of exercise). So, I read one of the books. It was disgusting filth. But two books remained, and how was I to know if the author hadn't repented of her ways, and written something worth reading – maybe not even at the beginning of the book, but more towards the end? Of course, it had the same sort of cover, but you know what they say about judging books by their covers. Anyway, the second book had me running for Big Bertha, my bathtub with the thirty-seven jet sprays, long before I reluctantly put it down. It was that bad. The third book was even worse. I fed Gabe oyster stew for dinner and made sure we got into bed an hour earlier than usual.

But back to my second cousin, young Peter, sitting innocently on my back steps. He was the picture of the scorned husband. Although his head was held high, his eyes told the story of love found, and love lost, both within five years – a breathtakingly short amount of time in my opinion. Why, I have leftovers in my fridge older than Peter's love affair with Delilah.

Peter rose quickly to his feet when I passed in front of my car. He was dressed in his sect's traditional garb: dark blue pants held up by suspenders, long sleeve denim shirt rolled up at the elbows and a straw hat with a navy cloth band. He waited until I was immediately in front of him before speaking.

'Magdalena, you have heard.' It came out as a statement, rather than a question.

I nodded.

'Yah,' he said sadly. 'It is all true. So now everyone knows that Peter Schmucker was a foolish man.'

'Don't say that about yourself,' I said. 'You were a young man, and everyone knows that young men don't think with their brains – uh, pardon my allusion. Besides, her name is *Delilah*. She was born to lead you astray. Plus, she was twice as old as you. What choice did you have?'

'One always has a choice, Magdalena,' the Devil whispered in my ear, but I refused to repeat that to Peter. Who was I to talk? There are those in Hernia who would be happy to point out that my nether regions were what led me into my disastrous first marriage wherein I became the infamous, inadvertent adulteress.

Peter stared at me; his dark eyes were luminous with tears. I wanted to hug him, but five hundred years of inbreeding in our family put the cut-off line at first cousins, and Peter was a second cousin. Plus, if I gave Peter a warm, enveloping hug, like my Jewish relations give me, that would only confuse him further.

He must have noticed my inner conflict. 'Magdalena, please do not judge me too harshly. Please let God be the judge, yah? Right now I need a friend.'

'Oh, cousin, I'm not judging you! I just wanted to give you a hug – a real one, with no slapping. But I thought you wouldn't like it and run into the wood screaming.'

Peter laughed as he wiped his eyes on his sleeve. 'A quick Englisher hug then, yah? But without slapping.'

So we defied our common tradition and performed an actual hug. Not one slap occurred. Not even one finger tap transpired. The hug may have lasted all of three seconds, but it got five hundred years' worth of ancestors turning in their graves, both in Pennsylvania and back in Canton Berne, Switzerland where our families originated. I read somewhere – the source seemed reliable – that barely detectable earthquakes occurred in both locations that day.

After we disengaged physically, Peter recovered from his embarrassment first. 'Magdalena, I am actually here on business. My brothers sent me to give you their verdict on the three candidates you brought out to be interviewed yesterday.'

'Yes?'

'As you know, most Amish have not had as an extensive period living out in the world as I have – well, it's not just that. There is a lot of sexism in scripture. Read what the Apostle Paul has to say.'

'Good grief, Peter. That was two thousand years ago, and had to do with women's role in the church, not their role as business partners. Are you saying that both of the women candidates that I took out there were passed over because they had ovaries, instead of testicles?'

'Ach! Why are you always like this? It is not so Mennonite.'

'What way?'

'Your language, Magdalena. It is always so graphite.'

'You mean graphic, dear, but your answer is that I say exactly what I think.'

'Well, then maybe you should think less sometimes. Besides, one of those women was very rude to my brother Solomon.'

'That would be Christine Landis. She definitely has a chip on her shoulder. But what fault did he find with the other?'

'He said that her accent reminded him of Delilah.'

'But it was a New Jersey accent, not a New York City one.'

Peter shrugged. 'East Coast. He doesn't know the difference. He did his rumspringa in Pittsburgh.'

'Tell me the truth,' I said. 'Was there ever a possibility of you three going into business with a woman?'

Peter chewed his lip before answering. 'No. I think not.'

'Then why did you bother to interview them?' I said, and I could hear the anger in my voice.

'Because these days we must appear to be compliant with the law. Compliant – that is the right word, yah?'

'Yes, if you're using it to describe sexist hypocrites,' I said.

Peter smiled. 'Anyway, Solomon said that he very much liked the tall, skinny man who served his customers out of miniature pig troughs. That made him laugh, and he is a very serious man.'

'As I well know,' I said. 'Unfortunately, Peter, that tall, skinny man went to be with the Lord last night.'

Peter appeared stunned. 'He *died*? Was it a heart attack?'

'No, Peter, he was murdered.'

'Here?' he asked sombrely.

I nodded.

'Oh cousin, there are some who believe that this is an evil place. I have heard it said that the best thing is for you to burn it down, and then move far away from here.'

Water boils at one hundred degrees Celsius, but my blood has been known to boil at room temperature. 'Burn my house down?' I shouted. 'Whose idea was that? I bet it was the Widow Gnagey!'

Peter shrugged slightly, which was the same as saying 'yes'.

'Well, it is *not* going to happen!' I said. 'That kind of talk is pure superstition, it's not even Christian, if you ask me.'

'But Magdalena, maybe what the Widow Gnagey whispers is not so bad – I mean, compared to what Tobias the Strong said during the barn-raising meal so that everyone could hear.'

My ears burned, as if I was there. 'What did he say?'

'He said that maybe it wasn't your place that was evil. Then he looked up and down the long table and smiled. Everyone there understood his meaning except for Slow George. Later his daughter explained it for him.'

'*Ach du Lieber!*' I said. 'If I wasn't a pacifist, I'd have half a mind to box Tobias the Strong's ears! That's slander, plain and simple. Before this day is out, I'll have another notch to put on my belt.'

'Huh?' Peter said.

'It's an Englisher expression. Don't worry about it. Anyway, you may as well be the one to share the good news with them.'

'Is that sarcasm?' Peter said.

'Yes. Sorry. But since they can't think any worse of me, say whatever you want. But I want you to know that I did *not* kill this Englisher.'

Peter grabbed my hands and held them firmly. 'Cousin, I believe you.'

'And the PennDutch Inn is not cursed. It isn't evil; only people can be evil. You know, like Hitler, or Mugabe.'

Peter squeezed my hands before releasing them. 'I believe the same as you, Magdalena. You must remember that we Amish do not go to school beyond grade eight. The purpose, as you know, is to keep our minds from getting contaminated with worldly viewpoints. But like you almost came right out and said before, an ignorant mind is fertile soil in which to plant superstition.'

'I said that?'

Peter winked. 'You are a wise woman, Magdalena.'

I stared at my second cousin, who had just recently chosen to be readmitted to the Amish faith as a professing adult. Some time when I had the chance, I would love to know just exactly how he'd spent his time in New York City. Many Amish youth spend their rumspringa experimenting with drugs, alcohol and sex. Peter had obviously followed a different path. It was common knowledge that he was exceptionally bright. Then again, so are many other Amish teenagers, which might explain why approximately twenty percent of them choose not to be baptized into the faith of their fathers when the time comes to make their choice, and are thereafter forced out into the world permanently.

'Well,' Peter said, as he stood, 'I have to get back to my brothers with the news. They were somewhat impressed with one of the candidates you brought out last month – a Mr Jeff Stevens, I believe. They'll probably choose to go with him. He seemed easy to work with, and he was – how should I put this—'

'Normal?'

Peter laughed. 'Yah, you took the word right out of my mouth. The pig troughs amused them, and going with the deceased might have made good business sense, but now I think that they will be more comfortable with their decision in the long run.'

'I agree,' I said. 'I guess I better go in and deliver the disappointing news to the ladies. Wish me luck; they've been up half the night, and one of them, as you know, doesn't have the nicest of personalities.'

'"Be strong",' Peter said quietly.

'"And of good courage",' I said, completing the scripture verse from the Book of Joshua. Then I slipped past him, and into the kitchen to face the music.

SIXTEEN

The music was loud and discordant. Although Toy was through taking brief statements from all three guests, all three of them were too worked up by what they had seen, plus copious amounts of caffeine, to go back to bed in our private guest cottage. They had all heard the hoof beats of Peter's horse, and watched at the dining room window as his buggy drew up the lane. They'd waited in the kitchen with bated breath, as they drank more cups of coffee – except for bathroom breaks. When I opened the kitchen door, they descended on me like a pack of ravenous wolves on a helpless fawn.

'Miss Yoder,' howled Christine Landis, 'where's the handsome Amish man? Why isn't he with you? Was he one of the Schmucker brothers?'

OK, so maybe she didn't exactly howl, but she did try and push past me, and I had to use my toothpick arms to block her from rushing outside. That I was able to stop her was a wonder, given the disparity in our ages, and phenotypes. Perhaps it was unpleasant memories from bygone days that provided the burst of adrenaline that turned spindly old me into a line-backer.

When I was a child, back in the good old days, before playground safety had yet to be dreamed of, teachers had us play a game called Red Rover. Two teams faced off at either end of a given space, in straight lines, and holding hands. Then, taking turns, the teams would chant, 'Red rover, red rover, we dare Magdalena [or whomever] over.' The child chosen would run as fast as he, or she, could and try to burst through a pair of clasped hands. If the player succeeded, they could bring a player from the opposing team back with them. However, if the line held firm, and the runner failed to break through, then he, or she, had to join that team. In summary, it was a good way for children to get sprained wrists, and sometimes even broken arms.

It took me a minute to catch my breath, but I let it stretch into two. Meanwhile Christine Landis backed off and joined Kathleen

Dooley and Ducky Limehouse at the kitchen table. Christine had a peculiar gleam to her eyes, which I hoped was new respect for me, and not murderous intent.

'Yes,' I said, 'the Amish man who was here was indeed one of the Schmucker brothers. He is the youngest brother, and his name is Peter. And yes, he came here to deliver their decision.' I paused on purpose just to punish Christine Landis. I know that was sinful of me, and I have since repented – but just to God, not to her.

All three of them leaned forward, even though Ducky didn't have a dog in the hunt. I folded my large, but well-shaped, hands in front of me, and shook my head solemnly.

'Folks, I'm afraid that the Schmuckers have rejected you as potential partners. They would have, however, gone with the recently deceased Terry Tazewell. I'm really very sorry about that, as I'm sure it must be extremely disappointing news.'

'What did you say?' Christine demanded at a million decibels.

'You heard me, dear. They turned down both you and Ms Kathleen Dooley.'

'That's so sexist!' screamed Kathleen Dooley.

'You should have warned us that they're anti-ovary,' Christine raged. 'I'm going to sue you for time spent out of the office, travel costs and accommodations – such as they are – and emotional damage.'

'Ditto for me,' Kathleen said, only a bit more calmly.

'Now hold it, ladies,' Ducky said, in his slow, Southern drawl. 'You may be jumping to conclusions here. I've seen pictures of Amish men and women working together in the fields, side by side, at harvest time. It's possible that they thought Terry really was the best man for the job, given his affinity for pigs.'

'Oh, shut up,' Kathleen Dooley said, with surprising vehemence. 'You men always stick together, and that irks the heck out of me. In fact, it makes me almost as sick as your accent.'

'Wait a minute,' Christine Landis said. 'I love a good Southern accent. It's you Easterners who drive me up a wall. Sometimes I want to stick a finger down my throat.'

Kathleen Dooley, who had never given me any trouble, held up a single finger. A middle digit. 'Go ahead then. Be my guest.'

Christine Landis lunged across the table, grabbed Kathleen's finger and bit down hard. Kathleen screamed in pain but managed to wrest her finger away from Christine's mouth. But then Christine grabbed the heavier woman by the shoulders and pulled her the rest of the way across the table and upside down into her lap. The chair immediately slid out from behind Christine, and the two women hit the floor. From that point on, for the next few minutes, it was like watching two cats scratching and biting each other. They did every move a cat would do, except kick their opponent repeatedly in the head with their back legs.

While this was going on Ducky Limehouse was jumping up and down flailing his arms. 'Cat fight,' he shouted. 'Cat fight in the kitchen!'

That left it up to me to do what any sensible adult would do under these circumstances. I got out my phone and filmed the entire scene. I stopped when Gabe snatched the phone out of my hand. From whence he appeared, I hadn't the slightest.

'OK, babe, that's enough.'

'But it will go viral on YouTube,' I said. 'We stand to make a ton of money.'

He ignored my money-making scheme. 'Ladies!' he bellowed. 'Enough!'

What a mild-mannered man, like my Sweet Baboo, did not understand was that when two people have that much adrenaline coursing through their veins, they may as well be wearing earmuffs. Once again, it was up to me to do what any sensible adult would do. I snatched an apron from a peg on the wall and wrapped it around my head to protect my ears. Then I slid open a drawer beneath a counter and extracted two large aluminium baking sheets. After donning protective oven mitts, I dove into the fray, holding the baking sheets on either side of my head and shoulders like body armour. Please believe me when I say that all that preparation took only a few seconds. The only thing that I didn't do right, and maybe should have done, was to think of a way to affix a funnel over my large Yoder nose.

The real problem was trying to force a wedge between the two women who were rolling on the floor, so consumed by fury that they didn't even stop long enough to catch their breath. I tried keeping up with them, but it was like chasing a zig-zagging ball of hate. Finally, in desperation, I threw myself atop the pair, and as they bucked in unison to dislodge me, I banged the two baking sheets together above their heads like a pair of cymbals.

That certainly put end to the 'cat fight' as Ducky had called it. Suddenly all their negative energy was focused on me. First, they jointly managed to throw me to the floor. Then the comely Christine Landis straddled my prone body, actually pinning me in place with her shapely ankles, while the less shapely Kathleen Dooley kicked the soles of my feet.

'You could have broken our eardrums,' Kathleen screamed.

'Speaking of which, dear,' I said. 'Take it down a notch, please.'

'And that's another thing, stop calling me "dear". I'm not related to you.'

'Thank heavens for that, dear,' I said.

Kathleen Dooley gave me a particularly hard kick to the sole of my right foot. I pegged her for a soccer player in her free time.

'You are absolutely incorrigible, Miss Yoder. I don't know how your husband puts up with you. He must be a saint.'

At that, Gabe guffawed. 'All right, gals, let the poor *dear* up, will you? She was only trying to keep you two from tearing each other apart.'

'Well, I for one enjoyed the floor show,' Ducky said. 'It was much better than pro wrestling. I was kind of hoping Miss Yoder would take on the winner.'

Gabe laughed even louder. 'That wouldn't even be a contest. My wife might be scrawny, but she sure can be scrappy. Of course, Magdalena is a pacifist, so that would never happen.'

I gave Ducky, and my husband, what were meant to be withering looks. However, I have a bad track record in that department. Once, what was intended to be a withering look, was interpreted by its recipient as a come-hither look. The last thing I wanted just then – or at any time – was for Ducky to think he was about to get lucky. And as for Gabe's chances, Miss Scrawny would need some alone time in which to lick her wounds, before she felt up to dancing the Two Sheet Tango.

'OK, folks,' I said, 'there has been far too much excitement for one day. I suggest that you return to your new rooms and take naps, or perhaps play board games in the dining room. Even in here, if you like. And of course, there is always the parlour, with its one amusing Apparition-American occupant. Do whatever you like. What you cannot do, is leave the premises, until you've been cleared to do so by Chief Toy Graham.'

'Does that mean that we're under house arrest?' Kathleen Dooley asked. 'Because you know that *I* didn't kill Terry Tazewell; I'm not the hot-headed one.'

'Yeah,' Ducky said. 'Miss Yoder, you can't deny that this other *certain* person is anti-social.'

'Being rude doesn't make one a killer,' I said.

'That's right,' Christine sneered. 'And neither does being ugly, because if it did, then you, Duck-Feet Limehouse, would be on death row right now.'

I threw my hands up in the air (don't fret, they were still attached to my arms). 'That does it! I'm out of here! I'm going for a walk. *You*, husband of the scrawny and scrappy woman, take over and babysit this bunch. Put them to bed, play Monopoly with them, make them lunch, or don't do any of those things. I don't care at this point. But you are going to be in charge here until I find my wits, because apparently, I've lost them.'

'I'll say,' Christine Landis said. 'You were two cards shy of a full deck even when I arrived.'

'Shut up,' Gabe said. 'Please. I'll not have you speaking to my wife like that.'

'Your scrawny, scrappy wife?' Christine said.

By then I was halfway out the kitchen door, but I knew from experience that Gabe's jaw was most certainly twitching. He is not a pacifist. If Christine were a man, he'd have invited her out behind the barn for some good old-fashioned pugilism. Gabe would most likely have been clobbered, because he's a retired heart surgeon, and his hands were always his stock and trade, so he never boxed. On the other hand, never underestimate the power of testosterone.

I hurried down the steps, practically stumbling, just to get out of earshot. From there I staggered in the direction of my little paradise on earth. What had once been a very large cow pasture, I have turned into the beginning of a woodland that encloses a small meadow. That in turn surrounds a fairly large pond that is fed by an underground spring and is drained by a gentle stream that winds its way across the meadow, into the woods, and eventually to my neighbour's farm. Cattails have naturally colonized one side of the pond, but in the shallow waters along the southern shore I have planted hardy water lilies. I'm an old-fashioned gal when it comes to 'natural' landscapes, so I stuck with the white variety of lily. Hardy waterlilies actually die back in the winter, and the pads begin appearing as the water warms.

Calmed now by being in my little paradise, I slowly followed the edge of the pond, peering into the crystal-clear water. My gaze was returned by several pairs of eyes, all belonging to small bluegills that darted into deeper water. I was hoping to see a bass or two, since I'd released some bass fry the summer before last. They should have been fairly large then. But no luck, just more bluegill.

But wait! What was that foot-long silver object hovering above one of my wadded-up kitchen towels? No, wait again, what was one of my kitchen towels doing on the floor of the pond, with a bass sticking out of it – except that wasn't a bass. That was a knife blade! Could that possibly be my missing bread knife?

What to do, what to do? If it was my bread knife, and it had been the murder weapon, I needed to retrieve it without leaving my fingerprints on it. I sure the heck (and I apologize for the swear word, brought to mind by stress) was not going to run back to the house for help. No siree, Bob. For all I knew the murderess, or murderer, was hiding behind the nearest large tree trunk, and would dash out to retrieve this piece of condemning evidence the minute my back was turned. Fortunately, as all good Christian women ought to do, I always wore a sturdy cotton slip under my dress (the Devil loves it when women wear silk – or even polyester).

My hands may look gnarled from age, all ropey and liver-spotted, but they have milked cows and slaughtered chickens. Any hand that can squeeze milk from a cow teat, and choke a chicken, is quite capable of ripping a swath of sturdy cotton off the bottom of a petticoat. I did this, by the way, in order to grab the knife without leaving any incriminating fingerprints, lest the towel should come loose during the retrieval process. At any rate, the next thing I did was to remove my shoes and hose. Then, accompanied by a few high-pitched shrieks, due to the water temperature, I waded out to the strange object. It not only was one of my dish towels, but it was one of my newer ones, imported from Portugal, and it sported a large cockerel on the front. You can bet your bippy that if it was ruined, someone was going to pay for it.

And of course, it was my bread knife. If it hadn't been, I would have said so sooner. But what really aggravated me about someone tossing my good bread knife in the drink, is that upon its retrieval, I could see that the towel, sporting the big cock, was only loosed wrapped around the handle. Had a duck, or a muskrat, or anything, caused any manner of turbulence, my expensive imported towel might simply have slipped further down along the slope of the bottom, and the knife itself would have sunk into the mud.

I hastily wrapped my petticoat bottom around the towel and carried the whole sodden, dripping bundle – blade held well away from me – to the nearest clump of shrubs, and hid it safely there. Then, and only then, did I feel comfortable enough to call Toy. I got a busy signal, which was not surprising, so I broke the sound barrier driving back into the village to speak to Toy in person.

I found Police Chief Toy Graham in his office, with his feet up on his desk, eating a cinnamon bun. On his lap balanced a sturdy paper plate with two more of the pastries. When he saw me, he almost choked on his last bite.

I gave him time to swallow before unleashing my agenda. 'Shirley, our mail carrier, has just been here, hasn't she?' I demanded.

Toy looked as if I'd caught him with his hand in the cookie jar. 'She delivers mail here every day,' he said quickly, in an unconvincing tone.

'Yes, but she's not working today, and she is baking cinnamon buns and slathering them with cream cheese icing.'

'I'm allowed to have friends, Magdalena.'

'What about accepting bribes?' I said.

'You can't be serious, Magdalena. Are you calling Shirley's buns a bribe?'

'They're big and tasty,' I said.

Toy laughed and gestured to the *Gazette* laying on his desk. 'You good at crossword puzzles?'

'I can't believe this, Toy. I'm solving a murder, and you're eating Shirley's buns and working on crossword puzzles.'

'This is my breakfast, if you will, late as it is. So anyway, what's a twelve-letter word, or phrase, for the following clue: "humourless book reviewer, works at . . ."?'

'Oh, that's easy,' I said. '*New York Times.*'

Toy jotted in the letters. 'That works. How did you know?'

'Because I once had a guest, a mystery writer, who wrote over forty hysterically funny novels, and none of them were ever reviewed by the *New York Times,* despite the fact that they also contained serious social commentary dealing with themes like religious bias and homophobia.'

'Gotcha. So now, tell me the real news that you've been dying to share.'

'I've found the murder weapon,' I said.

SEVENTEEN

Toy tore off a strip of cinnamon bun and popped it in his mouth. Given that he has impeccable manners, he chewed with his mouth closed, and swallowed completely before speaking.

'Tell me more,' he said.

'I was out walking by my pond, and I saw something strange about six or eight feet out. I waded out and retrieved it. It turned out to be my bread knife. My favourite Portuguese dish towel, the one with the big cock on it, was wrapped around the handle.'

'Where is it now? In your car?'

'No! I immediately hid it in the closest shrubs. If I'd carried it back to my car, one of the guests might have seen me. Aren't they all suspects?'

'Persons of interest,' Toy said.

'What's the difference?'

'Well, they all had opportunity, but we haven't established a motive for any of them yet.'

'Ah,' I said, 'but now we have the means, right? My bread knife. You can bet your bippy that knife has cut its last loaf.'

'Hmm. Don't get your hopes up too fast – on proving the means. Your favourite dish towel was wrapped around the knife handle for a reason, and that was to keep fingerprints off. Was it bloodstained?'

I tried to remember. 'Not that I could tell. Maybe it was. I didn't stop and examine it.'

Toy shook his head. 'The way that Mr Tazewell was butchered, that towel would have been soaked with blood.'

'Are you saying then that my knife, which I found in my pond, was just a diversion? That I lost a good knife and my best dish towel all for nothing?'

Toy shook his head at my stupidity. 'Think, Magdalena. If they were just a diversion, then you can still use them. Just wash them both, and they'll be good as new. But of course I'll check it out.'

'Good as new?' I wailed. 'My petticoat will never be the same! And you try getting pond water out of white cotton. As for my big Portuguese cock, it will always have green overtones.'

Toy smiled. 'Ah yes, that's what is known as the Barcelos Rooster. You'll see it everywhere in Portugal. Have you been to Portugal, Magdalena?'

'Does an international bazaar in Pittsburgh count? Toy, do you think that it could mean something that after I visited Shirley this morning – and feasted on her buns, by the way – she trotted down here and brought you a plate. What I'm trying to say is, do you think that—'

'These buns are a diversion?' Toy said, just before he popped the soft, gooey centre of the bun into his mouth. Then I had to wait until he held it there, savouring the sweet, cinnamon taste, a look of pure rapture on his face, until I poked him in the ribs.

'They're good,' I said, 'but not *that* good.'

'My tongue just had an orgasm,' he said.

'Eew! Yes, a diversion,' I said. 'For all I know, Shirley brought her own knife with her, and mine was a decoy. I looked around her place, and her knife set appeared to be complete, but who doesn't keep an old knife in the garage?'

'I don't,' Toy said.

'Well then, how do you cut through small roots in the ground when you're digging a hole?'

'That's why God created garden shovels. If a shovel doesn't do the job, I use a pair of clippers.'

'I'm not going to argue, dear; everyone needs a garden knife, and that's where old kitchen knives go before they die. Case closed.'

'Yes, ma'am,' Toy said, and saluted me. As much as I adore Toy, and I went so far as to have a crush on him before I discovered that he batted for the other team, the salute hiked my hackles. I was the mayor – Her Honour – and as such, Toy was my employee. Being snide was not in his job description.

'Toy, dear, I don't need your attitude,' I said. 'I'm stressed enough. Did you know that Gabe and I are thinking about selling the PennDutch and moving to Melbourne, Australia?'

His perfect features froze. 'You're kidding?'

'Only half kidding. Australia is too far from our children. But we are thinking of moving to Charlotte. After all, you do make it sound so wonderful. And it doesn't have the long, cloudy winters that we have up here.'

'Yeah,' Toy said, 'but good luck with finding a large, traditional Mennonite community.'

'At least there won't be a Church of Melvin there.'

Toy cleared his throat. Then he handed me the plate containing his two remaining cinnamon buns.

'Here, take one. You're going to need it.'

I could feel my own bun, the one comprised of my coiled braids, rising an inch off my scalp in dreaded anticipation. When someone offers you your favourite food as moral support, it's not a shoe that's about to fall – it's an entire shoe store, brick walls, roof, the whole shebang.

I snatched up a bun, licked off some of the excess cream cheese icing, and crammed half of it into my mouth. Unlike Toy, I wasn't raised by a genteel Southern lady, I was raised by a no-nonsense farmer's wife.

'Thock ith thoo me,' I said. Without the bun in my mouth, Toy would have heard: 'Sock it to me'. Either way, he understood.

'Magdalena, as you well know, freedom of religion was very important to our Founding Fathers. It's the First Amendment to our Constitution. The Pilgrims fled religious—'

'Get to your point,' I screamed. By then I'd swallowed, so Toy was spared a spray of soggy bun fragments.

'Yes, well, I hate to have to be the one to break this to you but both your cook, Anna Weaver, and her legally married wife, Shirley Valentino, are members of the Church of Melvin. Shirley told me that this morning.'

'My cook's a kook,' I croaked, and fell back in my chair in shock, 'and her wife is the Whore of Babylon.'

'Magdalena,' Toy said gently, 'refresh my memory, since I wasn't around here during the heyday of Melvinism.'

'Well, as you know, Melvin Stoltzfus, my arch-nemesis, was police chief at the time. Despite the fact that he resembled a praying mantis and had half the personality of a lobotomized sloth – and I say this with Christian love, mind you – a good many women in this village fell under his spell and literally began to worship him.'

'I have heard that before,' Toy said, 'but I always found that hard to believe. Do you mean that they thought Melvin Stoltzfus was God?'

'Some did. Some saw him as a great prophet, especially anointed by God. Either way, it was sacrilegious. Anyway, one of the women claimed to have discovered a scroll tucked in a crevice in a cave on her grandparents' farm. The scroll was called the Book of Melvin, and it foretold everything about Melvin, when and where he was to be born, even that he was going to be a policeman someday. But what really got folks to believe in its authenticity was that the scroll contained the following sentence: "Every word written herein is true". That sentence occurs in the Book of Melvin seventy-seven times.'

Toy shook his head. 'Someone was enjoying an elaborate practical joke.'

'A sacrilegious someone,' I snapped. 'These nutcases even met regularly for services. They sang so-called hymns praising Melvin, and then they'd take turns getting up and telling how their prayers to Melvin during the week had been answered. If you tried to argue with them, to show them how irrational their theology was, they'd just smile and say that they'd pray for you. Can you imagine that? These heathens pray for *me*? Me a *Christian*?'

Toy rubbed his hands together and took a deep breath. 'So, Magdalena, how can *you* prove that your Bible is true?'

'For one thing Mama told me, and her mama told her, all the way back to the time of Jesus.'

'You can't prove that,' Toy said, 'because the New Testament wasn't even written then.'

'Stop it!' I said angrily. 'The fact remains that Melvin Stoltzfus was the slime beneath the scum, beneath the muck, beneath the mud, on my farm pond, when I still had cows that pooped in it.'

'There it is,' Toy said. 'That's what I've been driving at; your hostility towards a religion that *you* have decided is illegitimate.'

'That's because it *isn't* a religion, for goodness' sake; it's a cult.'

'Magdalena, look up the definition of a cult; it doesn't apply to Melvinism. Bored housewives joined of their own free will. They weren't sucked into it. They weren't pressured to stay. They didn't have to cut off their relationships with families and friends while they were members of the Church of Melvin. They just enjoyed worshipping in a new way.'

'That's just impossible,' I said through gritted teeth. 'I'd rather die a thousand grizzly deaths than worship that man. He's a convicted murderer, for crying out loud. A disgrace to the people of Hernia. His followers sing, "Holy, holy, holy, Lord Melvin Stoltzfus". If you ask me, the worms that crawl out onto the sidewalk and die after it rains are holier than Melvin.'

'And again, there it is,' Toy said.

'There what is?' I demanded. I'd worked myself up into such a rage, that I was shaking. Since the Bible tells us that when we hate someone in our hearts, it is the same as actually killing that person, I might as well have been stabbing my nemesis with my newly located bread knife. At least then I wouldn't have to commit the same sin repeatedly like in that silly *Groundhog Day* movie that Gabe made me watch. However, there were two problems with actually committing the deed: 1.) Melvin was in the state prison, and 2.) I don't look good in orange.

'Magdalena, I was referring to your hatred for my predecessor. It's common knowledge. The vehemence that you just now spewed has been heard by others. The women – and he does have a few male followers – do not take this kindly. So far there has been nothing that any of them has been able to do about it, because we still have freedom of speech in this country.

'But it occurred to me, when Shirley brought me these buns, and ever so casually told me that she and Anna were members of the Church of Melvinism, that it could be – and the possibility of it being true is ridiculously, infinitesimally small – that the Melvinists – if that's what they're even called – killed this guest of yours, and are framing you for his murder.' Toy shrugged and laughed.

There have been times when something that I've read, or heard, strikes a chord deep inside me, and I immediately recognize that it must be true. I can't really explain it. But when Toy suggested that the Melvinists might be coming after me in a revenge scheme, it immediately felt right. The hair on my arms stood up, my stomach lurched, and my knees ached. All at once.

However, if it was as simple as me being the target of irate Melvinists because of my big mouth, then my tough old goose was cooked. Only the Good Lord knew how many of these heathens lived secret lives, disguised as everyday housewives. These were women with whom I exchanged friendly greetings at the grocery store. It could well be that some of the previous murders at my iconic inn had been perpetrated by members of this cult as part of a long game strategy, and that innocent people were now languishing in prison on *their* account. Not on *my* account, mind you. I refused to assume guilt for any crimes committed by any of those whackadoodles.

I grabbed the last bun before Toy could, but then after licking off some of the cream cheese icing, I generously shared it with him. After all, I'm not nearly as greedy as some folks make me out to be. We munched in companionable silence until we were both quite through, and then I spoke up first. I will admit that my voice quavered, and my thin shoulders slumped, for the scope of this investigation now seemed impossibly daunting. In Matthew 19:26, it states that 'with God, all things are possible.' But in order for that to happen, you and God have to be on the same page. I mean, millions of Christians have been praying for world peace for many centuries, but judging by His response, it seems that the Good Lord isn't interested in that idea, doesn't it?

'Toy-oy-oy,' I warbled unintentionally, 'now what do we do?'

'Hmm. Do you know how to do background checks? You got your private investigator's license a dozen years back on account of you being so – so—'

'Nosy?' I offered.

'I was going to say "inquisitive". Anyway, is your license still valid?'

'You bet your bippy,' I said.

'Great,' Toy said. 'So you can either start a background check on any of your three tourists – your pick – or swallow some of your vitriol and snuggle up to Anna Weaver. Casually ask her about her membership in the Church of Melvin. Make it sound like you've really forgiven Melvin, and that you want to keep an open mind on the church and its teachings.'

'You mean that you want me to lie?' I said.

'Prevaricate,' Toy said. 'That sounds ever so much better, doesn't it?'

'Quite. But before I decide, I want to know whether or not you believe in coincidences.'

Toy hiked his perfectly shaped brows. 'Of course. They happen all the time.'

'Yes, but are they natural phenomena, or are they something the Devil throws in our path to lead us astray?'

Toy chuckled, and I had the urge to slap the smirk off his cheek. Gently, of course. But that urge I felt was surely of the Devil.

'Oh, Magdalena. If I had a magic wand to wave, I'd wave it slowly over you, and erase all that literal-mindedness from you. Did you know that the Devil that is such a major player in your life, doesn't even make an appearance in the first half of the Bible? In other words, he doesn't show up until the New Testament.'

I stared at him. 'Don't confuse me with facts; I've told you that before.'

'OK then, yes! I believe that coincidences, as strange as they might be, are natural phenomena.'

'Un-huh. So what might be the chances that both Kathleen Dooley, and the Steeles' butler, Baines, who was from England, enjoyed tightrope walking? Doesn't that seem just a little bit too bizarre to be coincidence? To me that's like the proverbial red herring that a mediocre mystery writer would insert into her, or his, novel. You know the kind of writer I mean. The sort of author who couldn't write her way out of a paper bag.'

Toy laughed heartily. 'That type of red herring could only happen in a novel published in America. The Brits wouldn't put up with crap like that. But that is a very interesting coincidence, I'll hand you that. I knew that about Baines – that he really was a renaissance man – but I had no idea that Miss Dooley was a funambulist.'

Funambulist? I had to gather from context that he meant 'tightrope walker'. Normally it irritates me when an American – born and bred – drops an unfamiliar word on me, but since I'd licked his buns, I wasn't going to give him a hard time about it.

'I always wanted to be a tightrope walker,' I said. All the sugar that I'd consumed had put me in the mood to put my vulnerable self forward.

'Oh yeah?' Toy said kindly.

'You know, on account of my ginormous feet. Think about it, I could step to the left or right of the wire by a good eight inches, and still not miss it hitting the approximate centre of my foot.'

Toy chuckled. 'You *are* a hoot, Magdalena. Why didn't you pursue this dream of yours?'

'Well, I did – sort of. When I was ten years old. I was going to practice on Mama's clothesline, but Papa bought some rope from Miller's Feed Store, and then he and his cousin, Weak Chin Bernie, tied it between the two maples in the front yard. They used their tractors to pull it really tight.

'But we Conservative Mennonites aren't allowed to wear pants, not even little girls, so when Papa hoisted me up there I was wearing a dress. He handed me a long cane fishing pole, and I started walking. I did pretty well too. I got about halfway across the rope when Mama came running down from the house wielding a yardstick. The next thing I knew she was whacking at my ankles with the yardstick, and calling me a strumpet, and Jezebel-in-training. That got Weak Chin Bernie laughing, and he said that yah, he'd seen London, he'd seen France, even little Maggie's underpants. When Mama heard that, she grabbed me by one of my ankles and yanked me off the rope. If it hadn't been for Papa's quick action, rushing in to catch me before I hit the ground, I might have broken an arm or a leg. Then even though Papa and his adult cousin had been a part of my Jezebel-in-training session, it was only me who Mama whipped with the thin end of the cane fishing pole.'

Toy had a hand over his mouth, trying not to laugh.

'What's so funny?' I demanded.

'Nothing,' he said.

'Toy!'

'It's just that you sound like *my* cousin C.J. in Shelbyville, North Carolina, who claims to have some goat DNA. But enough about funambulism and cousins, here's what I want to know. What would you rather do? Stare at a boring computer screen while doing background checks, hour after hour, or would you prefer to do some actual sleuthing by getting to know some of the whackadoodles who worship your half-brother and nemesis, the evil Melvin Stoltzfus? Who knows, you might even be able to make a citizen's arrest.' Toy waggled his perfectly shaped brows seductively at me.

Silly man! He'd just offered a toddler the choice between Brussels sprouts and candy.

EIGHTEEN

The odds of me getting the chance to make a citizen's arrest were slim to non-existent. But I chose to hang my hat on the word 'slim'. Maybe Terry Tazewell's death really had been part of a plan to implicate me in a murder, or at least a plan to make my life more difficult. Perhaps I'd get lucky and overhear two Melvinists discussing this plot, so I could proceed with my citizen's arrest. However, lacking a weapon, or even a manner with which to restrain an individual, never mind two persons, I'd have to rely on my power of speech.

While I like to think that I am clear-minded, and have the voice of an orator, I have been told that I sound like a balloon that has been made to squeak by stretching the opening to a thin line. However, I do excel at prevarication, and it was within the realm of possibility that I could talk my way into the inner circle. After all, I was the monster's own blood, and I did know him better than anyone in the world, except for my sister Susannah, his ex-wife, who was in Vermont taking a Master Goat Yoga class.

The Church of Melvin rented a beautiful, newly restored Victorian house on Orchard Street. The house was grey, but the gingerbread trim was painted a crisp white. On the wraparound porch were strategic placements of white wicker chairs and side tables, and of course planters overflowing with Boston ferns.

The doormat, stamped from petroleum by-products, featured the silhouettes of two cats: one seated, the other stretching. The beautiful oak front door had a stained-glass window inset, which was marred by a cardboard sign, six inches high, that had been taped over it at eye level. Across it, someone with a steady hand had printed the following mission statement: 'Blessed are the Melvinists, for theirs is the Kingdom of Heaven. This is a holy place, open to all who seek the truth'.

Boy did that hike my hackles – all the way up into my armpits! The Melvinists had taken the first beatitude from the Sermon on the Mount, rewritten the first half, and left the words of Jesus intact for the remainder of the blessing. It was the single most sacrilegious thing that I had seen from them to date.

'Oh Lord,' I prayed, 'give me a peaceful demeanour, and keep my tongue in check. Thou knowst that thy daughter, Magdalena Portulacca Yoder, Miller, Rosen, Yoder – whatever, you know who I am – she tends to fly off the handle at times. If it be thy will, thou may strike me with temporary muteness, lest my loose lingua lash out viciously inside this beautiful Victorian. Amen.'

Then I slowly opened the door, to a surprisingly pleasant sound of cow and sheep bells attached to leather straps. In fact, I found the sound so melodious that I opened and closed the door several times in quick succession before stepping over the threshold.

'Stop that, you naughty kids!' It was the less than melodious voice of Plain Jane Brubaker.

I stepped quickly into an empty, peach-coloured room in order to identify myself. Plain Jane grimaced.

'Well, at least you're not one of the neighbourhood brats,' she said. 'They love the sound of those bells as much as you apparently do, and they're all the time opening and shutting the door just to hear them. Even though it's supposed to be a holy sound, it can get to be annoying after a while. No, I take that back; the sound can drive one up the wall.'

'Then why don't you lock the door?' I said.

'Duh,' Plain Jane said. 'Didn't you read the sign? This is a holy place, open to all who seek the truth.'

'Does this mean you have to be open twenty-four seven?'

'Duh again. One never knows when a truth-seeker might wander in off the street and open that door. That's why we have all those bells, Magdalena. If I'd been on the toilet down the hall, I could have heard you quite easily.'

I tried to nod and smile pleasantly, as I recalled that saying about catching more flies with honey, than with vinegar. The fact that I've never understood why I've needed any flies at all, much less *more* flies, has left me ambivalent about folksy sayings. That said, it isn't hard to look at Plain Jane and smile. I get a vicarious thrill of worldliness from her, without having to actually sully my reputation.

Plain Jane – her name has nothing to do with looks, but the

fact that she has no middle name. When she was born her mother announced that the baby girl's name was 'Jane – just plain Jane'. So the name stuck. Anyway, in the ways of the world, many men would consider her a 'knockout'. She started seventh grade as flat as central Kansas, and finished ninth grade with twin peaks. The Brubaker family was Baptist, so her mama let her wear makeup in tenth grade, and in eleventh grade Plain Jane dropped plumb out of high school and married Mr Walter Gawronski, our geometry teacher. Three years later she divorced Mr Gawronski and married Dick Watkins, the manager of Dick's Rent-a-Tool, over in Somerset. Five years later she divorced Mr Watkins and married Anthony Gastelli, of Tony's Pizza up in Bedford. That marriage lasted just twenty-six days.

To sum it all up, Plain Jane Brubaker is a thrice divorced woman. She is the only thrice divorced woman in all of Hernia's two-hundred-and-fifty-year-old history. As such, she is persona non grata to anyone with any social standing, as we are still (thank heavens) a village with a one divorce maximum rule. A canny soul might ask why it is that Plain Jane chooses to live somewhere that she is routinely snubbed. The answer is quite obvious to me: being snubbed is being noticed, and that is exactly what a person like Plain Jane requires in order to thrive. Plus, the topping on her metaphorical cake of attention-grabbing is her membership in the Church of Melvin.

All in all, I admire Plain Jane, despite her history of divorce. Unlike me, according to the Bible she is a *genuine* adulteress. It isn't her sin that I admire, but her ability to hold her head up, when the normally very gentle, Christian folk in our wee village hiss at her on the street. Plus, I have no doubt that there are more than a few of them who would be more than happy to toss a stone in her direction, if only someone braver launched one first.

'Plain Jane,' I said, 'I come in peace. I wish only to have a word with you – pseudo-adulteress to the genuine article.'

A hint of a smile passed across her heavily made-up face. Then again, it might have been just some of her war paint cracking.

'Well, all right. Don't just stand there; you're letting flies in. But since this is a holy place, you're going to have to turn off your cell phone and leave it in that little basket on the bench just inside the door. You can claim it on your way out.'

I did what I was told.

'Now, look at me,' she directed. Then she gasped. 'You're rail thin, for heaven's sake. In those drab Mennonite duds you're wearing, you look like a coat rack that someone has hung an old *shmatta* on. When's the last time you've eaten?'

'I've been gorging on fresh cinnamon buns all morning,' I confessed reluctantly. There was a fabulous smell wafting in from somewhere.

'That's not food! You need meat, lady. Come back to the kitchen with me, and I'll feed you a proper meal. I was just about to make myself lunch anyway.'

'Lunch? Isn't it a bit early for that?'

'Are you nuts, Magdalena? A faithful Melvinista rises faithfully at four every morning for prayers, eats a hearty breakfast at five, and then lunch at ten. I'm late this morning because some tourists wandered in, and I had to show them around.'

'Melvinistas?' I said. 'Is that what you call yourselves?'

Plain Jane laughed. 'What else would we call ourselves? Melvinists?'

'Actually, yes,' I said. 'That's what everyone thinks. Not just me, by the way.'

'How silly.'

'Plain Jane, before we have lunch, would you please show me around? Like you did with the tourists?'

She cocked her head and squinted. This time an enormous black false eyelash came partly loose, and dangled in front of her eye like a black tarantula. Plain Jane calmly plucked it the rest of the way off and stuffed it into her cleavage for safekeeping. Because of this I could safely assume that the floor-length, sleeveless, peach-coloured gown she was wearing lacked pockets.

'Well, yes,' she said, 'I suppose that I could give you a quick tour. So this,' she added, waving a surprisingly well-toned arm in a half circle to indicate the living room space, 'is the Great Hall. It is where our Divine Assemblies occur every Sunday morning at nine. On Sundays we are permitted to sleep until six, and then we eat at seven.

'And that,' she said, pointing to a bricked-in fireplace, 'is our high altar. Only our high priestess, Her Divine Eminence, is allowed to place the offering there.'

I struggled hard to keep my features in their regular, semi-sour position. 'Who is Her Divine Eminence?'

'Why me, of course. You see, the high priestess has to be a virgin.'

My slightly downturned mouth, an expression favoured by many Christians, turned a smidge upward. To my credit, however, I uttered not a sound. Keeping my cool certainly was not easy, as I pondered how in the dickens a woman who had been married three times could still be a virgin. That was as silly a scenario as a dictator claiming to win a landslide election in a one-party state.

Meanwhile Plain Jane stared at me for the longest time, which gave me a mega case of the heebie-jeebies.

'Look,' she finally said, 'there's a surgery for that these days. Plastic surgeons in New York and LA perform it for rich young women who come to the States to study, and who hail from certain traditional cultures where losing one's virginity before marriage can sometimes be a death sentence. At the very least, marriage for these young ladies is forever out of the question, unless they can regain their virginity. But yes, I am once again a virgin. Would you like me to prove it? I can show you if you wish.'

'Ach! A thousand times no!' I clamped my hands over my eyes, just in case she suddenly pulled a 'show and tell' on me. My sister Susannah, younger by more than a decade, used to take delight in exactly such antics. What's more, Susannah was also the love of Melvin's life, and he was hers, which just goes to show how big of a whackadoodle she was.

'Well then,' Plain Jane said, 'how about I show you the kitchen instead, and we can have a bite of lunch.'

'Absolutely,' I said gratefully. Confidentially, I've never even caught a glimpse of my own nether regions, and judging by the amount of time Gabe spends down there, he must surely find it bewildering to say the least.

So Plain Jane led me into a spacious kitchen that had obviously been remodelled in the last one hundred years. The appliances were all new, high-end models, and the counter tops were quartz. In the centre was a large island surrounded by six leather-covered stools with backs and armrests that swivelled. Although I was suitably impressed, and complimented Plain Jane, my thoughts were soon diverted to the delicious smells that emanated from a skillet set on a back burner which, by the way, had been turned off.

Plain Jane transferred the skillet to a front burner and relit the gas flame. Then she removed the lid.

'You've been smelling lunch,' Plain Jane said with a smile. 'Schmucker Brothers Morning Sausages fried with rings of green bell peppers and sweet onions.'

I stepped closer and peered in. 'Do you know that in Pittsburgh they call bell peppers "mangos"?' I asked.

Plain Jane laughed. 'Yes. Isn't that weird? Husband number two and I honeymooned in Belize. The real mangoes there, the fruit, were out of this world.'

I graciously refrained from comparing Belize mangoes to her state of mind. 'When do we eat?' I said.

'It's ready now.'

Plain Jane prepared an extra place setting while I washed my hands at the sink. Then she sliced open some hoagie rolls and filled them with the fried sausages and the accompanying vegetables. To both plates she added some crisps and carrot sticks.

'What would you like to drink?' she asked, as she handed me my plate.

'Sky juice is fine,' I said.

'Uh, I'm pretty certain that I don't have any.'

'Sure you do,' I said. 'Think about it. What kind of juice comes from oranges?'

'Duh. Orange juice, of course.'

'And what kind of juice comes from apples?'

'Duh. Apple juice. This is silly, Magdalena.'

'Bear with me, dear. Then what kind of juice comes from the sky?'

'Rain?'

'Duh,' I got to say. 'Exactly, and rain is water. I'm pretty sure that you have water, because I just washed my hands in some. So I'll take water.'

'Ugh,' Plain Jane said. 'You should try my grape juice.'

I nodded enthusiastically. 'I do love grape juice, but I seldom buy it, because it's usually more expensive than the other kinds.'

Plain Jane winked. 'I think that you will especially like this brand; it's sold just for adults because it has a little kick to it.' In my defence I must point out that she had her back turned to me as she poured my first tumbler full of grape juice.

That sounded like a challenge to me. Never one to insult my hostess, I swallowed my first gulp, even though it tasted more like vinegar than grape juice to me. Then when I saw that Plain Jane was looking at me quizzically, like she was waiting for me to say something positive about her juice, which was obviously being served past its due date, I took three more large gulps in quick succession. At that point, the weirdest thing happened. My tummy began to feel wonderfully warm, and my head felt – I don't know how to describe it – maybe, pleasantly buzzy?

'You might want to slow down with the juice,' Plain Jane said, 'until we've got some food in our stomachs. Magdalena, would you care to say grace?'

'"Grace",' I said, and then giggled.

'Magdalena, I can't believe you just did that,' Plain Jane said approvingly.

'I can't either,' I wailed. 'The Devil made me do it!'

'Hush,' Her Eminence said. 'We don't mention that name here. Now eat your sandwich before it gets cold.'

So I ate, and man oh man, was it good! To use one of Toy's Southernisms, it was so good that it about made my tongue come out and slap my cheek, that's how good it was. In fact, I had a second sandwich, and after that a couple of special chocolate brownies that Plain Jane herself had baked. To be frank, the brownies had a weird, sort of weedy texture to them, but they were very sweet, and very chocolatey, and that's what I craved. Had I been wearing a girdle, my belly, normally relatively small, would have busted right through that old-fashioned garment. But fortunately, I was suitably clad in my sturdy Christian underwear, which has about as much room for expansion as a suit of armour and is nearly as strong. The downside was that I felt that if I moved, my alimentary canal would explode at both ends.

'I don't feel so well,' I confessed. 'I mean, the food was to die for – not literally, of course . . . well, maybe if one was starving, but then what would be the point? Anyway, I stuffed myself. I'm not used to that. It's a sin, you know, to gorge oneself, and then waddle out of a restaurant, while there are people starving in this world.'

'Oh, pooh,' Plain Jane said. 'To you Mennonites, just about everything is a sin.'

'That's because everything can be a sin – if it's done to excess.'

'Bah. Nonsense. More is better, that's what we Melvinistas say. At any rate, let's not quibble over facts. Instead let me show you the "zoning room".'

'The *what?*'

Plain Jane wiped her hands on several paper napkins and grabbed my own large, but admittedly rather shapely, hand. 'Come along, sister.'

'I don't think that I can. I'll burst – in ways that aren't pleasant.'

'Oh, nonsense,' she said. 'Besides, I've been forewarned, so the onus will be on me. So come along then.'

She tugged me gently into an adjacent room, and bade me sit in one of six identical brown leather recliners. When I hesitated to sit, lest the downward movement disturb my equilibrium, Plain Jane intervened by giving me a firm push. I fell back, protesting loudly from both ends, but I felt not the least bit of embarrassment, because it was all Plain Jane's doing.

'Now then,' she said. 'Grab that thingy by your right hand and push the middle button to the left. That will bring your feet up and tilt you back slightly.' And so it did.

'Now what?' I said.

'This is what,' Plain Jane said. She had a bigger thingy, and she pushed several buttons. The first aligned her chair's position with mine. The second miraculously transformed all four walls in the room into a woodland meadow filled with wildflowers and butterflies that were actually moving from flower to flower. The third button that she pushed initiated soft, soothing music, even though I couldn't identify the tunes.

'Wow,' I said, overcome with wonder.

'Now just sit back and rest,' she said.

'That's a four-letter word,' I said. After all, there is no rest for the wicked, and the Bible teaches that we are all sinners, lost sheep who have gone astray.

'Well, I meant to say "relax". That's a five-letter word, Magdalena. I read a Norwegian study – and Norwegians are seldom wrong – that relaxation is the key to healing one's cognitive dissonance. That said, if you were to allow the beauty of this meadow, filled with wildflowers as it is, and this soft, soothing music, to penetrate that hard outer shell that you present to the world, you would find yourself so refreshed in a few hours, that you could be an even better wife and mother, than the awesome one that you are now. And I know that is saying a lot, because everyone knows that you are truly a wonderful wife to Gabe, and your children could not have asked for a better mother.'

'*Really?* You're not just saying that to make me feel good?'

'Magdalena, you're an awesome wife and mother. Even your most diehard detractors believe that. So all you have to do now is relax. And here, have another brownie.'

I took two more brownies. Then I relaxed like I never had before. I relaxed until the tendons in my body were the strands of overcooked spaghetti. I relaxed until the flowers in the meadow began to dance in time to the music. I relaxed until the music danced in time to the bobbing flowers. I relaxed until I felt compelled to reach over and take Plain Jane's hand in mine.

NINETEEN

'I love you,' I said. 'Not in the sexual way, of course, but if I did swing in that direction, you would definitely get a second look from me. On a scale of one to ten, I rate you an eight.'

'What a nice compliment, Magdalena,' Plain Jane said. 'Unfortunately, nature has not been so kind to you. I'm afraid I can't rate you more than a four.'

'Don't be ridiculous,' I said. 'I'm a two at best.'

We both giggled.

'It's too bad you're so ugly,' Plain Jane said.

'It's too bad you're so conceited,' I said.

We giggled again. After several minutes of giggling Plain Jane pulled her hand loose from mine. This was OK with me by then because her hand was so sweaty I was afraid that it might be leaking.

'Magdalena,' she said, 'do you think that I'm going to heaven?'

'Have you confessed your sins to Jesus, and asked Him to forgive you?'

'No. And I refuse to, because I know that the Bible is all a bunch of hooey.'

'Then you are going to burn forever in a lake of fire. You're going to scream in excruciating pain for all of eternity. Do you want me to demonstrate the screams? I've been practicing them on Gabe, you know, trying to get him to convert.'

'Magdalena, that is so vile,' she said, but she was laughing.

Suddenly I no longer felt relaxed, just weird. 'What else am I supposed to do? I don't want him to spend an eternity in agony.'

'But don't you see, your problem is that you take all that stuff literally. Why does God have to be a man? Why not a woman?'

'G-God is not a man,' I stuttered. 'God is a *male*. A male spirit.'

'Oh? What makes this spirit male then? Describe his maleness, Magdalena.'

'Stop it,' I cried. 'You're messing with my mind, and my mind is not its usual sharp self.'

'Jesus was a man,' Plain Jane said. 'You will at least agree to that.'

'Yes, but also God,' I said quickly.

'But did the man part of him get aroused when he saw pretty girls?'

I tried to jump to my feet, but instead stumbled into the flower-filled meadow. Unfortunately, there wasn't any soft bed of flowers to catch me, just a bare wooden floor, upon which I nearly broke my considerable Yoder proboscis.

'I want to go home,' I whimpered.

'Certainly,' Plain Jane said. 'Whom shall I call to say that Hernia's mayor, the Honourable Magdalena Portulacca Yoder, is lying on the floor of the Church of Melvin, drunk as a skunk and high as a kite? And of course, this after she propositioned me, and told me I was going to Hell.'

I tried to stand, but it took too much effort. Anyway, by then the cool floor wasn't feeling quite so bad, and when I stretched out one of my long, gangly arms, the wildflowers appeared to dance along it and into my palm. But no matter how fast I clenched my fist, I couldn't catch a single blossom. Still, I had the one rather large problem to take care of. Her Eminence had threatened to destroy my reputation, such as it was, and I needed to at least make nice with the wicked witch in the tunic, until I could safely manoeuvre myself back home, and maybe into bed.

'May it please Your Majesty,' I began, and trust me, I was well aware that wasn't her title. But surely anyone with the chutzpah to declare themselves the high priestess of a made-up religion, and then pay big bucks to get her virginity restored, has got to have a humongous ego.

'Go on,' she said.

'Well, the real reason that I popped by this morning was to ask you if any of your members still bore me a grudge. You know, for playing a part in getting your leader locked up in the slammer.'

'We all hate you, Magdalena. Every last one of us does.'

'But do some of you hate me more than others?' I asked.

She was silent for a moment. 'Yes, I'd say that there are a few who utterly despise you, and who would like to see you bound to a wooden post and eaten alive by a swarm of army ants.'

'That hurts my feelings,' I wailed. 'Isn't there anyone who feels a little more kindly to me?'

Another silent minute passed. Then another.

'Well, yes,' she said. 'There was Becky Steubenhoffer, who suggested that maybe you were just doing your job, but the membership took a vote. It was unanimous: we voted to excommunicate her.'

'God bless Becky Steubenhoffer,' I heard myself say, even though I had never particularly liked her. I take that back; I'd actually hated Becky ever since I was fourteen. Becky and I were the same age, and she had a reputation for being the class tattletale. I never, ever copied off another student's paper, but once – just once – during a World History quiz, when the answers were either 'true' or 'false', I turned my paper at an angle so that Agnes could get a glimpse of my paper. The poor girl had just returned from her grandmother's funeral in Ohio and had been too distracted to study.

At any rate, Becky Steubenhoffer saw what I was doing, and alerted Miss Leis in her whiny voice, which sounded even less pleasant than the top three keys of a toy accordion.

'Magdalena's cheating, Magdalena's cheating,' the little brat squeaked.

Well, Miss Leis was a burly, red-haired woman who'd been born and raised on a farm, and had had plenty of experience chopping wood. Rumour even had it that she had a tuft of orange hair peaking up at the V of her blouses, although I never saw it. The important thing that I wish to convey is that Miss Leis would routinely thrash a student, regardless of their gender, just as hard as Papa could. After Miss Leis thrashed me, try as I might, I could never summon up enough Christian love to forgive Becky Steubenhoffer. Every time I prayed about it, I would feel Miss Leis thrashing me again, so finally I just gave up.

I have no idea how long I'd been thinking about that brat Becky Steubenhoffer, and the muscular Miss Leis, when I felt someone poking me in the ribs. Hard.

'Ouch,' I said. 'That hurt!'

'Magdalena, are you in there?'

'No, I stepped out to get the evening paper, dear. I'll be back in five.'

'Magdalena, sarcasm does not become you,' Plain Jane said. 'I just wanted to know if you were all right – this being your first time to get high. And plastered. If only your peeps could see you now.'

'My *what*?'

'Never mind. What were you thinking about? You zoned out for an hour and a half.'

'No, I didn't,' I said.

'Yes, you did. Check your watch.'

So I did. I checked my watch, and then squealed like I did on my wedding night. My *first* wedding night, when everything was new and terrifying. Since then, I've never been able to look at a turkey neck again, and at Thanksgiving we make do with a standing beef roast.

'Did you mess with my watch?' I squealed again. 'Are you trying to drive me crazy? Is that how your cult works?'

Plain Jane smiled. 'That's how pot works. It messes with your sense of time. You were talking to yourself – rambling, really. Saying pretty bad stuff about Becky Steubenhoffer, who wanted to cut you a break, and you even laid into your pal Agnes for letting you take all the blame for it – whatever it was. By the way, what *was* "it"?'

'You know, dear,' I said, 'you have the most amazing eyes. Are they brown, or are they hazel?'

'Oh, no you don't! You don't get to change the subject like that. Besides, they're neither. Anyone can see that they're blue.'

'Well, I beg to disagree,' I said. 'Respectfully, of course. At any rate, tell me the names of your church members who hate me the most.'

'Now why would I do that?' Plain Jane said.

'Because I wish to send them each a fruit basket. And of course, I would send one to you as well. I respect folks who own their truth.'

'Would my fruit basket also contain a selection of cheeses and gourmet crackers?' she asked.

'Duh,' I said. 'Only the finest. What do you take me for? An ungrateful rube?'

'In that case, if you're looking for the person who hates you the most, look no further than your own home.'

'Anna Weaver?'

'Well, it certainly isn't your hunk of a husband – if one may speak thusly of an elderly man.'

'You may speak thus,' I said, 'because he will always be mine. Plus which, seventy-four is not even considered elderly these days. It's the new twenty, or something like that.'

'I wish. At any rate, you have a lot to be grateful for, Magdalena. Just about every woman in Hernia is envious of you, or at the least, puzzled about how you got where you are. How, they ask themselves, did such an unattractive, big-footed, flat-chested, mousey-haired farmer's daughter snag a big city heart surgeon? One who makes Cary Grant look like an English bulldog.'

'Cary who?'

'Oh, I left out the adjective "unsophisticated", so as not to be unkind. Cary Grant was a movie star who made over seventy films.'

'Hollywood is a den of iniquity,' I said. 'Not that *I'm* judging, mind you; it's all in some pamphlets that I have at home. I'd be happy to give you one if you ever stop by. Better yet, stop by Beechy Grove Mennonite Church some Sunday morning, and maybe I can return the favour to you.'

'What favour is that?' Plain Jane said guardedly.

'Turn you on with Jesus. You know, like you turned me on with pot today.' I chortled pleasantly.

'Oh, Magdalena, if only you could step outside yourself and hear just how pitiful you sound. If you think that you've been a faithful witness of your Christian faith today, well, you need to think again. While I swear that I'll never tell anyone what went on inside these sacred walls today, you better hope that you can keep your gossipy lips tightly sealed. If the rest of Hernia ever gets wind of what transpired here, not only will you lose your position as mayor, but Beechy Grove Mennonite Church will drop you as their head deaconess. You can count on that.'

I wrung my hands in despair. Then, since I still wasn't quite feeling like myself, I checked my hands for damage; they appeared to be none the worse for wear, but when did the nail on my ring finger get to be so long? Funny how some nails can grow up leaps and bounds overnight. And where did all those ropey veins on the backs of my hands come from? Did Mama's hands look like that when she was my age? Then again, how should I know? Mama would have been pushing up daisies long before she was my age, except for the fact that up there in Settlers' Cemetery the soil was too stony for daisies. But from the looks of her gravesite, Mama was very good at pushing up weeds.

'Magdalena, what's gotten into you? You look positively wretched. If you were a cat, I'd think you were about to hack up a giant fur ball. Didn't I just assure you that all you have to do is keep those thin, grey lips of yours shut, and that everything will be OK? If you can trust God, whom you've never seen, then surely you can trust me, what with my buxom beauty, and my soothing voice which, I've been told, is not unlike that of a nightingale on a summer's eve.'

Plain Jane turned and faced me straight on. Then she caught one of my big, ropey, but still uncommonly shapely paws in her petite, manicured hands.

'Just trust me, sweetheart,' she purred. 'Just as long as you and your chief of police leave me and my people alone, no one will be the wiser about what went on here today. I'll even throw in Anna Weaver as a freebie. I mean, I already told you that she hates you, so you're free to throw her under the bus – so to speak. You do understand that's just an expression, right? I mean with some of you conservative-type Mennonites, one should take care not to be taken literally.'

I smiled weakly. Anna Weaver was a hefty woman. It would take two of me just to *drag* her in front of the bus. Tossing her under it would require three of us, and then we would never be able to agree upon who grabbed which arm, and who got to pick up her feet. In a literal interpretation of the expression, Anna Weaver would come to no harm.

'Magdalena, what's going on in that oddly shaped head of yours? Are you sure that you're all right? Is there something that I can do for you?' Plain Jane asked. She sounded so kind, and patient just then, considering that I was acting like a doofus, that I could see how someone might want to belong to her church. Not the cult of Melvin's, but a church where someone like Plain Jane made one a sausage sandwich, and sat with one, and was remarkably straightforward, even if some of the things she said might hurt one's feelings. At least there wasn't anything fake about her.

'I'm fine, dear,' I said. 'I'm fine as frog's hair. Now don't be taking that expression literally. It's a Southernism that I first heard from our chief of police, Toy Graham, who uses upon occasion. You see, frogs don't really have hair – or maybe they do, and it's just so fine that one can't even see it.' I chuckled agreeably.

'I don't get it,' Plain Jane said. 'Once on an LSD trip I *did* see a giant frog with hair. And speaking of whom, the frog was about the size of Chief Graham. In fact, it had more hair on just one leg than you do on one of your arms, and that's saying a lot.'

Suddenly I was no longer feeling quite so kindly toward Plain Jane. Perhaps the mellowing effects of the marijuana I'd consumed were beginning to wear off. If I hung around any longer, I was liable to say something that I would forever regret. My tongue is a loose cannon as it is, but coupled with cannabis, any chance of me converting Plain Jane could be shot to smithereens.

I rose, perhaps somewhat unsteadily, to my feet. Don't get me wrong; I could still function. I could still touch the appropriate elbow if called upon to do so, just not by using the right hand to touch the right elbow, for instance. (Those days are long behind me!) And believe it or not, I was able to walk a straight line – if the line was wide enough.

'Well, I think that I'll be taking my leave,' I trilled, once more delighting in the sound of my own voice. So you see, I was feeling better by the minute.

'That might not be such a good idea just yet,' Plain Jane said, clutching at my skirt. 'You seem to be swaying atop your ugly black brogans.'

'Yes, dear, it's a wonderful idea,' I said, 'Because, you see, if I stay here a minute longer, I might undo five hundred years of pacifist inbreeding.'

'Oh, give me a break, you self-righteous twit.'

I reared back with an open hand, then swooped down, grabbed my pocketbook off the floor, and stumbled my way to the door. Fortunately – or was it my guardian angel who reminded me – I remembered to reclaim my cell phone from the basket at the front door.

TWENTY

When I turned my phone back on, I discovered that I was the most popular person on the planet. All told I'd received eight calls from people whose middle names I knew, and thirteen texts. The majority of those messages were from my dear, sweet husband, but four were from Toy, three were from Agnes, and two were from my daughter, who is a busy physician.

If I had been a wise woman, or at least a sensible one, I would have responded to Toy's messages first, and could have at least been forewarned about the Babester's escalating histrionics. Instead, I took the triage approach, and began with the Babester.

'Mags! Have you been abducted again?' he shouted. 'Toy won't tell me *anything*, which is, of course, telling me *everything*. I don't care what they say about not going to the FBI or they'll kill you, because you and I both know that you're too ornery to kill. If God wanted you dead, He's already had more than enough opportunities. What I want to know is, how the heck did that pencil-necked, dim-witted brother of yours manage to pull this abduction off, when he was locked up in a maximum-security prison? I know that you're against the death penalty, Mags, but I swear, if I had my hands around his Lilliputian gullet, I'd snap his praying mantis head off in a New York minute.

'Look, hon, we've got more money than we'll ever need, so make whatever deal that you can upfront with this cretin. I know, you're wondering why it is that I'm being so loose-lipped, when that imbecile is undoubtedly listening in to this conversation, but that's just it, babe: he's an imbecile. He probably thinks that I've been complimenting him.'

'It was a she,' I yelled, when the Babester finally came up for air.

'*What?*' Gabe gasped. 'Wanda Hemphopple is on the loose? Now that *is* bad news! Wanda is most certainly *not* an imbecile. Wanda is an evil genius.'

'You take that back,' I snapped. 'That woman is no genius. Wanda is a Bavarian shop where all the clocks are missing their birds. And anyway, I'm not being held for ransom, and even if I were, it wouldn't have been Wanda whom I spent the afternoon with.'

'Well, I called Agnes, and she denied that you were with her. In fact, I was so worried, that I promised her a seven-day Caribbean cruise if she would rat you out. Mags, she started to cry, that's how desperate she was for this cruise, but still, she didn't give your whereabouts away. That woman is a jewel. A true friend.'

'And you're a cad, Gabriel Rosen, because poor Agnes didn't have the slightest idea where I was. So you're still going to give her the cruise.'

'Then where the *heck* are you?' Actually, the word 'heck' is not in my dear husband's vocabulary. Enough said.

'I have just left the Church of Melvin and am headed over to Agnes's now – on foot.'

'Stop! No, don't stop! Get the heck away from there. Is that where you were all day?'

'That's right, dear. I had quite the elucidating lunch with High Priestess Plain Jane.'

'Did the Grand Screwball manage to convert you?'

'Bite your tongue. She served me a delicious lunch, got me drunk as a skunk, and high as a kite on Schmucker Brothers Sausages. Bet you didn't know that those sausages contain pot, did you?'

I waited for my urbane husband to guffaw. At the very least he could have showed me that he'd been paying attention by offering up a dismissive snicker.

'The Amish are putting marijuana in their sausages,' I said, speaking slowly, and loudly, as if I were speaking to a tourist who had only a passing acquaintance with the English language. 'Pot. In. Sausages!'

'Yes, babe, I already knew that,' my husband said.

'What? Since when?'

'Since that magical evening when we walked out to the pond, where everything was so – well-enhanced – on the walk back. Then later, in our boudoir – wow, wozee, wozer, if you get my drift. And that was after just an inch or two of that humongous sausage. If you recall, I really had to talk you into buying those Schmucker Brothers Sausages, because you objected to their advertising. You thought it was too suggestive.'

'Well, I still think that! Who knew that the Amish had sex lives?'

That is when Gabe decided to give me his dismissive chuckle. 'Apparently your ancestors did, or else we wouldn't be having this conversation.'

'Sex-shmex, you're missing my point. Why didn't you share that information with me? We're not supposed to keep secrets from each other.'

The expression 'can't walk and chew gum at the same time' will never be applied to me, because I eschew gum-chewing. Folks who discard their used gum on sidewalks and parking lots should be required to scrape it, and one hundred other pieces, off said sidewalk on the hottest day of the year. But what I apparently can't do, is talk on the phone and walk on an uneven sidewalk, while still being just a little bit 'buzzy'. While I did trip, I didn't fall. However, a very naughty word – much worse than what 'heck' stands for – came tumbling from my mouth. At least to my credit, I was horrified.

'I didn't say that!' I said.

That's when Gabe guffawed. 'Way to go, Mags. That's a first, isn't it?'

'Gabe, tell me you didn't hear that!'

'Oh, but I did, hon, and it was music to my ears.'

'Why would you say that? I am so disappointed with myself.' I meant it too. In fact, I began to cry, which I almost never do. I don't cry when I'm physically hurt, or even sad; I cry when I'm unbearably frustrated.

'Darling, I have to go,' I said.

'Go where?' he demanded.

'I mean that I have to hang up. I can't continue this conversation now. I need to talk to Toy and follow up on a lead.'

'But it won't be dinner time for another two hours. What will I do with the guests until then? They're antsy as all get out – that's the polite way of saying it.'

Some people have flashes of brilliance. I'm grateful for shimmers of mediocrity.

'Call Anna Weaver, and tell her to run into Yoder's Corner

Market and buy four packages of Schmucker Brothers' Dinner Sausages. They're the ones that mellow one out, and even make one sleepy.'

'Yeah, I know,' Gabe said with a chuckle. 'Babe, I can't believe you're doing this.'

'Wait, there is more. Anna also needs to buy hoagie rolls, and some cold slaw, and some tins of baked beans and potato chips. She also needs to pick up marshmallows and chocolate squares for making s'mores. Let's see, what else? A gallon of lemonade, and a gallon of iced tea – oh, and make sure that we have mustard, ketchup and relish on hand.'

'I see,' Gabe said, 'so I take it we're having a picnic down by the pond.'

'You got it. I suggest that as soon as you call Anna, you start rousing the guests and soliciting their help. You can use the riding mower to pull the garden cart back and forth full of supplies, but it's going to take several trips. Meanwhile, the guests can walk down to the pond. Make them carry light things, like blankets to sit on, and flashlights, and then once they get there, they can start hunting for firewood from the woods. Since these are city folk, you might want to warn them about poison ivy. Remember, leaves—'

'Babe, I've got this,' Gabe said. If I'd been FaceTiming him, I could have seen his eyes roll.

'OK, dear. Over and out,' I said.

By then my head was as clear as a mountain stream. I tried to call Toy, but his line was busy, so I called Amelia Morris, our part-time secretary, but the station line rang interminably. Then I remembered that today was her official day off, and that she had planned to attend a Zombie festival in Pittsburgh, dressed as one of those hideous things. I don't mean to be uncharitable, but there were days when a zombie could have performed better than Amelia at her job. However, Toy found that she interacted well with the young people in our community, so that was that. At any rate, I left Toy a message stating that I had learned something very interesting during the day, and my phone would be kept on for the duration. Then I resumed my walk to Agnes's house.

At the risk of spoiling everything that I love about my home-town, I just have to share the following: it is truly the most beautiful place on earth during spring. We in the Appalachian valleys of southwestern Pennsylvania, have the perfect soil conditions, and climate, for growing rhododendrons. To me the flowers are fluffy clouds of colour, blooming in yard after yard, in a variety of hues. I hope it's not sacrilegious to say this, but I hope that Heaven is more than just pearly gates and streets paved with gold. I would dearly love for there to be a garden that was at least as beautiful as the village of Hernia in early spring.

I was so overcome with emotion that I found myself skipping. Even in America there should be a law against seventy-four-year-olds skipping in public. Although I have never seen another person my age skip, from the flapping and jiggling of wrinkles and loose skin, I could feel that it must not be a pretty sight. Although I stopped abruptly after three skips, who knows how much damage I might have done to the young children out playing in their yards in the cool of the day? I might even have done psychological damage to the neighbourhood cats and dogs. Thank heavens for my sturdy Christian underwear that kept my breasts from falling out of their holder, like a pair of shrunken apples.

I was totally in control of my emotions when I arrived at Agnes's picturesque white Cape Cod house, set behind two glorious maple trees, and fronted by a bank of rhododendron in blazing red. One might think that a woman who had lived with two nudist uncles with dementia, might have become accustomed to living with her drapes drawn, or her shades pulled down. But oh no, not Agnes Miller. Agnes didn't mind, maybe even preferred, to live her life large and proud, where all the world could see – well, if they happened to drive past 815 Sycamore Street in Hernia, Pennsylvania. Of course Agnes wasn't a nudist; she was a General Conference Mennonite, and an upstanding member of her church.

But on that late afternoon, I could see quite clearly through her large picture window that she was a gyrating heathen. Now, I am not a judgemental woman, and I would never spread falsehoods about my best friend. But how else can I describe someone who is prancing around and twisting their body to the beat of rock and roll music? Mama said that rock and roll was the work of the Devil, and I am ashamed to say that when I was a teenager I doubted her, thinking her old-fashioned. But only the Devil could get a seventy-four-year-old woman, who was almost a hundred pounds overweight, to do the things that Agnes was doing to the loud beat of that music. What's more, my bestie was dressed in something they call a leotard, but I call 'Satan pants' because it leaves nothing to the imagination.

We Herniaites don't keep our doors locked on account of we're all good Christian folk, murderers and atheists excepted, so I walked in unannounced. I set my pocketbook on a living-room chair, but I remained standing, with my arms akimbo, my hands on my hips. Now, no Mennonite should ever stand with their hands on their hips, because that is a proud stance, and we are a modest people. But I did so because I was aghast, agog, and gobsmacked, by what my friend was doing. In a state such as that, one might be expected to abandon cultural mores that went back five centuries. However, I said nothing to Agnes as she pranced and jiggled around the room, and even if I had, she wouldn't have heard it over the Devil's own music.

Fortunately, all things must come to an end, even heathen displays of vulgarity. Finally, my bestie ran out of steam, and collapsed on the floor in a spherical heap, facing me. At first, she was breathing too hard to take note of my shocked and disapproving visage, but when she did, she let loose with a scream that would have summoned a sex-starved male panther, had there been any still living in the surrounding mountains. When at last she got it together enough to turn off what she thought passed for music, I knew it was time for me to face the music – so to speak.

'Magdalena Portulacca Yoder Rosen! How long have you been standing there spying on me?'

'Two years, six months, and three days,' I said.

'Ha, ha, very funny. Now, if you please, get me a bottle of cold water from the fridge. And while you're at it, bring me a roll of paper towels. All that exercise makes me *schvitz*.'

'You call that exercise, dear?' I said. 'I call it something that calls for an exorcism.'

'Water! Towels! Now!'

'OK, OK,' I said and trotted indignantly into my best friend's kitchen.

When I returned, I saw that Agnes had pulled herself off the floor, and was stuffed into her favourite recliner. Although the ceiling fan was on, she was also fanning herself with a hand-held paper fan with a Japanese motif printed on one side.

'Sorry I barked at you, Mags,' she said. She reached for the water, took a couple of gulps, and then held the bottle against her perspiring throat. 'I was just so uncomfortable. You know how it is, don't you? How being uncomfortable can make one irritable.'

'I do know how it is,' I said, and set the towels down beside her chair. 'In fact, I'm capable of being irritable even when I'm quite comfortable.'

'Isn't that the truth!' Agnes said with a grin. She took several more gulps of water and then looked at me questioningly. 'So to what do I owe the pleasure of your presence this late in the day, missy?'

'I'm here to find out when you discovered the truth about Schmucker Brothers Sausages,' I said.

Her eyes widened. 'What truth?'

'Don't be coy, dear. You know as well as I do that my cousins are seasoning their specialty sausages with marijuana.'

Agnes blinked and opened her mouth several times before uttering a syllable. '*How* did you find out?'

'No, no, no. I asked you *when* first. I mean, when you were outside dancing in the altogether, you were stoned, weren't you?'

Agnes grinned. 'Guilty. I can't believe I just heard you use the word "stoned".'

'Then you might find it hard to believe that I spent the afternoon stoned,' I said, 'and it wasn't for the first time, either.'

If Agnes's eyes had opened any wider, her eyeballs would have popped out and rolled across the floor toward my feet. As it was, her mouth fell open to such an extent that she almost dislocated her jaw. I realize that some would take me for a narrow-minded prude, but surely I can fall off the straight and narrow path just as easily as anyone else.

'Tell me,' she beseeched me. 'Tell me everything!'

'Well, the first time was with Gabe, and we ate the Dinner sausages. Then we took a lovely evening walk, and . . . uh, had a lovely, relaxing evening.'

'I just bet you did,' Agnes said with an envious smirk. 'And then?'

'And then the second time was just hours ago, and it was with Plain Jane, and she—'

'The same Plain Jane who worships the man who tried to kill you?'

'Yes, but she is actually a very good cook, and doesn't really believe that Melvin is anything special. She just enjoys the title of High Priestess and living in a nice house. And she's lonely.'

'Who isn't?'

'Maybe you two should get together,' I said.

Agnes tossed a wadded-up towel sheet at me. 'Bite your tongue! But not all the way off. Tell me more. I want to know all about your afternoon with the High Priestess of the Melvinists.'

'That would be Melvinistas, dear. That is what the High Priestess herself said that they are called.'

'Well, la-dee-da. Melvinistas sounds more like a guerrilla army than a bunch of religious nuts.'

'Agnes, maybe we shouldn't be so quick to judge.'

'Are you crazy? Did you drink the poison? Judging is what you do best. It's your strong suit. "Thou shalt not judge," the Lord said, "except for Magdalena, for whom I have made an exception".'

I backed away lest she be struck by lightning. Since God is all-powerful, I knew that he could send it through a plate glass window, even when there wasn't a cloud in the sky.

'That's sacrilegious at best,' I said. 'Putting words in God's mouth like that.'

'Oh Mags, loosen up. I can see that your second experience with Mary Jane didn't make you any less uptight.'

'Her name is Plain Jane,' I said tersely, not "Mary Jane".'

'Oh, my dear, dear, much beloved best friend, who has somehow managed to protect herself from the ways of the world, despite hosting a wide variety of its inhabitants. Mary Jane is a slang name for marijuana.'

I stared at Agnes long enough to see if she would crack a smile. But nope, she wasn't putting me on. Well, if being "worldly" is what it took to impress her these days, I'd give her "worldly".'

'Agnes, I know that you danced naked outside when you were stoned, and scandalized the neighbours, but Plain Jane got me drunk, and then she got me high on pot. She has this special room

with leather recliners, and projectors hidden in the walls that give
you the impression that you are in a field of wildflowers, and that
there are birds singing. And every now and then a butterfly floats
by that is so real you can practically just reach out and touch it.'

'My, aren't we something,' Agnes said, and rolled her eyes.

I've known Agnes since I was six weeks old. We will remain
friends until six weeks after one of us is dead, so getting mad at
her, and especially staying angry at her, is essentially pointless. I
have always forgiven her, and I always will.

'So,' I said, 'what I really came here to talk about is my cook
and housekeeper' – I glanced around, perhaps belatedly – 'you
know who.'

'Who?' Agnes said. Obviously, she was not as ready as I was
to play nicely.

'Martha Stewart, dear. I thought you knew. Anyway, Toy floated
the theory that the guest who was murdered, Terry Tazewell, might
have been picked at random, and his murder was a way of getting
back at me. That is to say, the killer's motive was to make my life
more difficult. He even suggested that a couple of the other murders
that happened at the inn might also have been committed by this
same person.'

'Stop looking at me, Mags! I don't hate you *that* much; I was
just irritated, because it seems like you always have to outdo me.'

'Well, I wouldn't kill you either, Agnes. Unless we were stranded
on a desert island. Without sustenance. And you begged me to kill
you. And a voice from Heaven—'

'Oh, stop it, Mags. So tell me, you headed straight to the Church
of Melvin because you thought that they hated you, am I right?'

'Right,' I said.

'And?' Agnes said.

'So what if those whackadoodles hate me? Consider the source,
I say. After all, they're mostly just a bunch of elderly women – and
a few men – who like to socialize once a week, and practice their
own crazy, mixed-up religion that makes not an iota of sense.'

'Like ours does, right?'

'Right as rain, toots,' I said. 'However, I did learn that one of
their number bears me a serious grudge, but for what, I haven't a
clue. I'm telling you, Agnes, no kind deed goes unpunished.'

'Amen. Who is this person?'

'Our dear, dear Anna Weaver,' I said. It was meant to be said ironically.

Agnes snickered and hoisted herself out of the recliner. 'Come with me,' she said.

She led me down the hallway to the back guest bedroom, a tiny space, which was painted a ghastly shade of antacid pink. Then she flipped on the light and pointed to a small table which had been crammed between a single bed and the wall. Covering the table was an old-fashioned lace doily, and on top of that, two items were on display. One item was a fist-sized analogue alarm clock, and the other, slightly more intriguing thing was a photograph of a woman, upon which someone – probably Anna – had drawn horns with a red marker. Wait a minute, not only horns, but red eyes and a goatee.

'That silly girl,' I said. 'How harmful could she be?'

'Take a closer look,' Agnes said.

I stepped closer. Then even closer. Then I gasped in alarm.

'That's me! She really *does* have it out for me!'

Just then the doorbell rang.

TWENTY-ONE

While I stared, transfixed, at the best photo of me ever taken, one that I had personally given to Anna when she came into my employ, Agnes excused herself to answer the door. This was the first likeness of me that I can remember in which I did not resemble a horse, but instead a baby jackass, and they are rather sweet looking. Yes, I know that a prominent psychiatrist once tried to tell me that I had body dysmorphia, and that I was actually quite attractive, but I'm as stubborn as a mule and that information didn't sink in. Nonetheless, giving my employee a photo of myself, for any reason, constituted the sin of pride, and as it says in the Book of Proverbs: 'Pride cometh before destruction, and a haughty spirit before a fall.' Even if Anna Weaver wasn't intent on destroying me, the future did not portend well for me.

While I was berating myself – a common activity – Toy burst into the room. Agnes followed on his heels, huffing and puffing, like a wolf trying to blow a pig's house down.

'There you are!' Toy cried. 'I've been looking for you all over!'

'Didn't you get my messages?' I asked calmly.

'Didn't you get mine?'

'Looks like your wires crossed,' Agnes said. There was envy in her voice. Even though she knew that Toy was gay, and a generation younger than her, she still harboured fantasies of the two of them running off into the sunset together and living happily ever after. In one of her ongoing fantasies, Agnes and Toy had a passel of children, one of whom was still an infant. Given the fact that Agnes and I are virtually the same age, I was pretty sure that her womb had a 'no longer in use' sign posted on it somewhere – so to speak. Still, a good fantasy can help one through a bad day, and I didn't begrudge Agnes hers.

'Agnes, sweetheart,' Toy said kindly, 'may Magdalena and I please have the room?'

'Sure thing,' Agnes said, but her voice was pitched higher than usual, and she shot daggers at me.

Honestly, I really did feel bad for her. While I used to have a thing for Toy myself, once he and his husband had been able to convince me that being gay was not a choice but that one was born that way, I dropped these daydreams like a hot potato. Besides, for me, as a married woman, those thoughts were akin to adultery.

As soon as Agnes's behind cleared the lintel, Toy closed the door. Then he counted silently to ten – I could see his lips move – and jerked the door open. Wouldn't you know, but my bestie had merely turned around. In fact, she was standing so close that if she sneezed, she could have slammed her face into the door.

'Yea-us,' Toy said, in his slowest Southern drawl. 'Kin ah hep you?'

I truly felt sorry for Agnes then, because she is a blotchy blusher. She looked as if she had contracted a weird alien disease from another planet, although of course there are no extra-terrestrial aliens, or the Bible would have told us so. And if there were such creatures, they would have had to have been born sin-free, because God only has one Son, and Jesus sacrificed himself for the sins of this world, not some other world in a far-off galaxy.

At that point there was no reason for Agnes to try and say anything, but of course that didn't stop her. 'Uh-uh . . . I think I left something in this room,' she blurted.

'Your dignity is back down the hall,' I said. 'That-a-way.' I pointed in the direction of her living room. One might think that I was being unkind, but au contraire. My little zinger was just enough to shift Agnes's internal compass needle from embarrassment to irritation, and believe me, the latter is always much preferred – especially if our love interest is standing inches in front of our faces.

Agnes shifted her weight to one foot so that she could look around Toy and give me the stink eye. 'We were cradle babies, Mags. You don't need to be so mean.'

'And you don't need to be so nosy, dear. I'll fill you in later with what I can,' I said.

'Promise.'

'Pinkie promise,' I said.

Toy closed the door. 'Whew! Should I open the door again? If so, what do you think I'll find? Her ear pressed to a glass?'

'Nah,' I said. 'She's learned her lesson. Go ahead; yank it open.'

So that is what Toy did. But already Agnes was nowhere to be seen, which meant that unless the rapture had suddenly taken place, and Agnes had been swept up into the clouds with Jesus and his angels, she really *had* booked it down the hallway, and then into the living room, which was out of sight.

'OK,' Toy said, turning back to me, 'where have you been?'

'Getting stoned on Mary Jane with Plain Jane all day. Did you, or did you not know, that the Schmucker brothers put pot into their big, fat, succulent sausages?'

'*Succulent*, Magdalena? That's a strange way to describe meat.'

'Well? Did you?'

Toy shrugged. 'Well, as you know, my husband and I are pescatarians.'

'I thought you were Episcopalians. And what does that have to do with sausages?'

Toy laughed. 'A pescatarian is vegetarian, except that they add fish and seafood to their diets. We haven't eaten the flesh of mammals for the last six years. And I don't mean to be preachy, but we do feel better for it.

'However, I have suspected from some of the reports I've gotten that these very upright, religious Amish men may have been adding a little something-something to their recipe. I base that on the fact that calls about domestic violence have dropped to near zero in the last couple of months. The folks who used to be drinkers appear to go to sleep after dinner, and the only complaints coming into the department have been that cars take forever to start moving again after they get to our stop sign. Oh, well there was the time Agnes danced in the nude, and Donald Neubrander went shopping at Sam's Corner Market in his pyjamas. And remember you were telling me about Shirley Valentino acting drunk? Maybe it was the sausages. But no felonies, not even any misdemeanours, and of course, no murders until now.'

'Harrumph,' I said. 'You still could have shared what you suspected with me. As mayor, and as the sole source of funds for our minuscule police force, I *am* your boss.'

'Yes, ma'am,' Toy said, and saluted.

'Don't get smart with me, Toy,' I said, 'or I'll dock your pay.' Of course, I wasn't being serious.

'Yes, ma'am,' he said with a wink. 'So did you really get high? I haven't gotten high since my college days. Personally, I didn't care for it. I didn't like the feeling that I wasn't my natural self.'

I nodded. 'Yes, I got as high as a kite in a tornado and, unfortunately, it was one of the highpoints of my life – no pun intended. But how was I to know?' I wailed. 'That Plain Jane is a wily woman. She seduced me with wine first, telling me it was grape drink.'

Toy laughed so hard that he had to hold his stomach, taut as it is. 'I'd have given my right arm to see that,' he finally said.

'And I'd have taken your right arm and given it to Agnes. That poor woman still hasn't given up on you.'

Toy sighed. 'I consider her a dear friend. My husband and I do spend a lot of time with her because she's lonely, now that Doc is dead. Do you think that our making time for her is contributing to the problem?'

'Possibly,' I said. 'But that doesn't mean that you should stop being friends with her altogether. Maybe just scale back slowly, and let your husband handle the social calendar, so that she doesn't see you as the instigator.'

'Thanks,' Toy said. 'That sounds like wise advice. Maybe the pot didn't kill any of your brain cells this time.'

I flicked my tongue out at him. 'So, what did I miss at your end?'

'Interesting stuff,' Toy said. 'I ran background checks on three of your surviving guests. The two ladies have no priors and are pretty much what they purport to be. Christine Landis won a number of beauty pageants, including Miss Illinois, but she immediately lost her title by unleashing a nasty tirade on a backstage reporter who stepped on her toe.

'And speaking of reporters, that is exactly what Ducky Limehouse is – a reporter for the Charleston, South Carolina *Post and Courier.* He'd heard about Schmucker Brothers Sausages from a cousin living in Harrisburg, Pennsylvania. His cousin swore to Ducky that the sausages contained marijuana, so Ducky got clearance from his editor to come up here, and do a feature on the story, if the rumour panned out. That's why he was literally sniffing around behind that shed on your little field trip. He was searching for marijuana plants.'

'Did he find any?'

'He did. Those clever Amish are growing them interspersed with their corn crop.'

'Are you going to bust them for that?'

Toy laughed. 'Bust? My, aren't we up on the lingo. Well, for the moment I haven't been out there sniffing around their corn fields, so all I have is hearsay.'

'So you're not going to bust my cousins?' I said.

'You heard me,' Toy said. 'Now what is even more interesting is what I discovered about our murder victim. This is information I got from both the internet and by calling around to other police departments. Most of what I've learned is confidential, but some of it I can share with you.

'For instance, you can forget about how Terry Tazewell looks now – he was actually a very striking-looking man when he was younger. I've seen the photos. He had a very successful modelling career in New York before going into the restaurant business. It was in New York where Terry met Peter Schmucker, who was just knocking about during his rumspringa years. Both men were potheads at the time – that means smokers of marijuana – and they met through their dealer.

'Anyway, they became friends, as unlikely as it might seem. I think Terry had a crush on Peter, because Peter is so good-looking, but that didn't work out, because Peter is heterosexual. In fact, he was working for an upscale escort service and was highly in demand.'

'I don't get it,' I said. 'So he helped old ladies get across the street. How upscale can that get?'

Toy grabbed my hand and led me to the only chair in the guest bedroom. 'Sit down, please, Magdalena. I'm going to be blunt with you. Peter was a prostitute. A male prostitute. He slept with very rich ladies for huge amounts of money. Some of these were very old ladies from prominent families. Some of these were even the wives of the diplomats, or Washington bigwigs visiting New York.'

'Shut the front door!' I cried. 'But Peter is Amish. Even on rumspringa, I have never heard of an Amish boy doing such a thing. Yes, occasionally an Amish youth sows one wild oat, and some poor girl has to be sent off to another Amish community in a distant state for six or seven months, but I've never heard of an

Amish boy sowing an entire field of wild oats in the Big Apple.'

Toy patted my shoulder affectionately. 'You have such a way with words, Magdalena. I swear, sometimes you remind me of my mother.'

I jerked my shoulder away from his touch. 'Well, sometimes *your* way with words leaves something to be desired.'

'Sorry about that,' Toy said. 'But you need to remember that there are outliers in every religion, in every group of people. I bet you that there has got to be at least one Episcopalian pescatarian who has enjoyed Schmucker Brothers Sausages.'

'Maybe even a Presbyterian pescatarian,' I said.

'So we're cool, then?'

'Yes,' I said. 'Please just don't compare me to your mother again.'

'Gotcha. So, how tired are you right now?'

'That all depends. Does whatever you have in mind come with a warm cinnamon bun and a mug of hot chocolate?'

'It involves driving out to Bill and Linda Steele's house.'

'At this hour?'

'They asked for you specifically. They said it was urgent; that it couldn't wait.'

I sighed. 'Given that Gabe is already a mite put out that he has to entertain our guests tonight – I told him to do a cookout by the pond—' I gasped in alarm. 'Oh my gracious, oh my soul.'

'There goes Alice down the hole,' Toy said.

'What?'

'Never mind. That's just something from *Alice in Wonderland*. What's got you so worked up?'

'Well, someone is bound to discover the murder weapon. You know, the knife that I discovered in the pond, wrapped up in my dishtowel from Portugal.'

'OK, here's what we'll do,' Toy said calmly. 'You drive out to the Steeles' and see what's going on, and I'll hurry over to your place and crash the cookout so that I can retrieve the knife.'

'You sure you don't mind? What will your husband say?'

'As it happens Steven is working late in Bedford tonight. It was just going to be me and leftovers in front of the television tonight anyway.'

'Then it's a deal,' I said, 'but they're roasting sausages, so you won't get much to eat.'

'Will there be s'mores?' Toy asked.

'You betcha,' I said.

'I can live on s'mores until I get home,' he said with a grin. 'No problem.'

He opened the door and Agnes literally fell into his arms. Poor Toy staggered backward under her weight, and the momentum propelled him until he collapsed on the bed with Agnes on top of him. I could almost feel his breath being squeezed out of him.

'Oomph!' he moaned.

Agnes, clever woman that she was, remained atop him a couple of seconds longer than she needed to. 'Oh, I'm so sorry,' she finally said, as she slowly rolled off him. 'I was coming to ask you something, and then I tripped.'

'A likely story, dear,' I said. I grabbed Toy's hands and pulled him into a sitting position. Then I helped get him to his feet. I was glad that I had helped Agnes select that mattress the year before, and that we'd chosen one of the very soft models, otherwise I'd have had to fluff Toy out, like a stuffed animal that had been packed in an overfilled suitcase.

'Well, that was fun, wasn't it?' Toy said, but he was not amused. Toy hates eavesdroppers. 'Well Agnes, what is it that you were going to ask me?'

'Oh yes, that. I wanted to know if you would like to have dinner here tonight, given that Steven has to work late tonight in Bedford.'

I jumped in before Toy could speak. 'Agnes, I think I see a wood splinter in your right ear.'

'What?' Agnes clutched her ear and rolled into a sitting position. 'Why would I have a splinter in my ear?'

'From pressing it so hard against the door,' I said.

'Don't be silly,' Agnes snapped. 'I used a glass. It's here on the bed – oops, did I just tell on myself?'

Toy chuckled. 'I'm afraid so.'

'Be sure your sin will find you out,' I said. 'That's from the Book of Numbers, chapter thirty-two, verse twenty-three.'

'Eavesdropping is *not* a sin, Mags,' Agnes said. 'I doubt if it's even a Heavenly "no-no".' She giggled.

'I hate to burst your bubble,' Toy said, 'but it's not a cool thing to do. Police work is serious business, and there are things that civilians should not be privy to.'

Agnes appeared both crestfallen and green with anger. It twisted her otherwise pleasant face into an almost unrecognizable shape.

'Then how come Magdalena gets in on all the good stuff? She's nothing but a civilian. In fact, she's the civilian that seems to attract murder victims like the Pied Piper attracted rats. Explain that to me, will you, Chief Toy from North Carolina?'

Wow! In three sentences my best buddy had managed to roll me under the bus, plus remind Toy that he was ultimately an outsider.

To his credit, Toy smiled pleasantly. 'Magdalena is a certified private investigator and has a long history of partnering with this police department. She has proven herself to be fearless, innovative and willing to go the extra mile when it comes to pursuing justice. As to my origin, as the old song goes: "nothing could be finer than to be in Carolina in the morning". So I will make no apologies for not being born in Hernia, Pennsylvania.'

I couldn't help but applaud. Truly, I couldn't. Perhaps it was the Devil that grabbed my large, but shapely, mitts, and slapped them vigorously together repeatedly until Toy gently laid a hand on my shoulder and whispered in my ear that maybe it was best that I stop.

'Well, we'll be off then,' Toy said softly. 'Thank you for your hospitality.'

'Yes, thanks oodles,' I said. 'Now tootle, dear. I have police work to do.'

Agnes gave me the stink eye again as I brushed past her. She would forgive me of course – in time – just as I would forgive her anything. Well, maybe I wouldn't forgive her if she stole Gabe away from me, but I'd forgive her anything else.

As I drove along the winding, rural road that led to the Steeles' mansion, Agnes, Plain Jane and Toy were the last thing on my mind. I was totally focused on the road ahead, and even more importantly the vegetation on either side. In Pennsylvania there are thousands of auto and deer collisions annually, many of them fatal.

Gabe said that he read that the problem is that deer evolved along with predators such as wolves, and that deer instinctively know how close a wolf can get to them, before they should bolt and run. Gabe also said that since deer did not evolve with automobiles, they misjudge the speed of cars and that is why they leap in front of them at the last minute. Just between you and me, I think that this theory is a bunch of baloney, since neither wolves nor deer *evolved*. They were *created* by God on the sixth day of creation, and if you don't believe me, just read the Book of Genesis.

By the way, most experts agree that if you encounter a deer in the road, take your foot off the gas pedal and hit it. You will do less damage to your car, and yourself, than if you swerved and hit a guardrail, or another vehicle. The one exception is if the deer happens to be a large buck with antlers. They have been known to crash through windshields and impale those in the front seats.

Dawn and dusk are the worst times to drive through deer country, and I was driving at dusk. The entire drive I prayed that I would not see a single deer, but if I did manage to hit a buck, and was impaled, death would come quickly. I also took the liberty of asking the Good Lord to send my sweet Aunt Grace to the Pearly Gates to greet me, instead of Mama and Papa. Papa might have been OK – once he got to Heaven – but I sincerely doubted that Mama, even after sitting at the Lord's feet, plucking at a harp for half a century, would have been able to hold her acerbic tongue.

TWENTY-TWO

T hank heavens I made it to my destination without running over even an opossum. The Steeles' circular drive was well lit. However, since they are so far from civilization, I didn't want to take any chances meeting up with creatures of the night (whether human or animal) while I waited on the front steps of the mansion for someone to answer the door, so I called from my locked car before venturing out. This time Linda opened the massive door before I was even halfway to the house. What's more, she threw her arms around me as I entered.

'I'm so glad that you're here, even though you're so very tardy.'

'About that,' I said. 'I came as soon as I got your message. I was unfortunately incommunicado for the bulk of the day.'

'Well, I hope it was police business,' Linda said. Her tone was only slightly accusatory.

'Indeed it was,' I said. 'It couldn't be helped, and I'm sorry about that.'

'All's well that ends well,' she said and patted my arm. It was a curious thing for her to say. At the time I assumed that she was referencing her feelings of annoyance regarding my 'tardiness'.

'So then,' I said, 'what is it that I can do for you?'

'Magdalena,' Linda said, taking my elbow, 'unlike His Highness, Chief Graham, you didn't dismiss out of hand our belief that our son's friend Brian was telling the truth. He did, in fact, swerve to avoid hitting an Amish farm wagon that was not displaying either tail lights, or any sort of reflectors.

'Now, what I'm about to tell you next – to actually show you – may, or may not, be related to that tragic incident. But then again it might. Bill and I both have a hunch that it does. Unfortunately, Bill had to attend a business dinner in Pittsburgh tonight, and couldn't wait until you made your tardy appearance, so you're stuck with just me. But anyway, we both feel that since you tend to think outside of the box – given that rather quirky mind of yours – you're just the person for this case.'

'Was that supposed to be a compliment?' I said, getting straight to the point. 'We quirky-minded folks have feelings too, you know.'

Linda's hand slid off my elbow and clutched her pearls. 'Oh my, yes! Indeed, it was a compliment of the highest order. Only geniuses have the level of quirkiness that you possess. Think of Sherlock Holmes! Think of—'

'Think no further,' I said, my hurt feelings assuaged. 'I'm the woman for your job.'

'Fabulous. Then follow me.'

On my previous visit the Steeles had indicated that their butler, Baines, had lived in another wing of the house – er, mansion. That was rather an understatement. He actually lived over their four-car garage, in a private apartment that was roomier than Agnes's Cape Cod cottage. The garage, with its several gables, was built at right angles to the house with its numerous gables. Had Baines been so inclined, he could have strung a cable between the house and the garage and tightrope-walked to work.

Whereas I supply Anna Weaver with a simply adequate cottage, that is tastefully, and quite functionally, furnished, the Steeles went overboard in spoiling Baines. Perhaps he felt unbearably lonely because he was forced to sleep in a king-size, four-poster, mahogany bed. And who wouldn't feel overwhelmed by an eighty-five-inch, flat-screen television in every room, except for the three bathrooms? In the bathrooms the televisions were just a mite smaller. And the plethora of plump sofas and automatic recliners – the poor man probably had a nervous breakdown just trying to decide where to plop his weary body at the end of the day.

'Tut-tut,' I said in disapproval.

'I beg your pardon?' Linda said.

'*King* Tut,' I said quickly, 'would have loved this place; it's so well appointed.'

'Magdalena, why do you lie so much?' she asked.

'I do?'

'Everyone knows that about you. Pinocchio Yoder, they call you. It's such a shame, because you'd have many more friends if people could just take you at your word.'

'*Pinocchio* Yoder? Just because I tend to embroider the truth?'

Linda nodded. 'Still, I like you. I like to think that you don't lie about the big stuff.'

'Most certainly not!' I said. 'Cross my heart and hope to die, stick a needle in my eye – well, not literally. That's just a silly childhood saying; it doesn't count as lying.'

'I suppose you're wondering why we give our butler such lavish quarters,' she said, giving that sentence the Canadian inflection.

'I'm only human, dear.'

'Well, you try coaxing a genuine English butler to cross the pond to the wilds of southwestern Pennsylvania, where no one has ever heard of Marmite, and where so few gay men are out of the closet. We thought the applicants needed some extra perks.'

'Not all butlers are gay,' I said. 'Whatever gave you the idea that they are?'

'Well, in the movies you never see their wives.'

'Oy vey,' I said. 'And here I thought that I jumped to conclusions. Can you please just show me what I drove all the way out here to see?'

'Well, you don't need to be insulting,' Linda said with a shrug. Then she led me back into one of the guest bedrooms, where she stopped in front of a large, framed print.

'Marc Chagall,' I said aloud.

'How do you know that?' she said. She was clearly quite surprised.

'My husband is Jewish. He has a book of Marc Chagall prints.'

'This isn't just any Marc Chagall print; this one is signed and numbered.' She deftly removed the print from the wall and laid it carefully on the king-size bed, revealing a safe. Then with three practiced turns she unlocked the safe and opened the door wide.

'Look in there,' she said. 'Tell me what you see.'

'It looks like a passport. And also, a black leather pouch.'

'It *is* a passport, and there is a black leather pouch. Now take them out and examine them, starting with the passport.'

I hesitated. 'Shouldn't I be wearing latex gloves?'

'Oh, Magdalena, you're so tiresome.' She sighed. 'Well, if you insist.'

What I hadn't noticed before, when she'd laid the print on the bed, was that there was already a pair of white latex gloves lying on the bed, atop the white duvet cover. These she picked up and thrust at me.

Unfortunately, the gloves she gave me were a size medium, and I wear extra large, so I thrust them back at her with the exact same intensity. I wasn't being mean; I was merely doing unto her, as she had done unto me.

'I'm sure that handling them just one more time won't matter,' I said. Frankly, touching them with my bare hands probably didn't matter at all, but I felt like being officious.

Having said that, I removed the two items and examined each carefully. The first one that I scrutinized was the passport. It was British, and the holder was none other than Baines. It was well used, indicating that Baines was able to visit his husband frequently. And speaking of surprises, that black pouch contained twenty-five thousand US dollars.

'Very strange,' I said aloud. 'How could he have gone back to England without his passport? And who in their right mind is going to leave that much money behind and not say a word?'

'Exactly,' Linda said.

I replaced the items in the safe and headed back to the master bedroom where there was a walk-in closet. Linda pranced after me in her pair of designer pumps. It didn't take me a minute to discover another alarming fact: there were no clothes hangers anywhere.

'Don't they use clothes hangers in England?' I asked aloud.

'What?' Linda said.

'Well, look around. There's not one in sight. Either he made off with all of your clothes hangers, or someone just lifted the clothes off the racks, because they were in a hurry to make it look like Baines had cleared out. Where did he keep his suitcases?'

'Follow me,' Linda said. She led me out of the apartment and into the indoor hallway that connected it to the main house. Just before we reached the entrance to the main building, she paused in front of an unobtrusive door that lacked any visible hardware. It opened just by a firm touch to reveal winding wooden stairs.

'*Voila*,' she said. 'The attic. Although as you will see, it is pretty clutter free up there. We learned from watching Oprah Winfrey that if you haven't seen, touched, worn or enjoyed something for a year, it is time to pass it along to someone else.'

'I don't suppose that you have any diamonds up there that need passing along?' I asked hopefully. Of course, I could afford my own diamonds, but it never hurts to ask.

'Don't be silly,' Linda scoffed. 'Your type of Mennonite is supposed to dress simply. You couldn't get away with wearing diamonds, and you know it.'

'Harrumph. Well, lead the way up these impossibly steep stairs, perhaps even worse than my own, but don't expect me to catch you, if you fall backwards. I have long spindly arms, and I'm in the last quarter of my life to boot.'

Linda snorted. 'Magdalena, there isn't a staircase on the planet earth that is worse than yours. But since you are, by your own call, so ancient and decrepit, I insist that you go first. That way if you fall, I will simply stand aside, and let you tumble all the way to the bottom, whereupon you will break your scrawny neck and pass over into whichever of the two eternities awaits you: Heaven or Hell.'

I cackled with delight. 'You can certainly give tit for tat. If I weren't old enough to be your mother, I might consent to be your friend.'

'My thoughts exactly,' Linda said. 'If you weren't old enough to be my great-grandmother, I too would explore the possibility of us being friends.'

'In a pig's ear,' I said sweetly and, gathering up my skirts, scrambled up her impossibly steep stairs.

When my horsey head had cleared the attic floor I stopped abruptly and looked around. The space was illuminated by a single LED light, but I could see for quite a distance. However, the first thing that caught my eye was a pair of blue vinyl suitcases.

'Who owns the blue vinyl suitcases?' I called down the stairwell.

'Oh no,' Linda said weakly. 'You were right. Those suitcases are Baines'. He never left here on his own at all; he was abducted.'

'I'm coming down,' I said. But it was only when I turned around that I truly appreciated how steep her staircase was. I felt like I was in a treehouse, and about to descend a ladder face first. Nope, this wasn't going to cut it. I turned around again and inched my way down.

'You better give me a soft place to fall,' I hollered, 'after all that I've done for you.'

'*Done?*' shrieked Linda. 'An hour ago Baines was in Bognor Regis polishing off a buttered scone, and thanks to you, he's been kidnapped, and we haven't even received a ransom note.'

'Or maybe you have,' I said.

'Make sense, Magdalena. Has pulling your hair back into a pile of braids on top of your hair for your entire life finally addled your brains?'

'Don't be cruel, dear,' I said. 'You may regret it when you're standing in front of the Pearly Gates.'

'You Mennonites drive me crazy. I bet you believe that every word in the Bible is literally true.'

'Look, toots,' I said, 'you're the one who just got on my case for some harmless prevarication. But if you're so bent on the absolute truth, then read your Bible, because the Good Lord doesn't lie. Every single word in there was dictated from him to the men who wrote it down.

'Now, let's not waste another second discussing something which has already been proven. Instead, we need to run back into the main house and re-examine the clues that Baines' kidnapper has so thoughtfully left for us.'

'Magdalena, you're crazy, you know that?' Linda said.

'I'm as nutty as an almond tree, but come on, time's a'wastin.' I inched past her, and when I finally got to the floor, I hoofed it back to the main house just as fast as my seventy-four-year-old legs could take me. Linda, who was two decades younger, could barely keep up with me.

'So where are the clues?' she panted when we got there.

'Where are the letters you got from Baines?' I said.

'What does that have to do with anything?' she demanded.

'Well,' I said, 'he obviously didn't leave the country, and we both agreed that he was kidnapped, so those letters had to have been forged. I would like to examine them – please.'

'All right,' she groused. 'But they had British stamps and post marks on the envelopes.' She walked over to an end table adjacent to an enormous white sofa, and from the table's drawer extracted the letters. She didn't actually hand them to me, rather she made me snatch them from her hand, which was hovering over mine.

'See here,' I said, pointing to the postmark on one of the enve-lopes, 'it doesn't quite match up to the stamp, and the colour is off. This stamp was probably purchased over the internet, already postmarked from a collector – which meant it was used – and then pasted on this envelope. But look at its denomination. Why would Baines put just two, one penny stamps on it, and expect it to get here? Moreover, how did it manage to get here? I'll tell you how: it never went through *any* postal system. All the kidnapper – or kidnappers – had to do was to look up British postage, and simply dropped the envelope in your mailbox. This was all part of a ruse to maintain the fiction that your beloved butler had departed on his own volition.'

Linda snatched the envelopes back. 'You think you're so smart, don't you?'

'Yes.'

'But I still don't like those severe hairstyles you Conservative Mennonites wear. Hair braided and twisted into buns. And those silly white prayer caps you insist on wearing. It's all very unflattering. Without any make-up at all, you tend to look so mousy. Tell me, do you Mennonite women think that dressing this way makes you better Christians than we Presbyterians?'

'I refuse to answer such a provocative question. But I will say this: I think your appearance would be greatly enhanced by a pile of braids, and maybe even by a black Amish travel bonnet. You know, the sort that covers the entire back of the head and neck, and even the sides of the face and throat.'

'Magdalena, get out of my house this minute!'

'Well, I declare! And here I was hoping for a warm cinnamon roll, and mug of hot chocolate, as thanks for a job well done.'

'Out! Get out now!'

'Linda,' I said calmly, 'you might want to pay attention to the words of Hebrew chapter thirteen, verse two: "Be not forgetful to entertain strangers: for thereby some have entertained angels unawares".'

Linda snorted. 'First of all, although you're strange, you're no stranger. And second, you're definitely not an angel.'

'So that's it, huh?' I said, over the rumbling of my tummy. 'Not even one thin biscuit? I haven't had my supper, you know.'

'Not even a teensy, weensy crumb,' Linda said.

'OK, but if I starve to death on the way home, my death will have to be on your conscience. And just to show you how good a person I actually am, I am going to see to it that Chief Toy reopens the investigation into the accident that took your son's life. A hunch from a woman is worth two facts from a man, and I have a very strong hunch that what your son's best friend saw that fateful night is directly linked to Baines' disappearance.'

Linda laid a cold hand on my forearm. 'I could microwave us a pizza in no time at all. How about it? With a nice toss salad. And there's chocolate cake for dessert.'

'Thanks, but the more I think about it, I really can't stay. There's something that I need to do. Have you any munchies that I can eat in the car?'

'I've got some packets of peanut butter and crackers. You can have as many as you like.'

'Great. I'll take four.'

Having gotten my snacks, I drove, following the Devil on a black steed into the gathering gloom.

TWENTY-THREE

'In for a penny, in for a pound.' That phrase might have originated in the United Kingdom, where pounds are a form of currency, but we Americans co-opted it centuries ago. As long as I was that far from home, I might as well keep going and see if I could make it a red-banner day. I was pretty sure that I knew who had kidnapped Baines, and who had murdered Terry Tazewell. But first I needed to run a few things past my second cousin, Peter Schmucker.

Once one has driven as far from Hernia proper as the Steeles' mansion, then it is just a few miles more to Peter's farm. If I timed things right, I might even get a delicious home-cooked dinner out of my impromptu visit. Peter wouldn't have cooked it – he wouldn't have had time to – but surely a relative would have dropped a hearty meal off for him to enjoy. On the other hand, Peter could well have been dining out at a relative's house. That's just the chance I had to take when dealing with a group whose faith forbade the use of cell phones.

When I arrived, it was easy to tell that Peter was home because I could see his buggy, although his horses had obviously been stabled. There was a light shining through his kitchen window, although the rest of his house was dark. Now a wise Magdalena would have called Chief Toy and ran her newly acquired theory past him, and maybe even told him where she was. A considerate wife would have called Gabe and asked him how the picnic and sausage roast out at the pond was progressing. While I do my best to be considerate, I will admit that I haven't gained much wisdom with age.

Since the Amish don't use electricity, they don't have doorbells. That is no problem for me; I have knuckles that are the envy of prize fighters.

'Knock, knock,' I said as I gave my knuckles a good workout on the kitchen door. 'Knock, knock. It's me, Magdalena, your second cousin.'

'Just a minute, Magdalena.'

The door swung open presently to reveal Peter dressed in a 'wife-beater' undershirt, as Gabe calls them, and a pair of blue jeans. A 'wife-beater' undershirt, by the way, is a white, sleeveless, ribbed, cotton garment often associated with drunken husbands who beat their wives. At any rate, for a nanosecond I thought that I might have gotten the wrong house. I had never seen an adult Amish man, one who'd been baptized into the church, wearing so few, and such worldly clothes. The sleeveless undershirt revealed a sculpted body, one that was rippling with muscles. I was dumb-founded. What's more, in those clothes, Peter was a dead ringer for the hunks on the sexy paperback novels that I had read in my research to keep filth out of the PennDutch Inn.

'Magdalena,' Peter said warmly, 'how good of you to drop in. What brings you all the way out here?'

'Well, I was driving around – sort of – and happened to think of you. How have you been coping?'

His eyes teared up immediately. 'Not so good. But come on in, Cousin. Don't stand out there like a stranger.'

I didn't even need to step into his kitchen to tell that dinner was in the oven. 'Is that a roast I smell?' I asked as I entered.

'Your incredible Yoder nose does it again,' he said. 'Yah, it is a roast. A rump roast with potatoes, carrots and onions. Can you stay for dinner? The roast is big enough for six, so that there would be enough for leftovers during the week.'

'That's very kind of you, but I've been snacking all day,' I said. 'But I do need something to drink, please; I'm parched.'

'Of course,' Peter said, appearing somewhat cheered. 'I have cola, milk, orange juice and apple juice. Now sit.'

I sat at his kitchen table, which was lit by a Coleman lantern. 'Apple juice, please,' I said. 'Peter, you are a very intelligent man. Do you know that one needs a passport just to get on an international flight?'

He hesitated for maybe two seconds. 'Yah, I have read about this. This is true.'

'Have you ever met Bill and Linda Steele?'

Peter, who was getting a clean glass down from a cupboard above the sink, turned to look at me. 'Bill and Linda Steele,' he repeated. 'I have never met them, but I know who they are. They are the Englishers whose son was killed in a car crash last year. The driver of the car was his drunk friend, but he claimed that he was swerving to miss an Amish farm wagon at three in the morning. Yah, am I right?'

'You're right as rain,' I said. 'Of course, what most people don't know is that there was a third person in the car, someone who was safely buckled in, riding in the back seat. That person was unharmed, and that person also saw the hay wagon. The reason that this person didn't come forward and testify is because this person was living here on a visa that had long expired. Can you guess who that person was?'

Peter shrugged and turned away. He had his back to me for a minute or two as he opened the propane-powered fridge and poured the apple juice. He also opened another cabinet, as if he was absentmindedly looking for something. The poor man was operating on empty, so I hated putting him through the third degree.

'I can't guess, Magdalena,' he said, handing me the apple juice. 'So please just tell me. I'm really exhausted tonight.'

'I'd be glad to,' I said. First, I took a sip of apple juice. What in the tarnation had my second cousin served me? That apple juice was so bitter, so vile, it must have been squeezed by our first ancestors to arrive on this continent in 1738. Given that Peter was taking the departure of his wife so very hard, I didn't want to burden him further with my weak constitution, therefore I gulped down the entire six-ounce serving without pausing to breathe.

Peter watched in amazement. 'Would you care for some more, Magdalena?'

'No, thank you,' I said. 'What I was about to say is that the witness to the accident was Baines, the Steeles' English butler. Did you ever meet him?'

'No. Magdalena, you made it sound like something has happened to him.'

'Did I?' I asked.

'Yes,' Peter said. 'You used the past tense.'

'So I did. Well, I do think that something has happened to him. He disappeared – went who knows where, but he left his passport locked securely in a safe. Along with fifteen thousand dollars.'

I've had Lasik surgery, and I've also had my cataracts removed.

My vision is superb for an old biddy like myself, so maybe it wasn't my imagination when I saw a vein throb along Peter's right temple.

'Well, that is very strange,' Peter agreed. 'But have you wondered if maybe God took him?'

I stifled a laugh. 'You mean just sort of zapped him up to Heaven, like he did Enoch?'

'Yah, why not?' he said, looking a bit hurt, and making me feel guilty for my blithe response.

'I'm not saying it's impossible, but *if* God took Baines up to Heaven, wouldn't God also be able to supply him with a Heavenly wardrobe? I ask this because all of Baines' clothes are also missing, even the clothes hangers. Surely Heaven isn't in need of earth-style clothes hangers.'

Again, Peter shrugged. 'The ways of the Lord are mysterious, Magdalena. You were taught that, just like I was.'

'God knows the truth, Peter.' What I really wanted to say is that I came to his house to suss out a confession. I was one hundred percent sure that Peter Schmucker had kidnapped Baines, the Steeles' butler, despite struggling to come up with a credible reason why. The part about there being a third person in the car, and that person being Baines, that was just a hunch – from me. A woman. I also wanted to get Peter to confess that he was the person who murdered Terry Tazewell. Peter was one heck of a good actor – and there, I just used the 'h' word – but it was so true. Even though God doesn't make mistakes, Peter should not have been born Amish. I am convinced that Peter would have made a fine career out in Hollywood, although frankly, he might have been too good-looking. A lot of famous actors have stayed at the PennDutch, without their make-up, and they are not nearly as good-looking as you might think.

These were my intentions, but the best laid plans of mice and women sometimes go awry. There I was, one of those hardy souls who bragged (a sin, I know) that she didn't poison her body with unneeded medications. In fact, I rarely even took an aspirin. Because of that, I had zero tolerance for any chemicals, other than the ones that comprised my body. Apparently, something in the apple juice was quick acting, and try as I might, I was unable to fight the need to just lie down and sleep. But where?

'Excuse me, Peter, but I need to get to my car,' I said, as I swayed in my chair.

'You look sleepy, Magdalena. You're in no condition to drive. Why don't you take a nap here first? Just a short one. Or let me drive you home. Gabe can drive you back tomorrow to collect your car.'

'Gabe can what?' I said, as I laid my head to rest on my crossed arms on his kitchen table. That was my last memory of that night.

TWENTY-FOUR

I awoke with a slight headache, but an overwhelming need to urinate. I sat up immediately and then realized that I wasn't in my own bed. In fact, I was chained to a bed, in a room I had never seen. Beside the bed was a bucket, and a roll of toilet tissue, both of which I urgently availed myself. It wasn't until after I'd relieved myself that I realized that I was still wearing my original clothes, and most importantly, was in possession of my sturdy Christian underwear. The latter I pulled up quickly, before examining my surroundings further.

I examined the chain. One end was attached to a steel ring that encircled the rear bar of the metal bed frame. The other end was attached to a metal cuff that fit snugly around my slim right ankle. The chain itself was about a dozen feet in length. The bed, much to my dismay, was bolted to the wooden floor. I gathered from this that I was not the first guest whom Peter had entertained in this fashion.

Whereas the toilet bucket was located at the foot of the bed, adjacent to head of the bed there was a small, sturdy wooden table (it too was bolted to the floor). In front of the table was a cooler. Atop the table was a thermos bottle, a mug, a plate, a bowl, a stack of paper cups, two spoons, and a box of sugar-frosted cornflakes. Laying across the bowl was a business-size envelope.

Beside the cooler, on the floor, was a small stack of books. I examined the titles by the bright light of one of four LED lanterns: The Holy Bible; *The Ultimate American Gardening Book; Leonardo Da Vinci* by Walter Isaacson; *The Norton Anthology of English Literature; Official Rules for Card Games*; and a travel book called *Down Under* by Bill Bryson. In addition to those books there were two of those so-called bodice-ripper books, you know, those trashy romance books with Peter on the cover. After having seen him last night in jeans and a sleeveless undershirt, I was one hundred percent convinced that Peter was indeed the model for these covers, as well as the covers for the books that I had found in my guest rooms.

Anyway, the next thing that I did was open the envelope. Inside was a single piece of paper folded in thirds, with the following scrawled message:

> Magdalena,
> Had to go to work. Be back to give you supper. We will talk then.
> Peter.

'It was mighty kind of you to sign your name,' I growled. 'Now I can quit wondering if the government is behind this.'

I lifted the lid of the cooler. Inside was a quart of milk, two quart bottles of water, an ice pack, and on top of that two sandwiches, one cheese and tomato, the other peanut butter and jelly.

'Well, at least I won't starve,' I said aloud.

Just for the record. It is perfectly normal to talk to oneself. We all do it. It is also perfectly normal to answer oneself. It is, however, a wee bit odd to take umbrage at your own answer. Therefore, it is best to play it cool when engaged in solo conversations. In other words, don't tell yourself anything too controversial.

Knowing that I had a full day in captivity – if my pleas to God for deliverance didn't pan out – I decided to begin my day as normally as possible. Thus, I picked up the well-worn Bible, read some scripture, and said my morning prayers. Then I poured myself a heaping bowl of frosted flakes and a mug of steaming hot coffee.

One might think that I wouldn't have any appetite, having just discovered that I'd been chained to a bed by a mad Amish man, but au contraire. I believe that my ravenous appetite was the first part of my prayer for deliverance being answered. I believe that this was the Good Lord's way of telling me that I needed to keep up my strength for what lay ahead. As I ate, I considered what possible weapons of self-defence were at my disposal.

The cereal bowl, the plate and spoons were all plastic. The milk and water were also in plastic containers. The mug, however, was ceramic, so that was a slim, but still possible, contender for the weapons of self-defence category. Now the thermos, that was definitely worth considering. But by far, the most obvious choice would have been the lid to the cooler, or even the cooler itself, had they both not been made out of Styrofoam.

One might rightly draw the conclusion by my musings that I had abandoned my pacifist heritage, and one would be right. My Amish ancestors refused to defend themselves when they were attacked by a Lenape raiding party in 1750, and my six times great-grandmother was scalped, and my five times great-grandfather was taken captive. When I grew up I was taught to admire their bravery and their strong commitment to their Christian ideals. However, I can assure you that it is one thing to be a pacifist, when life is chugging along at a normal pace, and you are feeling safe in your usual environment, and it is quite another thing to be a pacifist when you have been chained to a metal bed frame by a raving lunatic who was undoubtedly a murderer.

Of course, said raving lunatic had not supplied me with my purse, which contained my cell phone. I did, however, wear a small, inexpensive wristwatch, and thus had a way to mark the hours. It was only half past nine – in the morning, I assumed – when I'd finished breakfast, so I decided that the best way to occupy my mind was to read one of the bodice-rippers. I figured that I would be so disgusted by the filth that I read, that my mind wouldn't have room for fear.

My first selection was the book entitled *Endless Ecstasy*. The cover pictured a tanned, shirtless Peter with his brawny arms around a woman in a low-cut peasant blouse, her ample assets threatening to go rogue. As atrocious as the writing was, as sinful as the characters in the book acted, I am afraid that I have to say the following: the book was a real page-turner. And yes, I did find myself aroused from time to time, and of course I stopped and prayed about this confusing state of affairs. But consider this, falling for a fictional character is not the same as falling for a flesh and blood man. One cannot commit adultery in one's heart, just because one got aroused when they read the words 'Jeremy's (censored) manhood'. If indeed that's exactly what happened.

My point is that it was time for lunch before I knew it, and again I was ravenous. I was also furious with the ditsy blonde heroine for temporarily (I hoped) dumping the handsome Jeremy (who was also a peasant) when the cruel duke proposed to her. I selected the peanut butter and jelly sandwich first and ate it while

I read, and quite accidentally smeared peanut butter on the word 'Duke'.

Although I am a fairly fast reader, Satan made me savour every sentence in this trashy book, to imagine myself in the role of Deborah with the long blonde hair that hung so low that it brushed her firm, round buttocks. In the early afternoon the story reached a satisfying climax, and left me lying breathless on the bed, ready for a nap.

When I awoke, I saw that an hour had passed, so again I got down on my knees and spent at least another hour praying for deliverance. But barring the appearance of an angel with a flaming sword, I didn't see how that was going to happen. Instead, in another three or four hours a very sick man was going to pay me a visit, and possibly even kill me. Now I could have read the Bible during those hours, but I had read the Bible from cover to cover, at least once a year, ever since my baptism at age twelve. I was familiar with its contents, and my very active mind was sure to stray back to Peter's imminent return, and my certain doom. Therefore, the only solution to tamp down my terror was to tackle the second book, the one entitled *Captive Bride.*

Although the title of the second book scared me a bit, I told myself that there was no way that even a lunatic like Peter could think of me as bride material. Surely that was not why he had placed that particular book in the room for me to read. After all, I was old enough to be his mother, and we weren't of the same or even related faith. Peter was clearly no longer a practicing Amish. Still, with his looks, Peter could have had any woman that he so chose. On the other hand, his wife Delilah had been older than him, but still young enough to bear children. Anyway, after reading two pages I was completely drawn into the storyline and was identifying with the heroine. This time I was an eighteen-year-old girl, with flaming red tresses that spilled over my milky-white shoulders. I was also the youngest daughter of a king, and my name was Princess Maeve. I was kidnapped by a masked bandit while on a journey to visit relatives in the country. Well, I shan't bore anyone from here on, or lead them into sin, because the plot left me breathless at times, even lying back upon my pillow and gasping. Who knew that fiction could be so stimulating? And here I thought that the Nancy Drew books were as good as it got.

Princess Maeve had just realized that she was in love with the masked bandit and was finally going to give herself to him fully when the door to the room that I was in opened with a bang. I thrust the books under my pillow and sat with my knees together, my feet flat on the floor. I looked straight ahead at a windowless, unadorned wall.

'Hello, Magdalena. I'm sorry that I had to be gone all day. How are you?'

'"Yea, though I walk through the valley of the shadow of death, I will fear no evil",' I said, quoting from the twenty-third Psalm.

Peter laughed. 'I didn't come to kill you, Magdalena.'

'You *didn't*?'

'Of course not. I like you, Magdalena; you're my friend. You're the only person in all of Hernia who gets me.'

Actually, I don't, I thought. Far from it. But I have to play it cool.

'Yes, we are friends, Peter. I've known you since you were a baby. And we're second cousins, as well. You can tell me anything.'

'*Anything?*'

'Absolutely. Peter, tell me why I'm chained to this bed.'

'Oh that,' he said almost casually. 'That's so we can talk.'

'Can't we talk without the chain?'

He scratched his head. 'Yah, maybe. In a day or two. But now I need to clean up in here so that I can bring you your supper.' Thank goodness he began by removing the bucket as it had gotten a lot of use. Then he returned and took away the cooler, the thermos and the dirty dishes, cups and spoons. I saw him glance to where the paperbacks had been, and then I saw him smile.

'I'll be back soon with supper,' he promised.

During his absence I picked up the Holy Bible again and read some Psalms. I also prayed for the wisdom to say the right thing, so as not to anger him. Above all I prayed for the knowledge to extract myself from the situation in which I found myself. The Bible has plenty of stories of mad men, and wicked men, and of course Peter was both. I believed that the answer would come to me if I was faithful and listened to that 'still, small voice'.

When Peter returned he brought a dinner tray that was thought-fully arranged. Besides the entrée, it contained a side salad, a cloth napkin, salt and pepper shakers, and this time, stainless steel cutlery. He set the tray on my side table.

'I'll be right back,' he said, and indeed he was, with a plastic gallon container of store-bought water.

'Please eat,' he said. 'I thought I'd keep you company while you ate.'

Ah, so that's why there was steel cutlery this time; Peter might be crazy, but he was also careful. Well, there was certainly no harm in appeasing the whack job by eating while the food was still warm. I would also make a point of complimenting him on his cooking skills. The entrée appeared to be leftovers from the pot roast with root vegetables that he'd made for himself the night before. There is nothing wrong with leftovers in my book; they often taste better on the second day.

I cut a piece of the tender meat and smelled its unique, but tantalizing aroma. What cut was it, and what spices had he used?

'What cut is this?' I asked.

'It's a rump roast,' Peter said with a grin.

'But is it pork, or is it beef?'

'It's Baines,' Peter said, looking me straight in the eye.

My stomach lurched and I dropped the fork. 'Could you repeat that?'

'It's the Steeles' butler. Baines, the Englisher.'

I prayed for the strength to talk to Peter calmly, like a real detective might. But first I had to set the tray back on the bedside table.

'You need to taste it,' Peter said. 'Otherwise you might offend the cook.'

'Well, I can smell that it's been cooked to perfection, but I forgot to tell you that I'm a vegetarian now.'

'There are plenty of vegetables on that plate,' Peter said. 'You can eat them.'

'Actually, I can't, Cousin. You see, because they have been cooked with meat, they have absorbed meat juices, and that makes them no longer suitable for a vegetarian diet.'

Peter's handsome face hardened.

I hastened to distract him from my dietary lie. 'Peter, I'm sure that you had a good reason to kill Baines, because knowing you like I do, I know that you wouldn't do anything lightly.'

He nodded and looked away. 'Yah, it had to be done. It wasn't just the boys – the butler also saw me late one night with the wagon carrying marijuana plants. But I made him a deal: I would supply him with high quality marijuana, the very best, if he would stay quiet. But then he gets greedy and starts asking for money. Magdalena, when someone starts to blackmail you, there is no end to their demands, unless you stop it. Let that be a lesson for you.'

'Thank you. I will bear that in mind. Cousin, since we're having this heart to heart' – I paused to take a deep breath – 'I hope you're not offended by this question, but did Delilah also end up as a delicious-smelling roast?'

Peter started and turned back to me. 'Delilah? Magdalena, I'm not a savage! I wouldn't eat someone who I once loved. Delilah, I had to dispose of through our sausage machine at night, when my brothers were sleeping. Well, most of her. You can't make sausage with bones. The bones I had to feed to the hogs; they'll eat anything.'

I needed to throw up so badly; it was all I could do not to reach for my potty pail. Remember that you're Detective Rosen, not Magdalena, I said to myself. Keep getting information, while he's still willing to talk.

'This means their heads too?' I asked, with only the slight quaver in my voice.

'Skulls are bones too, cousin, yah?'

'Yes, of course, how silly of me not to think of that. Cousin, is this what you plan to do with me?'

'Oh Magdalena, I could never hurt you. You are blood of my blood, and flesh of my flesh. We share the same great-grandparents. Our grandparents were brother and sister.' He covered his face with his hands and emitted a weird sort of howl. 'I wish that you would not be so nosy all the time. Why do you work with the police, Magdalena? Do you not see what a dilemma you have caused me? You have put me between a rock and a hard place, yah?'

Well, that took the cake. The cannibal cousin of mine was blaming *me* for discovering just how far around the bend he'd gone. 'Just keep him calm,' the still, small voice inside me said. 'All things work together for good to those who love God.' That is a quote from the Book of Romans. Gabe hates it when I recite this verse. He says, 'Didn't any of the six million Jews who died in the Holocaust love God? Or what about a widowed, Christian mother who died of cancer, leaving behind three children under the age of ten?' I didn't have answers to those questions, so I stopped quoting that favourite verse. But that evening, when I was chained to the bed, and everything seemed hopeless, I just knew that as long as I kept Peter calm, everything would work out to the good for me.

'Cousin,' I said gently, 'I want to be a soft place where you can land. A place where you can bring your troubles, and I will help sooth them away, because I will not judge you. Because like you said: I am blood of your blood, and flesh of your flesh. And what's more, I have known you since you were a baby, I watched you grow up into a fine young man, and we have been friends for many years.'

Peter smiled weakly. 'Yah, this is true. Although we are second cousins, you have always been more like an auntie.'

'Auntie Magdalena,' I said. 'I like that. So here's what I suggest. You take this lovely meat tray back down into the kitchen and bring me back some cinnamon buns and a full thermos of hot chocolate.'

Peter scratched his full mop of black hair. 'I don't have any Cinnabons, and I just used the last of my cocoa powder. But I could make you some cinnamon toast and a thermos of Ovaltine.'

I clapped my hands excitedly. 'Even better. I haven't had Ovaltine since I was a child! And I love cinnamon toast. Will you be putting butter on it, or just margarine?'

Peter rolled his eyes playfully. 'Please, Auntie Magdalena, I am still Amish, remember? The butter was churned by my sister Lydia. She is my favourite sister, my baby sister.'

'Oh, and one more thing, *nephew* Peter,' I said, 'Bring up a couple more of those books with your picture on them. They are actually quite entertaining.'

Peter blushed deeply. 'Auntie, I posed for those books when I lived in New York. An agent saw me on the street and approached me about the job and I – uh – well, I needed the money. It didn't pay very much at first, but then I got a contract for seventeen covers altogether, and more money rolled in than I could imagine. Job offers too, including modelling jobs with my clothes off!'

'New York is where you met Terry Tazewell, am I right?'

'So you have connected the dots on that one too, yah?'

I nodded.

'He wrote me a letter before coming here that sounded a lot like blackmail about my past – things he knew that I suspect you've found out too – but then again it wasn't. Do you understand?'

'Do you still have it?'

'Yah. In the safety box downstairs. Do you want me to bring it up?'

'Yes, please. Bring it up with the toast and Ovaltine, and at least two of those flighty, but quite enjoyable books. We'll have a pleasant time sussing out the meaning of that letter as we munch the toast smeared with Lydia's home-churned butter and sprinkled liberally with cinnamon and sugar.'

Peter finally smiled. 'I'll see you as soon as I can,' he said.

The man obviously multi-tasked; perhaps, while waiting for the Ovaltine water to boil and the toaster to pop up with slices of perfectly light-browned bread, he'd also gotten the books and the letter. I'd barely had time to use the bucket and clean my hands with the moist, anti-bacterial cloths that my captor had so thoughtfully provided, when he was back.

The first thing that Peter did was bring in the tray, which was indeed loaded with enough cinnamon toast to last two people for a long time. Also on the tray were a pair of fresh mugs, and a stack of six bodice-rippers. Clearly, at some point I was going to be doing a lot of repenting if my plan didn't go right.

'Hold on, there's one more thing,' Peter said, and hurried to the open door. 'I don't want you to think that I forgot this.' He returned carrying a thermos jug that was twice as large, and twice as heavy, as the original thermos.

'Praise the Lord!' I said.

Peter laughed, as he set the jug on the floor in front of the bedside table. 'I knew that would make you happy. Would you like me to pour you a mug right now?'

'That would be wonderful,' I said. 'But first, please do me a huge favour.'

'What is that? Auntie Magdalena, you know that I can't release you – not until we've come to more of an understanding.'

'Of course,' I said, although I shuddered to think what that might be. 'No, you see, I wear contacts, and I dropped one, and I think it might have slid under the bed.'

'Contacts?' Peter said in astonishment. 'You are kidding! But of course, how foolish of me to think that someone of your age, who did not wear glasses – well, you know what I mean.'

'Nephew, will you please look for it? It's for my right eye, and without it, I can barely see your face.'

'Sure thing.' Peter got down on his hands and knees in the general area pointed to and peered under the bed. He may have seen an army of dust bunnies, but one thing is for certain, he did not see a contact lens belonging to Magdalena Yoder. That woman had just lied through her teeth.

While Peter was so helpfully searching on my behalf, I was stealthily picking up the thermos jug, and waiting for just the right moment. That moment came just as Peter's head started to emerge from beneath the bed. My arm was already raised, and I didn't even think twice about swinging that fat, heavy jug alongside Peter's head. Down Peter went, blood pouring from his wound. Did I care? Yes, I cared! But I cared more about finding the key to my leg cuff.

It was clear that I'd knocked Peter unconscious, but for how long? He was wearing a navy-blue shirt with a pocket. Many Amish communities forbid the use of buttons, but fortunately, Peter's did not. First, I had to turn him over, which was no easy task, then out of guilt I decided to pull him up in a sitting position and prop him against the side of the bed. The entire time I prayed that he wouldn't come to and grab me with one of his strong farmer hands. But fear is a great motivator, and the adrenaline it produced was downright amazing. Once I had him seated, I could easily unbutton the pocket. Inside I found a small key. It was the key to my ankle lock.

'Hallelujah!' I shouted. 'Praise God!' Then, fearful that my shouts might bring him back to consciousness, I hustled to free myself from my chain.

Then when I checked, Peter was still unconscious, so I immediately put the ankle grip on one of his hairy, but sturdy, ankles.

It just fit. Then I poured half a bottle of water over the side of his head to see what was what. Contact with the jug had produced a laceration no more than an inch long on his left temple well above his eye. As the mother of three children, I knew that scalp wounds of any kind bleed profusely. While I was tempted to search his house (if indeed that's where I was) for something to stanch the bleeding, or even to dress the wound, I ran the very real risk of becoming his prisoner again.

So no, I would put my trust in the Lord that He would take care of Peter. Meanwhile I would hike up skirts and run for my life. Which is exactly what I did. But I guess I shouldn't have been surprised when I got outside to see that my car was gone. Someone as bright as Peter was not going to leave such a tell-tale sign of my presence out in the open. A quick check of his barn revealed the infamous wagon without reflectors, but no car. And it wasn't parked behind the barn, or his house either. He could have rolled it into his farm pond, but if he had, that wouldn't have done me any good in any case.

Fortunately, Peter had yet to unhitch his horse from his buggy. Either he had been in such a hurry to attend to my comfort, or else he had plans of his own after feeding me. Perhaps he'd been invited to eat dinner at one of his sisters' or brothers' houses. Not that it mattered now. I knew how to drive a horse and buggy, because for years we at the PennDutch used to have one for the tourists' amusement – for which they paid a hefty fee, of course. Oh, how greedy I had been then. Could the Good Lord possibly be getting back at me *now* for that? Was God really that punitive? Did He hold a score card in His holy hands? Nah, that didn't make sense in this case, because this horse and buggy was my salvation, not some divine punishment.

Now the question was where should I ride in the waning light of day? I knew that the nearest house belonged to Lydia, Peter's youngest sister, and that she was married to Gideon Burkholder. But the Burkholders do not use telephones, so I could not call for help from there. Besides, there would be questions, and how was I to explain to Lydia that her favourite brother was a serial killer, who had chained me to a bed and tried to feed me his latest murder victim?

My best hope was to head back the way Peter had brought me

in, out to the highway, and then take it straight in to the village of Hernia. The buggy, unlike the wagon, thank the Good Lord, did have blinkers. Still, I didn't like the idea of driving it on a highway at dusk, especially since Hernia numbers some real speed demons amongst its citizenry. The good news is that its fastest, and reputedly the most reckless driver would be the one holding the horse's reins.

TWENTY-FIVE

As it happened, I encountered only one car before I reached the first house. That vehicle belonged to Thelma Kraybill, who drives so slowly that snails have been known to overtake her. She was coming from the opposite direction, of course. Perhaps the sun was in Thelma's eyes, or her mind was elsewhere (it *has* been wandering lately), but despite the fact that I waved so hard that I practically dislocated my shoulder, she didn't even take any notice of me. Driven to desperation, I even resorted to shouting obscenities into her open car window as she passed, hoping to get her attention. But words like 'excrement' and 'copulation' did not faze her.

I continued towards the nearest house, and much to my great relief the horse and I both got there unscathed. It was a modest, but tidy, bungalow belonging to Zachary and Edith Troyer, a young couple from my church, Beechy Grove Mennonite. I'd known both of these twenty-somethings all of their lives, and I'd known both sets of their parents, all of their lives as well. The Troyer side was also related to me, but that fact is inconsequential here.

They had one daughter, a five-year-old named Little Edith. Some people described Little Edith as 'precocious', others called her 'a real pistol', and yet there were those who referred to this kid as a 'spoiled brat'. It was not yet chilly when I arrived, and the front door was open to allow the screen door to let in fresh spring air. Because it was such a small house, I could see the family sitting around the kitchen table. I rang the bell.

'I'll get it!' screeched Little Edith and pushed her chair so hard it fell backwards on the floor. When she reached the door, she pressed her pug nose into the screen and just stared.

'Who is it?' called Edith.

'It's that woman from church,' Little Edith said.

'Tell her it's Magdalena Yoder,' I said urgently.

'It's the lady with the big nose,' Little Edith said.

'Which lady with the big nose?' Zachary yelled. 'Magdalena Yoder, or Irma Graber?'

'The one with the *really* big nose.'

'Look, toots,' I said, under my breath, 'you don't exactly have a button *shnoz*.'

'Mama,' Little Edith hollered, 'Miss Yoder is calling me names.'

'Oh, for heaven's sake, let her in,' Big Edith said. 'Your food is getting cold.'

Little Edith unlatched the screen door and stepped back imperiously. 'Ooh, she stinks,' the ill-mannered child said as I passed her.

'Let's be charitable, dear,' Big Edith said, but when I stood before her, she brought her napkin up to her nose. 'Magdalena, what is it that you want? It *is* the dinner hour, as you can plainly see.'

'I need to use your phone. Please. It's incredibly important. In fact, it's an emergency.'

'What's wrong with your phone?' Zachary said. It was a legitimate question, and I wouldn't have been offended, but then he too used his cloth napkin to cover his mouth and nose.

'I don't have it.'

'You mean you lost it?' Big Edith said. 'Magdalena, I must say that I'm very disappointed in you. After all, you're the mayor, and a senior deacon at church.' She shook her head vigorously to indicate her level of disappointment.

'Now, now, dear,' Zachary said to Big Edith, 'we mustn't judge Miss Yoder too harshly. She is, after all, what? In her eighties? She could be experiencing dementia.'

'I'm seventy-four, for crying out loud,' I shouted, 'and I'm starting to feel like Gulliver. Look, folks, I don't have a phone because the day before yesterday I was kidnapped by a psychotic Amish man and chained to a bed. He ditched both my purse and my car. I just now escaped by borrowing his horse and buggy, and if you don't believe me, have your bratty daughter check for it outside.'

Big Edith's cheeks were flushed with anger. 'Did you just call our daughter "bratty"?'

'Did I?' I said. 'I'm sure I meant to say "precocious".'

Big Edith said nothing as the colour drained from her face.

'I think it would be helpful if you apologized,' Zachary said.

'I'm sorry,' I mumbled.

'I couldn't *hear* you,' Little Edith said. She was holding her nose, and still had not sat down.

'Look, people,' I said, 'the reason that I may be a mite redolent is because I haven't been able to either wash or brush my teeth for a while. And like I said, that's because I've been kidnapped and chained to a bed.'

'Little Edith,' Zachary said, 'go outside and see if there's a horse and buggy in the driveway.'

'Aw, do I hafta?'

'Pretty please,' Big Edith said.

'With a cherry on top,' Zachary said.

'Oh, all right!'

Little Edith stomped off, but she reinforced her displeasure by banging the screen door behind her. In a second, she came running back in hollering her head off.

'Ain't no horse and buggy out there! Lady with the biggest nose is lying!'

I ran to the door to see for myself. Well, what do you know, the child was right. I hurried back inside.

'I forgot to tether the horse,' I said, 'because I was too anxious to get to a phone. Trust me, this is an emergency. You call the police, yourself, if you don't believe me. Meanwhile the killer is on the loose.'

'Maybe we should call the police,' Zachary said. 'At the very least Chief Graham can come and get her off our hands.'

'But he's a *homosexual*,' Big Edith whispered, and motioned to their daughter with a tilt of her head.

'Homosexuality is *not* contagious,' I said.

'Please be quiet,' Zachary said, 'I'm dialling.'

We all waited quietly for Toy to answer his phone. Meanwhile Little Edith stuck her tongue out at me. I don't believe in the notion of 'spirit animals', but if I did, Little Edith's would have to be the anteater. That child could possibly wash behind her ears with it, given the motivation.

Then Zachary began to speak. 'Chief Graham, this is Zachary Troyer at 1128 West Somerset Road. Magdalena Yoder is here – yes, that's what I said. *The* Magdalena Yoder, you know, the mayor, owner of the PennDutch Inn. The lady with the big nose – well, it looks big to me. And not just to me, but also to my wife – yes, sir. I will. No, sir. No one else.' Then he hung up.

'So what did he say?' Big Edith demanded. 'You didn't get to tell him very much. Why didn't you tell him about her crazy kidnapping story? He would have had a good laugh, I'm sure.'

Zachary shook his head. 'It must be all true. She's been missing since the day before yesterday. And we're not supposed to say a word about this to anyone. Not *anyone*. Not even your mother. You got this, Big Edith?'

Big Edith nodded, before shooting me the evil eye, which if you ask me, isn't very nice for a Christian lady to do.

'How about you, Little Edith?' Zachary said. 'Do you promise to keep Miss Yoder's visit a secret? I'll buy you a new doll if you do?'

'From the mall in Pittsburgh? It's gotta be from Pittsburgh. I don't like the stores in Bedford.'

'No, from the stores in Bedford.'

'And with extra clothes for the doll,' Little Edith said, her arms crossed.

'What a precocious child,' I said, although I meant something quite different.

'Miss Yoder,' Zachary said, 'would you care for something to eat?'

'Actually I would.' I moved to seat myself at the extra chair at the table, which would have put me opposite the one used by Little Edith. Before I could plonk my bony patooty down on the padded seat, Big Edith jammed a stack of newspapers between my behind and the chair.

Little Edith resumed her rightful place. 'You have to eat your vegetables, or you won't get any dessert,' she said. 'Not even one bite.' Then she stuck her tongue out at me.

I returned the favour.

'Mama!' Little Edith wailed. 'Did you see what she did to me?'

'Miss Yoder,' Zachary said, 'would you like me to fix you a plate?'

I nodded. 'That would be very nice.'

'Zachary,' Big Edith said sharply, 'she's a grown woman for Pete's sake; she can fix it herself.'

Nonetheless Zachary fixed me a decent plate, with a chicken breast, mashed potatoes and gravy, peas and a dinner roll with butter. He also gave me a small, tossed salad. Unfortunately, I was just able to chew and swallow one bite of chicken when the sound of a police siren could be heard. I slapped some butter on the dinner roll and crammed the entire thing into my mouth, knowing that my meal was quickly coming to an end.

'Mama, look at what she did! If I did that, you'd spank me. You need to spank Miss Yoder. Spank Miss Yoder, Mama!'

Big Edith was flushed again. 'I don't spank you, Little Edith. In fact, I have *never* spanked you.'

Little Edith got out of her chair and patted her buttocks dramatically. 'Ouchy, ouch, Mama, sometimes you spank me so hard that I can't sit down for my whole life!'

Zachary laughed. 'Isn't she a pistol? For her whole life, indeed.'

I swallowed the roll and shoved a forkful of mashed potatoes into my mouth, even as Toy thundered up the steps and into the house. When he saw me, his face broke into a grin.

'Magdalena!' he cried joyfully.

As I stood up to greet him, I purposefully pushed the pile of newspapers off the chair. They slid hither and thither, just not quite yon, but they still made enough of a mess to upset Big Edith. I know, that wasn't my finest moment, but given how stressed I was, I might have behaved far worse than that.

Although I am not a touchy-feely person, and Toy knows that, we both knew that a hug was inevitable. 'Be warned,' I said, 'the Troyer family thinks that I stink. But if you think that you can handle it, I'm coming at you.'

'Bring it on,' Toy said.

That was the longest hug that I ever shared with someone not related to me by either blood, marriage or adoption. We hugged so long, in fact, that Little Edith grew envious and wanted in on it.

'Hey, no fair,' she whined. 'Why does Miss Yoder get to hug the policeman, and I don't? She stinks and has a big nose, and I don't have neither.' She stamped her little foot.

Toy stopped hugging me and bent down. 'Maybe I hug Miss Yoder because she's my very special friend, and because she doesn't call people names.'

'Hmm,' Little Edith said. 'Does that mean if I said Miss Yoder had a regular nose and didn't stink, you'd hug me?'

'Sure,' Toy said with a twinkle in his eye. 'You betcha, then I would.'

'Well, I ain't supposed to lie,' Little Edith said. 'So that means I ain't never gonna get no hug.'

'Grammar, dear,' Big Edith said. 'Remember, dear? We ain't – I mean we *aren't* supposed to say "ain't".'

'Well, that's just silly,' Little Edith said, and stuck her tongue out at her mother.

I slipped back to the table, grabbed what remained of my chicken, and a handful of rolls from the breadbasket, and wrapped them up in my cloth napkin.

'I'll wash the napkin and give it back to you at church,' I said. 'Zachary, thank you very much for calling Chief Graham. Big Edith, your chicken was a tad rubbery, and there were a few too many lumps in the mashed potatoes for my liking. But the dinner rolls are awesome – they must have come from a tube. Thanks very much for dinner, by the way. And as for you, Little Edith, you have a lot to learn about respecting your elders. Let's hope that someone teaches you that before you start public school in the fall.'

Then Toy had no problem hustling me out of that house and to his waiting cruiser. Once his door had closed behind him, I turned to him and said, 'Toy, do you mind if I cry?'

While that might seem like an unusual request, the truth is that I had never once cried since the day my parents were buried. That, by the way, was fifty-four years ago.

TWENTY-SIX

Toy held me while I cried. Perhaps I cried for fifteen minutes. He did not tell me that I stank. I might have boo-hooed even longer, but the Troyer family was lined up on their front porch watching us and eating popcorn. I did not judge them for behaving thusly. Like many Conservative Mennonite families, the Troyers did not own a television set, so we were their evening's entertainment. However, I was annoyed when I disengaged from Toy's embrace and Little Edith tossed popcorn into the air and shouted, 'Yippee!'

From the Troyers' house Toy drove me straight home. He had called Gabe immediately after getting my call, so Gabe had been waiting on pins and needles. Thank heavens the guests had already had their evening meal, so as per Toy's instructions, Gabe ordered them to spend the evening inside the guest cottage. Of course, that went over like a lead balloon until Gabe, acting on his own initiative, told the guests that he was cancelling all of their fees for the week. This made them so ebullient that even said lead balloon, if it had existed, could easily have sailed off into the stratosphere.

On the drive home I'd managed to give Toy an outline of my ordeal, and the atrocities Peter had so calmly related to me. Toy kept a cool head, but he did have a disturbing piece of information of his own to share.

'Unfortunately, Peter Schmucker's residence is not within the village limits of Hernia, and so it doesn't lie within my jurisdiction. This means that—'

I finished his sentence. 'Sheriff Stodgewiggle will have to handle the case. He has the finesse of a bison on a bulldozer. When the dust settles the local Amish community is going to be flattened by guilt by association. Peter's brothers will undoubtedly end up in prison, because they were too – too what? Ignorant? Innocent? – to know what was going on? But according to the law, that is no excuse. And what do you think the village of Hernia is going to be known for in the future? The two Cs: cannabis and cannibalism.'

Toy reached over and patted my arm. 'There may be a way around this.'

'How?' I demanded. 'I'm sorry, but this is one thing that I don't think that God is going to fix!'

'Now, hush your mouth,' Toy said gently. 'Don't you ever give up on your faith, Magdalena. That's what makes you, *you*. Listen to me carefully. A couple of months ago my husband and I were down in Pittsburgh on a Saturday night, and we stopped in at the Goat and Hen.'

'The what?'

'The Goat and Hen. It's a gay bar. Guess who we saw there?'

'No, you did not!'

'Yes, ma'am. And guess what else? He was slow dancing with a guy we know – well, I won't say his name. But the guy is definitely gay. I called him later, and he said that he and the sheriff had been seeing each other for some time.'

'Toy, does this mean that you're thinking of blackmailing the sheriff?'

'Magdalena, I must protest against even an insinuation that I would do so. I would never blackmail Sheriff Stodgewiggle. That would be so unethical, and of course, illegal. No, I will simply remind him that I saw him at the bar, and then tell him your story, and then lay out the ideal way for this case to be handled. And then as I take my leave, I will say that I hope to see him and Ronny again at the Goat and Hen. Oops, I didn't mean to say that name.'

'What name?'

'You're a peach.'

'Do you think that your plan will work?'

Toy shrugged. 'The sheriff is ostensibly a very religious man. He goes to church every Sunday where the preacher rails against homosexuality. Also, Sheriff Stodgewiggle has been supposedly happily married for over thirty years. I would only gently hint that there is a disconnect between how he lives openly, and his secret life.'

'Pull over,' I directed, as we had almost reached the PennDutch. Toy had chosen the back way, avoiding driving through the village, even though this was a slightly longer route, but I was grateful for the privacy that it afforded me. Therefore, Toy was able to oblige me by stopping in the widened part of the road in front of a cattle crossing.

'So what is your ideal way for this case to be handled?' I asked.

Toy answered at once. 'As quickly as possible, and without hoopla. Sheriff Stodgewiggle loves nothing more than being in the limelight. I'm sure that if he had his way, this story would make its way to the front page of every newspaper in the United States, every talk show, both radio and TV, and even into *Time Magazine*. Heck, I wouldn't be surprised if even some British newspapers and magazines could dine on this for weeks.

'I would tell him how devastated the Amish community would be by this news, and how any unnecessary publicity would compound that. I would suggest that in this case, he was like a shepherd, and that the Amish were his flock, and that it was his job to keep them safe from the hordes of reporters, not to mention the curious kooks who like taking selfies in front of infamous places.'

'Your plan has merit,' I said, much relieved. 'I know Sheriff Stodgewiggle pretty well, and your shepherd reference alludes to Jesus. I think old Stodgewiggle will be mighty pleased to assume that mantle, given that his ego knows no bounds.'

'Thank you,' Toy said. 'I'm glad you approve. The second I drop you off, I'm heading up to see him.'

Five minutes later he delivered me into Gabe's waiting arms, and off Toy went, red light rotating, and siren blaring. Presumably he drove that way the entire twelve miles into Bedford.

Meanwhile my darling husband scooped me up and carried me into the kitchen. If he found my body odour repugnant, he said not a word. I did, however, excuse myself to use a real toilet and wash my hands and face. When I returned to the kitchen, Gabe had set the table, and was busy making my favourite omelette: sharp cheddar cheese with sliced green olives.

'Look inside the microwave,' he said.

'There's a plate of cinnamon buns,' I said happily.

'Agnes made them this morning. She said that she had to stay busy. I swear, that woman loves you like a sister.'

'Better than a sister,' I said. 'Agnes treats me much better than Susannah ever has. Sweetheart, is there any chance that I could have hot chocolate to top off this feast?'

'Gotcha covered, babe,' my darling husband said. 'That's what's heating up in the glass-covered pot. Stir it if you would, please, so that it doesn't scorch. That's also courtesy of Agnes.'

Gabe claimed to have already had a bite to eat with our guests, but he did help himself to a cinnamon bun. Between bites of my scrumptious feast, I told him about my ordeal. He alternated between being properly horrified, appropriately angry, and most importantly, comforting.

'I can't imagine how terrified you were,' Gabe said. 'It creeps me out thinking of you shackled to that bed. I just want to rip that man apart with my bare hands.'

'Well, a great amount of time spent in prayer, and an almost equal amount of time reading soft porn, helped keep my mind off my situation.'

'Come again?' Gabe said.

'Bodice rippers. You know, romantic novels of the lowest order. Apparently, Peter's wife – may she rest in peace – worked for that particular publishing company, and she got Peter to pose as the model on the cover of dozens of them. So they had a huge collection of those books with their scandalous covers at Peter's supposedly average Amish farmhouse, and there were a couple of those books next to the bed to which I was chained. Sweetheart, I know it was wicked of me to read them, but they kept my mind occupied.'

'Oh hon, I adore you,' Gabe said. 'The mere fact that you call romance novels bodice rippers, and think that they're wicked, well, that's so Magdalena Yoder of you.'

I took a huge gulp of sweet, rich, hot chocolate. 'What is that supposed to mean? So Magdalena Yoder of me.'

'It means that I haven't corrupted you entirely – *yet*. But I'll keep trying.' He winked.

'Harrumph. Anyway, I did do something that I read in a nonfiction book, and that was to try and keep *him* calm, and it seemed to have worked.'

'What was that?' Gabe said, leaning forward.

'Well, the advice was to try and make your captor relate to you on a personal level. Talk about your children, or something like that. Since Peter and I are second cousins – our grandparents are first cousins – at one point, I stopped calling him Peter, and only referred to him as Cousin. I even said that he was blood of my blood, and flesh of my flesh.'

'Ouch.'

'Yeah, but that was before I knew how sick he really was.'

'You know,' Gabe said, 'in a secular society, someone like Peter might have received the help that he needed a long time ago, maybe even as a child. While they are not foolproof, there are certain danger signs that often point to the possibility that a child could grow up to be a serial killer.'

'Such as?' I said.

'Well, one of the most commonly agreed upon ones is if the child tortures, or kills animals,' my darling said.

'Do you mean like pulling the wings off flies?' I asked.

Gabe swallowed. 'That one I wouldn't get too excited about, but it is still disturbing behaviour. I was thinking of something more along the lines of throwing rocks at kittens and puppies, or trying to drown them. Or picking up baby birds that have fallen from their nests, and cutting their wings off while they are still alive.'

I shivered. 'Peter did that very thing at a family picnic. His mother quickly killed the bird, threw it deep into the bushes, where a dog retrieved it and then gulped it down. Peter just laughed.

'But you know, other than that, he was always a shy and pensive boy. I remember that he didn't seem to have any friends – not even among our myriad of first and second cousins gathered at our family reunions.'

Gabe swiped another one of the cinnamon buns, which was fine with me. Agnes has made too many for one meal, and my husband's cheese and olive omelette had been enormous. Plus I needed room for all that delicious hot chocolate.

'Mags, isn't it unusual for an Amish family like the Schmuckers to associate with you Yoders, given that your family had left the true faith? Weren't they supposed to shun you?'

I nodded, unable to answer until I swallowed my next bite. 'You're right. But each church community has its own rules, its own Ordnung, which is overseen by the bishop. In biblical times Jews had to free their slaves after seven years. Our bishop was a kindly man who believed that shunning should not last any longer than slavery.'

'Kudos for him,' Gabe said. 'Mags, you know that Agnes is chomping at the bit to speak to you. Are you up to it, or would you like me to call her, and tell her that you need your rest, and to try again tomorrow?'

'Actually, tell her to come on over. It's always better to visit in person.'

'Are you *sure*? I should think that you're exhausted.'

'You're right, I should be, but the funny thing is now that I'm free, I have this adrenaline rush, and I need to get the adrenaline out, or I won't get to sleep. So, if you don't mind, after you call Agnes, please fill the tub with bubble bath. Make it extra hot. And when you call Agnes, tell her that if she wants to hear my story, she has to scrub my back.'

'Will do,' Gabe said.

I was still sitting at the kitchen table eating when Agnes arrived. She let herself in, and then came running at me with open arms, only to stop a meter from me.

'Eew, you stink,' she said.

'That's why you're here,' I said. 'Besides, it's only been a couple of days since I showered, so just think of me as French.'

'Just as long as you don't try to talk with a Parisian accent. When you do, you sound like Donald Duck with a bill full of marbles.'

'I love you too, dear.'

True to her promise, Agnes went with me to the bathroom and proceeded to lather my back. Then I playfully lathered her face (which did not go over well) as I began to elaborate on my ordeal. She was properly sympathetic, and practically climbed into my massive tub to hug me (I was tempted to pull her in). Although she is no relation to Peter, she did know him better than Toy did, and so some of her questions took a different tack.

'Peter was just about the best-looking guy I've ever known,' she said. 'Even that crazy, cereal-bowl haircut that Amish men wear didn't diminish his dark brooding looks one iota. And he had the longest lashes I've seen – on a man, or on a woman.

'When I'd see him at the store, and there would be Amish girls there, they'd suddenly start whispering and giggling behind their hands. And blushing. Even some of their mothers would get into the act. He had to have known that he was something special, don't you think? Mags, why do you think that he came back from rumspringa? Did he tell you?'

'He said that he came back to Hernia because he missed his family. But I don't know if that's true. I read somewhere that serial killers are unable to form emotional attachments.'

'But in a documentary that I saw on TV,' Agnes said, 'they tracked down and caught this guy who killed like fourteen people, but he was married and had two children whom he supposedly loved very much.'

'Supposedly,' I said. 'How are we to know what really goes on in people's minds?'

'Whatever the case may be, he seemed to have a certain fondness for you, in that he kept you alive for as long as he did. And Mags, I'm so proud of you. I want you to know that.'

'Proud of me for what?' I said.

'For being so brave,' Agnes said.

I have long slender toes that can function as fingers, so I utilized them to turn the tap to hot water. Then, still using my toes, I picked up my cruet of bubble bath and added a dollop under the hot stream.

'Mags,' Agnes said, 'you could have asked me to do that.'

'I like to be self-sufficient,' I said. 'Now back to what you said about being brave. I was not brave. One is brave when one acts nobly in spite of being afraid. I just lay there, shackled in bed, reading titillating books – no pun intended.'

Agnes twittered. 'But you were brave when you conked him on the head with the thermos jug. There's no telling how that could have gone wrong.'

'Well, I beg to differ even there. That was all the Good Lord's doing. I'd prayed for guidance, and even though it was a violent act, I did what the still, small voice inside me was telling me to do.'

'Or maybe you were just acting nobly when you were afraid. Maybe God doesn't actually talk to us one-on-one or do individual favours. That would turn Him into a puppet master, wouldn't it?'

I gave Agnes a righteous splash. 'What are you now? An Episcopalian?'

Agnes splashed me back, getting soap in my eyes. She also got some of my hair wet. It had not been my plan to wash my hair that evening, given its great length and the time it took to dry it.

'No, I just think for myself,' Agnes said vehemently. 'That's all. I will be seventy-five in November; it's time I came to my own conclusions. Look Mags, if you want to believe that a still small voice inside you, meaning God, gave you the idea to clobber that whackadoodle on the noggin with a thermos, then be my guest. But if God was the instrument of your salvation, then I want to know this: why did God allow Peter to chain you up in the first place?

'And don't trot out that old "free will" argument, because an omniscient God already *knew* that Peter would chain you up, so Peter had no choice but to do it. Besides, Peter Schmucker is so mentally ill, that he probably can't be held responsible for his actions. So again, we see that Peter had no free will, because his disease forced him to chain you to the bed. Therefore, God could have – no, *should* have – prevented the whole darn thing from happening in the first place!'

I was gobsmacked, maybe even *God*-smacked, by my best buddy's sacrilegious vitriol. Sure, I was raised in a more conservative branch of the Mennonite Church, but we were both baptized, faithful Christians. How had I not seen the cracks in Agnes's faith develop? How was it possible that we could talk to each other every day, and then suddenly in my dotage, I discover that my very best friend, whom I had known since I was three months old, was now spiritually a stranger?

'Get behind me Satan,' I croaked.

'Oh, stop it, Mags,' Agnes said. 'You use that phrase too often. You know I'm not Satan. You also know that you still love me. I feel that I've matured in my thinking, whereas you now view me as a heretic. We shall just have to agree to disagree, because the one thing that we can both be certain of, is that the other one is as stubborn as a brace of mules.'

I smiled wanly. 'That is certainly true in your case.'

'Also,' Agnes said quickly so that I couldn't interrupt, 'if you're really worried about my soul, then you will just have to worry silently, because you know I'll just push back against any efforts on your part to re-convert me.'

'Aha,' I said. 'So you were converted once!'

'You know I was,' Agnes said. 'You were with me at the time.'

At that point we were interrupted by Gabe rapping on the bathroom door. I knew the Babester wouldn't have disturbed us unless it was a truly urgent matter, like the house was on fire, or he'd won a million dollars on a scratch-off lottery ticket.

'Come in,' I called.

'But you're naked,' Agnes whispered.

'He's my husband, dear,' I said. 'Trust me, it's old hat by now. Old, old hat.'

When Gabe entered he brought with him his cell phone. 'It's Toy. He's calling from Maryland.'

'Put it on speaker,' I said. 'Hey, Toy, Agnes is here with me. Is that all right?'

'Agnes,' Toy said. 'Swear yourself to secrecy.'

'I hereby swear,' Agnes said.

'Magdalena,' Toy said, 'I met the sheriff at Peter's house, but he had already cleared out. I had a hunch that he'd headed south to Maryland.'

'Where one must always take provisions,' Agnes said.

'What?' Toy said.

'That's what Magdalena claims. I like Maryland; I think that it's possible to find food there.'

'Anyway,' Toy said, 'I put an all-points bulletin out at the border for his arrest, and we got him! There was just one small, unforeseen hiccup.'

'Oh, no,' I said. 'Tell me.'

'Well, the junior officer in the arresting team discovered a Tupperware container in the trunk that contained a very tender ham – or so he thought. His girlfriend was coming over shortly, and he was going to propose to her over a candlelight dinner of pasta.'

'He didn't!' I said.

'That's right,' Toy said. 'We were able to stop him in time, but only by telling him why. The good news is that Baines is coming back to Hernia, and we can give him a proper burial here.'

'But in a regular size coffin, not in a hat box. Right?'

'Or you could cremate him,' Agnes said. 'He's already got a head start.'

The three of us were horrified. 'Agnes!' we said simultaneously, and then one of us snickered.

Then to punish Agnes for her macabre attempt at humour, I lunged up and grabbed both her arms, and pulled her into the tub. Given her size, she couldn't avoid but to land directly on top of me. Water and bubbles overflowed on both sides, and dear Gabe yelped as he tried to flee the sudsy tide in his expensive moose-hide moccasins. Who cared if the floor got wet – that's what the drain was for. As for me, I was feeling ever so happy to be home again.

TWENTY-SEVEN

Peter Schmucker pled guilty, but of course he still had to stand trial. How could he not? There was a mountain of DNA evidence to back up my story, including Baines' cooked remains, and I think that he was finally relieved to get caught. He was, after all, a human who had acted inhumanely – just another poor lost soul in need of salvation. Well, perhaps there is a wee bit of difference between mooning one's neighbour and turning them into one's Sunday roast, but you get the picture.

At any rate, what was revealed in the trial was that he had entered the PennDutch through my unlocked kitchen door, taken my bread knife and Portuguese dish towel and planted them in the pond. Then he returned to the inn, slit Terry's throat with his own knife, which he'd worn on a holster, returned the knife to the holster, and then let himself out the upstairs window by hanging from the sill, and then jumping to the soft grass. His horse was tethered in the barn. He was quite lucky that he did not cross paths with anyone coming into the kitchen to raid the fridge. Peter's reason for murdering Terry was that he was terrified Terry might recognize him from his days as a male prostitute.

As the grizzly details emerged, the media attention exploded exponentially. Soon the peaceful little village of Hernia, Pennsylvania gained international notoriety. The PennDutch Inn, and myself in particular, were singled out. My neighbours succumbed to bribes, and vans of reporters and trucks bearing state-of-the-art cameras and sound equipment lined both sides of our property and were stationed across Hertzler Road from us. The no trespassing signs didn't stop their occupants from crowding our front steps and back steps, and peering into every window where there was a crack between the drapes. To put it succinctly, we were under siege.

However, in the long run, I had it relatively easy. It was the Schmucker brothers, their sisters, and their extended families who *really* had hard rows to hoe (to use one of Toy's Southernisms).

Although both of Peter's older brothers were acquitted, because they hadn't the faintest idea what Peter had been doing to make their sausages taste so good, the stigma attached to the family name was too strong to allow them to continue to live within their church community. Of course, their sausage enterprise went kaput.

Both of the older Schmucker brothers uprooted their families and moved to Kansas. There had been twelve adult children in the Schmucker family at that time, three men, including Peter, and nine women. Eight of the women and their families also elected to move to Kansas. The youngest Schmucker sister, now a Burkholder, who had been closest to Peter, committed suicide. She was found hanging in Peter's barn three days after she'd gone missing. It happened four weeks into the trial. After her death, her husband joined the other family members in Kansas.

Bill and Linda Steele were, along with the rest of Hernia, traumatized when they heard what had happened to their former butler Baines. They insisted on contacting Baines' husband of twenty-four years to see how Hank wished to dispose of his loved one's remains. Hank Gibbons asked if the Steeles could see to it that Baines was cremated and that his ashes were scattered in some sylvan setting, as Baines was quite fond of nature.

One problem that Toy and I had not initially anticipated was the trauma that sausage consumers in Hernia suffered. Our citizens panicked. Had they inadvertently cannibalized one of Peter's victims? If they had, would that send them on the shortcut to Hell? Since it wasn't a common occurrence, our clergy were not prepared to counsel so many distraught parishioners, especially when they, themselves, were in need of help.

Children were surprisingly less bothered by the news. Some of the boys even thought it was 'kinda cool' to be known as cannibals. The girls, of course, thought it was gross, and pretended to vomit whenever the word was mentioned. The school psychologist, a young man in his late twenties, sided with the boys, and said that the best way for the children to get over their 'icky feelings' was to embrace them. Taking a page from his playbook, the school football team shed their old name, the Hernia Hedgehogs, and renamed themselves the Hernia Heathens. That's when they won their first football game in a generation. Alas, the school board made them change the name again, several times, but finally agreed to let them call themselves the Hernia Hornets. They still haven't won any more games – but it's only been a year since then.

As for me, I'm doing just fine and dandy – well, not really. I have nightmares now and then, accompanied by leg thrashing. Each day, however, passes with fewer intrusive memories. On a really good day I don't think about Peter and those shackles more than two or three times. Gabe wants to take me on an eleven-day Mediterranean cruise, and I want to go – but just not yet. I'm working with a therapist three days a week so that Gabe and I can go on the trip as a *couple*. In other words, without Peter.

Speaking of Peter, it was determined by a panel of three psychiatrists that he knew what he was doing when he committed his heinous crimes. Peter was convicted of pre-meditated murder in the First Degree, and sentenced to life in prison, without parole.

AFTERWORD

Although I have never been an inadvertent adulteress like Magdalena, I have been an inadvertent cannibal. At the time, I was thirteen, and living in the Republic of the Congo, which had until recently been the Belgian Congo. Meat was scarce, and when our cook went to the black market to buy some, he returned with what he believed to be elephant meat. Three days later we read that the supposed elephant meat actually came from fresh graves (there was a civil war raging all around us).

I don't remember feeling particularly sickened by this knowledge, because it was now in the past. There was nothing I could do about it. Also, having grown up in the Belgian Congo, with a tribe of headhunters, there wasn't much that could faze me.